A MESSAGE WRIT IN BLOOD

Gideon drove the hay sled to the hollow the next morning. Accompanied by Pillow and Patrocino, he looked ahead and saw blood on the snow near French Creek. Horse tracks showed where a critter had been encircled by riders—and roped, likely. Gideon urged the team ahead. He followed a trail of frozen blood. A mature bull, wounded, had staggered down the bank of the creek. Dropping in his tracks on the ice, the big animal had rolled onto his side and bled to death.

Gideon halted the team and jumped off the sled. He jogged through the snow to the carcass. Kneeling, he saw a gaping wound. The underside of the bull's thick neck had been slashed open at the jugular.

Gideon stood. "Looks like Ben Anderson left a message." He turned to Patrocino and saw the *viejo*'s face distorted in anger. Mills Pillow was silent. No translation was needed.

Pillow asked: "What are you going to do?"

"Make him pay," Gideon said.

COLD WIND

STEPHEN OVERHOLSER

LEISURE BOOKS NEW YORK CITY

A LEISURE BOOK®

January 2002

Published by special arrangement with Golden West Literary Agency.

Dorchester Publishing Co., Inc.
276 Fifth Avenue
New York, NY 10001

ISBN 0-8439-4961-9

The name "Leisure Books" and the stylized "L" with design are trademarks of Dorchester Publishing Co., Inc.

Printed in the United States of America.

Visit us on the web at www.dorchesterpub.com.

COLD WIND

Ranchers

"Men who live in the open
who tend their herds on horseback
who go armed and ready to guard their lives
by their own prowess
and who call no man master."

—Theodore Roosevelt

Chapter One

Late in the night of his long ride the moon went down. Midnight temperatures dropped below zero by the time he reached Columbine, and the endless snow paled in starlight, turning gray as death and twice as cold.

Gideon Coopersmith crossed the rutted street from the livery, dry snow creaking under his boots. He looked up. By the faint light of stars he saw jagged peaks. The Never Summer range of the Rocky Mountains marked the end of the trail.

This mining camp lay in the bottom of a steep-sided cañon, nine thousand and eight hundred feet above sea level. The log and false-fronted buildings could have been tossed randomly amid granite boulders by a giant's hand, but, in fact, the shops, saloons, and rooming houses had been built on any patch of ground that was more or less level.

As Gideon expected, Columbine was virtually shut down in the grip of mid-winter. The largest gambling hall, Ore Deal, was boarded up. Closed, too, was Dinah Might, a two-story, dark-windowed house marked by an oil lamp with a red chimney.

Like mythical snowbirds, most miners had departed after the first big snowfall and hard freeze, men heading homeward for employment in towns or seasonal work on far-flung ranches in warmer climates. More a place to endure than to seek a fortune now, this snowbound cañon beyond the reach of law offered something better than riches to a man on the dodge—refuge.

Gideon stomped snow from his boots. He moved toward the lamplight glowing through the ice caked on the window of Miner's Delight. Pulling off stiff mittens, he paused to unbutton his sheepskin and adjust the Remington holstered on his hip. Then he opened the saloon door.

A gust of hot, stale air washed over him. He stepped inside and closed the door behind him. Clouded by tobacco smoke, the narrow room was rank with odors—coal fumes from a heat-cracked potbelly stove, soggy chew in tarnished brass spittoons, and many seasons' worth of rum, rye, and dark beer sloshed onto the puncheon floor.

He moved to the bar, eyed by three townsmen standing elbow to elbow there. Beyond them, under a kerosene lamp hanging by a strand of wire from the ceiling, half a dozen cowhands were seated at a round gaming table, hats cocked back on their heads. The men regarded him before turning their attention back to the cards in their hands.

He turned to the barkeep. Cigar stub clenched in yellowed teeth, she was a stout woman wearing a threadbare Mother Hubbard dress of gray and black fabric. She planted both hands palms down on the plank bar in a gesture of ownership as she met Gideon's eyes, but offered no other greeting.

"Double shot of whiskey," he said, shouldering out of the coat. "And coffee, if you got any."

He stood far enough away from the townsmen to discourage conversation and close enough to the stove to thaw. After draping his coat over the bar, he dug into a trouser pocket for his wallet.

The barkeep brought a shot glass and long-necked amber bottle, took her pick of coins Gideon had tossed onto the bar, and then retreated to a back room. Presently she returned with coffee in a chipped mug of white porcelain. She set the steaming brew in front of him, and turned away.

Gideon noted her face was deeply pocked. A broad scar angled across her cheek, causing one eyelid to droop. Even so, in sidelong glances, he felt a sense of recognition. The blunt nose and heavy chin reminded him of the pimpled youngster whose trail led here. From the home place Gideon had pursued that kid, first traveling to Buckhorn where he rented a fresh saddle mount, and then riding into the mountain cañon on this frigid night.

Now he drank slowly, ate a cold sausage, a pickle, and made one trip to the outhouse. He ordered more coffee after the cowhands trooped out. Half an hour later, when the townsmen departed, the barkeep announced her establishment was closed.

Gideon watched the last man pull the door shut. He turned to face the big woman and state his business—too late. In that moment she had stooped down behind the bar, and now she came up with a Greener—a .20-gauge shotgun with double barrels cut down to twelve inches, the stock sawed off at the pistol grip.

"I done told you," she said. "Miner's Delight is closed."

He nodded at the scatter-gun. "You make a habit of running off your last customer every night?"

"Customer, no," she replied. "Robber, yes."

"Robber?"

"Mister, when I first seen you stomp through that door with your coat open showing a gun, I knowed you was trouble. You aimed to rob me until you seen this here mantamer, and that's the Lord's truth, ain't it?"

Gideon kept his hands on the worn planks of the bar. "I'm no bandit. But you're right about one thing."

"What's that?"

"Trouble," he replied.

"How do you mean?"

"A month ago a youngster appeared at my back door," he said, "afoot, dirty, as cold and hungry as a lost pup. I put him on the payroll for barn and corral chores, even though my wrangler had to teach him everything from the dirt up."

She gestured impatiently with the gun. "Mister, it's been a long day. I got no time for yarns. . . ."

"After payday," Gideon went on, "the kid pulled stakes in the middle of the night. Now I'm missing one good cutting horse and tack, and a winter-born pony my daughter hand-raised from a foal."

"What're you getting at?"

"I figure you know by now."

Thick lips pressed together, she made no reply.

"That youngster," Gideon said, "is your son, isn't he?"

"Get out," she whispered. "Get out."

"Ma'am, all I'm after are my horses and gear. Return my property, and I'll ride out."

"I dunno what you're talking about."

"Then I'll put it to you this way," he said, ignoring the shotgun as he leaned across the bar. "When I get my mind set on a thing, I don't let up. You need to know that about me before you get some notion to run me off."

She met his gaze for a long moment. Then, as though suddenly weary, she lowered the gun. "My boy. . . ."

"Where is he?"

"Mister, you gotta understand about Tommy. . . ."

"Tommy? Is that his given name? He told me he went by George, George Larsen."

A smile crossed her face. "George Larsen was a roomer of ours. I ran a little boarding house in Denver back when Tommy was a sprout. Guess he remembered the name." She paused. "Say, if you didn't know his right name, how'd you find me?"

"The kid's boastful," he answered. "Claimed he made an ore strike in the Columbine gulch, sold out before the silver crash, and bought a share of Miner's Delight."

Her eyebrows arched, as though she was proud of a clever tale concocted by her son.

"I lost his trail outside Buckhorn," Gideon went on, "but it was a safe bet he was headed for this cañon."

She repeated: "You gotta understand about Tommy. . . ."

"Ma'am" he broke in, "I don't have to understand one thing about him. All I have to do is find him, and all you have to do is tell me where."

She threw her head back and cast an indignant look at him. "You come stomping into my place of business like some desperado. I know nothing about you . . . not your name . . . nothing. Why should I tell you anything?"

Jaw clenched, he said: "Coopersmith. Gideon Coopersmith. I own a cattle outfit up in North Park, a long, cold ride from this place. In winter I've got my hands full just keeping critters alive. Chasing down a thief is the last thing I need to be doing. Now, I'll ask one more time . . . where is he?"

"Not here, not in Columbine. I dunno where to find him."

He studied her. "You sure about that?"

"Calling me a liar?"

"When did you see him last?"

She glowered at him. "Four, five months ago."

"Where?"

"Laramie, Wyoming," she said. "You have to understand about Tommy. I found out he was in prison up there, convicted of robbery. Tommy swore he's innocent. That boy

11

don't lie to his mother. Lawdogs and some crooked judge stacked everything against him."

Gideon shook his head, and she reacted angrily.

"I don't care what you think of my Tommy, Mister Coopersmith. You don't know him like I do. I'm telling you, he was railroaded into the territorial prison."

Gideon saw a determined look in the woman's eyes, and figured she was stubborn enough to stick to her story. He drew a deep breath. Fatigue swept through him as the rigors of long hours in the saddle and shots of whiskey caught up with him.

"What did you say your name is?" he asked.

"I didn't," she replied, "and I got nothing more to say to you."

Reaching for his coat, Gideon said: "Columbine's not a big camp. If your boy's here, I'll find him."

He hoped he sounded sure of himself. He had doubts. This granite cañon had been picked and shoveled and dynamited in the two decades since the gold strike of '74. First mistaken for lead, silver was found later. This discovery revived a gold camp in decline until '93, when the government declared an end to bimetallism. Honeycombed with mines and prospect holes now, Tommy had plenty of places to hide if he put his mind to it.

With a last glance at her broad face, Gideon put on his sheepskin and headed for the door. Pausing there, he buttoned the coat and pulled on his mittens. Then he opened the door and stepped into cold darkness.

That much he remembered. That, and sudden pain exploding in the back of his head. Later he would know he had been hit from behind, very hard, and dragged around the corner of Miner's Delight. His assailant left him in a snow bank without his wallet, revolver, and cartridge belt—

left him to freeze in sub-zero weather.

A stranger in these parts, local folks would figure, he had stumbled out of the saloon skunk drunk, passed out, and hit his head when he fell, and that was how he froze to death.

Labored snorts and sour breath awakened him. With consciousness came the sensation of being trapped. He felt confined under heavy quilts, trapped by a large, warm creature. Stripped to his woolens, he attempted to move, but was pinned by a thick bare leg and two fleshy arms.

Gideon blinked. He tried to collect his thoughts as he separated bizarre dreams from reality. Then, wincing against the pain throbbing in his head, he saw the barkeep's pocked, scarred face inches from his own, eyes squinted shut.

She breathed raggedly as though sleep were hard work, her grasp tightening when she inhaled and then loosening with every gusting exhalation. Her breath, foul as a bear's den, wafted into his face.

He pulled back abruptly, and her eyes opened.

"You're alive!" she exclaimed. With this discovery, she lifted her leg off him and raised up on an elbow. Her nightgown fell open to reveal massive breasts.

"You got feelings, Mister Coopersmith?"

"What?"

"Feelings? You got any?"

"What . . . what happened?"

"Hammered," she said with a snort that sent quivers through her chest. "That's what happened. Oldest damned trick in the world. Step into darkness, and some feller hammers you, steals your goods." She added: "One of them cowhands, maybe. I'd never seen 'em before, and they seemed nervous."

Aware now that they shared a narrow bunk, he tried to edge away, but found, if he moved another inch, he'd be on the dirt floor. He glanced around the small cabin, seeing a battered trunk, wood stove, pine table and one chair, and walls insulated with layers of newspapers glued onto warped planks. In a corner his sheepskin, boots, and clothing lay in a heap.

"After I swamped out the Delight," she said, "I started for home. That's when I seen you laid out in the snow. If not for that big coat, you'd have froze solid, likely. I dragged you here. Figured you'd either live or die by daybreak, and tried to keep you warm as best I could, hoping to hell I wasn't sleeping with a damned corpse." She eyed him. "Feelings? You got feelings?"

"Feelings," he repeated, looking at her large body.

"Is you numbed up?" she demanded. "You got feelings in your feet, legs, and so on?"

Quilts fell away when Gideon sat up. His toes ached and his ears hurt from exposure to the cold. Except for a pounding pain in the back of his head, he was all right.

"I owe you," he said, turning to her. "You saved my life."

Strands of stringy hair fell across her face. She brushed them aside with the back of her hand and suddenly pulled the front of her nightgown together, covering mountainous terrain mapped by blue veins.

"Yes, sir, Mister Coopersmith, I reckon you do owe me. Yes, sir, reckon you do, now that I think on it. You could return the favor. If you was of a grateful mind."

"How?"

"By riding out."

He studied her scarred face. "You've seen your son in the last day or so, haven't you?"

She lowered her gaze.

"The way I add this thing up," Gideon went on, "your boy busted out of a Wyoming prison and headed south for Colorado, dodging lawmen. That's when his trail crossed mine. He hid out on my Double Circle C. Then he stole from me, cashed his paycheck in Buckhorn, and made a beeline for Columbine."

She made no reply.

"You saved my life. I'll do what it takes to even the tally."

"Well, then I'll be obliged, Mister Coopersmith, if you leave. Soon as you're able."

"Only one thing slowing me down."

"What's that?"

"Facing Annie," he answered, "when I get back to the home place without her yearling."

"Annie?" the woman repeated.

"My daughter's nine," he said. "She loves that prancing jughead, loves him the way only a girl can love a horse."

"Annie," the barkeep whispered.

Gideon stared at her. He had not expected to see tears in a rugged face.

She cleared her throat, eyes blinking. "Mister Coopersmith, I lost my baby girl sixteen years ago. Sixteen years and three months. Outbreak of influenza claimed her. Ain't a day goes by that I don't think of my Annie. Not one day."

"You amaze me, Gideon Coopersmith. You truly do."

Maggs Coopersmith sat with her legs folded under her robe while holding the sleeping baby in her arms. Her smile beckoned from her heart to his, never failing to draw him close.

Gideon gazed at his wife, seeing delicate features framed in long, blonde hair, free and uncombed. Her favorite chair, an upholstered platform rocker, was turned to the fireplace. Light from the flames played across her face.

He told her what had happened—or most if it. From Columbine he had ridden to Buckhorn where he reported the assault and robbery to the county sheriff, Nate Clarke, and his day deputy, Oliver Moore. After a trip to the bank to withdraw cash, he ate dinner with the two lawmen in the café at the Colorado Hotel. Then they accompanied him to the gunsmith's shop.

Gideon had hefted several hand guns and tested their action before heeding the advice of the sheriff and his deputy. He purchased a new Colt revolver, oiled and fresh out of the box. The .45 caliber pistol—six-shooter, double action, blued steel barrel and walnut grips—was the most dependable, heavy-hitting hand gun ever made. Along with a holster, cartridge belt, and three boxes of ammunition, he bought a tooled leather wallet.

Back on the home place, Gideon handed the reins of his played-out saddle horse to Patrocino, the wrangler of the Double Circle C. His long, cold journey ended when he trudged from the log barn to the house, pulled off snow-stiffened boots, and found Maggs by the crackling fire with Andrew in her arms. In the telling, he left out unimportant details such as waking to discover he'd spent half the night and most of a morning in the embrace of a woman whose name he did not know.

"Amazed?" he repeated

"I saw that look in your eye when you rode out at a gallop," Maggs said.

"What look?" he asked while gazing at Andrew. Heart-shaped mouth half open, the five-month-old baby's eyes were closed in sleep.

"The one that says you'd sooner take a beating or a

bullet than come back empty-handed," she replied.

He shrugged as though he had no notion of what she was talking about.

"That kid got you as riled as I've seen you in a long while," she said. "I'm glad you're safe and back home where you belong . . . but I'm truly amazed you rode out of that mining camp without your horses and gear."

"Like I told you," he said, "the lady barkeep dragged me out of a snow bank. She's the reason I'm here. Settling the score cost me everything Tommy stole . . . along with my wallet and cash, and my Remington and cartridge belt. I'm left with a sore head and a daughter who's going to be sore-headed when she finds out about her pony."

"I'm thinking about those tears," Maggs said.

"Tears," he repeated.

"That woman shedding tears over her lost baby," Maggs said. "A baby named Annie. It's touching, but. . . ."

"But what?"

Gideon watched her eyes for a clue to her meaning. Her given name was Margaret, a name hated almost as much as Margie. As a child in school, she was nicknamed Magpie by girlfriends, a name finally shortened to Maggs. That last one stuck, used by everyone now except her mother.

She did not answer his question directly. "We've been married for ten years and two months."

"Who's counting?"

"I am," she said. "All this time I didn't know you were sentimental."

"Sentimental? I'm not sentimental."

She laughed softly. "Your face is apple red."

"I'm chilled to the danged bone, Maggs," he protested, looking past her at flames dancing in the fireplace.

Alone here until his marriage, Gideon had single-handedly built that firebox and chimney. He mixed mortar one bucket at a time, selected each granite stone from French Creek eight miles away, and constructed the fireplace rock by rock. Then he dragged pine logs from the slope of Deadman, hired carpenters in Buckhorn, and built a house far too large for one man.

"The flames might be coloring me up some," he allowed now.

Maggs gazed at him. She leaned closer and kissed him. The baby stirred, but did not awaken.

Chapter Two

A great, humped shadow in gooseberry bushes exploded to life when the grizzly growled and charged out of the thicket by the creek. With no time for escape, the trapper had only a split second to raise his musket and snap off a shot. He saw the ball raise a puff of dust in the grizzled coat, and in the next instant the bear was on him.

Shot through the lungs, blood foamed in the beast's mouth when his teeth closed over the man's throat. The long-barreled musket clattered in the rocks as they slid down a bank and splashed into the creek. The dazed man came to rest under seven hundred pounds of dying bear.

With glacier-cold water rushing over him, the man's mind and body were soon numbed. He felt a strange stillness when the grizzly breathed his last, eyes open. The great jaws did not relax. By nightfall the lone trapper was dead, too, his empty gaze fixed on the brown eyes of the beast.

Most names from this era are lost to history, along with hand-drawn maps and daily journals. Chroniclers of the American West believe French trappers were the first Europeans to see North Park, the first to tromp through lush meadows, the first to scale forested slopes. In a region unmapped and unknown to them, they followed meandering waterways in search of pelts—beaver, muskrat, fox—and found them aplenty.

From prehistoric ages to that moment of death in the gurgling stream that came to be known as French Creek, this natural park of ninety square miles was ringed by mountains, home to ptarmigans and pack rats, bobcats and bears, wolves and wolverines. Grizzlies feared none of them, never backed away from any two or four-legged creatures.

On open ground and in shadowed forests the trappers came upon herds of moose, elk, deer, antelope, and even mountain bison. Creeks teemed with greenback trout. Overhead, eagles and hawks circled in their hunts for sunning prairie dogs and carefree field mice. Insect-laden marshes were home to coveys of birds.

According to one French trapper, Pierre LeDuc, the midday sunlight was dimmed by flocks of ducks and geese winging their way through cloudless skies. His words survive in a pocket-sized journal with pages listing pelts, flora and fauna, and detailed phases of the moon with weather calculations and compass readings.

Most memorable, however, is LeDuc's description of his party of four trappers following a creek from the grassy floor of North Park up the side of a forested mountain. Thirsty from their climb, he reported, the men kneel at water's edge. They drink heartily, and become aware of a unique taste and peculiar sweet-sour aroma. That flavor and a tinge of color inspires LeDuc to compare this chilled water to a rare, light wine. A discovery! Who knows what wondrous, curative properties this elixir of nature brings to them—good health and long life?

Attributing the bouquet to a profusion of ripe gooseberries along the bank, they fill canteens before moving upstream. A dozen paces farther the men make a discovery LeDuc calls putrid—rotting carcasses in the water. A buckskin-clad man lies under a grizzly bear, both long dead, both corpses, seeping the yellowish-brown fluid that stains and flavors the water.

★ ★ ★ ★ ★

On the map two words were pushed into one: Deadman. Not Mount Deadman. Not Deadman Mountain or Deadman Peak. Just Deadman.

The great mountain thrust high into the sky ten miles north of Double Circle C range, a peak framed in the panes of Maggs's kitchen window. As she often pointed out, other mountains in North Park bore honorable and properly descriptive names: Never Summer and Medicine Bow and Rabbit Ears.

"Why do we have to be saddled with Deadman?" she asked. "Who cursed that regal mountain with such an awful name?"

So began her one-woman campaign. Letters bearing a Buckhorn, Colorado postmark traveled by coach and rail car to Washington D.C. In her precise handwriting Maggs composed reasoned arguments to elected representatives and political appointees in the Department of the Interior, so many missives that the very sight of the distant postmark must have brought dread to the recipient. Finally, Maggs received a curt reply.

It came from a government cartographer, a man with the unlikely name of Mills Pillow. He had translated Pierre LeDuc's journal, and related the trappers' putrid discovery on the headwaters of French Creek half a century ago. The men were sickened, LeDuc wrote, and worse, from that day on, their canteens bore a rotting stench of death. The French-to-English translation was "dead man," a name later shortened to one word by a map maker. Pillow further informed her that, once entered on the official map of the United States, the peak out there in the wilds of Colorado would forever be known by that name.

Forever? A fighting word if there ever was one to the

woman known to politicians and government officials as Margaret Stearns Coopersmith. In fact, she was personally known to some of them. As the daughter of Ezra Allan Stearns, the Centennial State's second U.S. senator and a one-time vice-presidential candidate under the Republican banner, half a dozen of her childhood years had been spent in the nation's capital.

Her father had been deceased for more than a decade, but the Stearns name was favorably remembered. Quoting his words in letters, she evoked his memory and cited his achievements in her quest to re-name the mountain peak she had greeted through kitchen window panes every morning for the last ten years.

Wasn't it only right and proper, she asked politely and persistently, to honor the memory of a towering American by naming this great Colorado peak Mount Stearns?

"Daddy! Daddy!"

Gideon heard his daughter's excited shouts from the verandah. Still tired after his ride back to the home place, he had risen after dawn, late for him, and had eaten a breakfast of scrambled eggs, bacon, and warm biscuits spread with honey stirred into butter freshly churned. Rested and stomach full, he was headed for the bunkhouse when Annie called out.

Turning, Gideon backtracked through half a foot of powdery snow.

"Bad news, darlin'," he said as he reached her.

Barefoot and still wearing her flannel nightdress and matching nightcap, she leaped into his arms. "Mommy told me. I'll get another pony, won't I?"

Before he could answer, she said: "I'm glad you're all right."

He looked at her face, at lively eyes, and saw a hint of Maggs's side of the family—at once hearing a mother's coaching in the child's voice.

"I love you, Annie."

"Love you, too, Daddy."

"Come spring you'll have your pick of the foals. . . ."

Fighting tears, Annie hugged him. "Mommy said you were hit on the head and robbed and left to die."

"If I was a dead man," he said, "maybe someone would name that big mountain for me."

"Daddy, don't tease," she said in a youthful imitation of a wife reprimanding her husband. As an only child until five months ago, Annie had always seemed older than her years, taking on adult concerns in ways that amused her parents.

"Better scoot back inside before you take a chill," he said, and put her down.

After watching her cross the snow-dusted verandah in graceful, toe-pointing strides, he retraced his steps in the snow and went on to the bunkhouse.

It was a low, frame structure, equipped with half a dozen bunks, a woodstove, pantry and long table, and a back corner stacked with dime novels, *Police Gazette*s, and outdated copies of the *Rocky Mountain News* from Denver and the *Boomerang* from Laramie. It was home to Patrocino.

As one who had earned his place, Patrocino was the ranch's sole year-'round hand. In winter he had the bunkhouse to himself, a place free of body lice and body odor for now, free from the cuss-and-discuss of cowhands on the Double Circle C payroll. The full crew would be hired in the spring—three cowhands, possibly four, depending on how many cattle survived the winter and how many head Gideon would purchase for a season's fattening. From springtime until autumn roundup Patrocino would tend saddle stock and assist Maggs with meals for the hands.

Gideon stomped snow from his boots. He greeted Patrocino in the bunkhouse. The two men shook hands, Gideon a head taller, their eyes meeting in unspoken respect. Patrocino referred to himself as *"el viejo,"* the old one, but despite snow-white hair and a curvature in his back, Gideon did not believe this man was old by the calendar— on the young end of fifty, he reckoned.

Maggs believed Patrocino was bent not by time but by life's burdens. The nature of these burdens she could only guess. In three years they had never engaged the man in an extended conversation. Language was a barrier. When Patrocino first landed on the ranch he claimed to speak no English—*"No comprende, no comprende."*—were his only words back then. But from the art of breaking horses to doctoring cows, he knew livestock and quickly proved himself to be an asset on the ranch.

In time, Gideon discovered this man understood a little English. Whether Patrocino did not converse from a lack of confidence, or simply out of secrecy, Gideon did not know. As a Western courtesy, he respected a man's right to cover his back trail, and did not question him. Annie got more out of him than anyone else on the Double Circle C, their soft-spoken exchanges springing from a mutual love of horses.

Patrocino possessed two great gifts. His skill in gentling a kicking, head-tossing, sun-fishing, biting beast into a responsive saddle horse was unsurpassed. Gideon joked privately to Maggs that Patrocino talked more to the horses than to him. But whether this *viejo* ever communicated in English more than a word or two at a time was of no concern. He spoke fluent Horse.

The other gift was sculpting.

Entering the bunkhouse now, a fresh odor of cut wood

filled Gideon's nostrils. Curled shavings were scattered across the bunkhouse floor. He looked at carved, larger-than-life-size faces on the bunks and window sills, some of the carvings with head and shoulders and upper chests, all of them looking at their creator through empty eyes.

"My face?" Gideon said, pointing to the newest bust.

Patrocino smiled at the familiar joke. "No, *señor*. No, *señor*."

With nothing but a mallet and a few hand-forged chisels, he carved faces out of logs. Raw material came from the woodpile where thick sections of pine and aspen had been buck-sawed into eighteen-inch and three-foot lengths. Before they were split for firewood with a sledge and a wedge, Patrocino would inspect each one. After selecting the ones he wanted, he'd shave away bark to expose smooth wood, and lug them into the bunkhouse.

On occasion Gideon watched him, seeing the man's hands sweep over each chunk of wood, his expression intense, searching. Then the cutting began. Mallet *tap-tap-tapping,* he drove the blade of a wood chisel up and down the grain, or straight in for horizontal cuts. Shavings fluttered to the floor like feathers while larger chips dropped at his feet. Within an hour the broad outline of a face peered out, a presence set free. Finish work was done with the ant-ler-handled knife sheathed on his belt or the razor-sharp blade of the Barlow pulled from his trouser pocket.

Each figure was different. Yet the large carved eyes under heavy brows and the long, squared noses over thick lips made all of them look as though they were born into the same family.

Family. Maggs admired the carvings and even brought a few into the house after convincing Patrocino she was not seeking firewood. Alone with Gideon and those staring faces, she ventured her theory. Patrocino left his family for a reason, she said, a compelling reason. Perhaps he had been falsely accused of a crime. Maybe he had suffered a great lost love. Or his family succumbed to a disease or a fire. Alone in the world now, he carved these faces, surrounding himself with them as a bulwark against the loneliness and sorrow that bent his back.

Thinking of the many novels Maggs had read on cold winter days, Gideon figured her theory was an imaginative tale. For himself, Gideon rarely gave thought to the motives of others. On the ranch, there was always work to be done, and he occupied himself with how best to tackle the most pressing jobs.

"Colorful yarn," he said.

She frowned. "Colorful."

Gideon conceded Patrocino might be living with a dark secret or a tragedy impossible to bear. Patrocino may have even committed a crime and fled New Mexico Territory or somewhere south of the border. But here on the ranch, the Coopersmiths would never know even bare facts of his background. Gideon was convinced of that. Language barrier aside, in the last three years Patrocino had guarded his privacy. The forces or circumstances that drove him to abandon home and hearth for a cattle ranch in a land of long winters and short summers would never come from that man's lips.

Maggs considered her husband's opinion, and dismissed it with a single comment: "The past gives birth to the future."

In a way he never expected, Gideon soon discovered the wisdom of her words. Five days later the rattle of a heavy wagon drew him out of the barn. Patrocino followed, shouldering the scoop shovel he had been using to muck out horse stalls. The two men squinted against sun-glare on a vast field of snow. A big wagon approached on frozen wheel ruts. That road forked some ten miles away, with one branch leading south to Buckhorn and the other angling north off the shoulder of Deadman to Laramie across the Wyoming line.

This was not a ranch vehicle or a surrey or spring wagon from the Buckhorn livery stable. It was large and sturdy, drawn by two out-size black mules. The wagon was empty, too, judging from the loud rattling of floorboards. A pony was in tow.

Gideon blinked. With high sideboards, that was an ore wagon, out of place here in cattle country. When it rolled closer, he recognized the chocolate-colored pony tied to the tailgate.

"Oh, no," he said aloud, drawing a curious look from Patrocino.

Perched high on the bench seat of the ore wagon, a stout figure was bundled in tattered blankets, covered by a ratty buffalo lap robe, a scarf, and thick woolen cap.

Gideon winced. There could be no mistaking the driver when she pulled the scarf away from her face. His visitor was the barkeep from Miner's Delight.

Chapter Three

"Hell's fire, Mister Coopersmith, I've been called a lot of names. Plenty of names, good and bad. Mostly bad, now that I think on it. Yeah, mostly bad. You don't wanna hear 'em. Not worth repeating, not in polite company. Ma, she named me when I was birthed. Ruth, she called me. From the Bible, you know. Ma was a Bible reader. Oh, she just about committed the whole entire Good Book to memory, she did. Read the verses ever' night. Read 'em aloud, figuring the holy word had no power without giving strong voice to it. Yes, she was a Bible reader, Ma was."

Gideon listened, jaw clenched. His only crime was to ask her name so he could properly introduce her to Maggs. He got a rambling speech for punishment, a diatribe punctuated by sudden stabs of an unlighted *cigarillo* in her hand. In Columbine, this barkeep had spoken tersely, but, standing here now in the great room of the ranch house, Ruth Logan rattled on. And on.

The more she talked, the greater his discomfort. If she spouted long enough, Gideon figured this woman would reveal her bear-hug, life-saving technique. He was relieved when she abruptly demanded to see Annie. In the next moment a squeal of delight and a slammed door told them the discovery had been made.

Gideon strode after Maggs and Ruth as they hurried outside. Shivering, they stood on the edge of the verandah watching Annie sprint through the snow to her pony. Patrocino was already there, untying the lead rope from the tailgate.

"Brownie, oh, Brownie!"

Gideon moved to Maggs's side and put his arm around her.

"Your daughter," Maggs said to him, "should have her coat on."

He smiled as they watched her stroke the pony's blaze face while Patrocino held the rope taut.

"She's a beautiful girl," Ruth said around the cigarillo. "Just beautiful, your Annie."

She turned to them. "I left the Miner's Delight in the care of a man who'll drink the profits and rob me plumb blind, but, seeing that girl so happy, makes it all worthwhile. Damned if it don't."

"Speaking of robbing . . . ," Gideon began.

Maggs shot him a cautionary look.

Gideon would not be silenced. "Bring anything else that belongs to me?"

If it was possible to be angry and embarrassed at once, Gideon thought he saw both of those conflicting emotions register in the scarred face. Ruth yanked the cigarillo from her mouth and glowered at him as though he had violated a trust.

"What about Tommy?" he went on. "Did he give you my horse and gear to return to me?"

Ruth answered with a shake of her head. "I brung your pony in, Mister Coopersmith. That's the best I can manage under the circumstances."

"What circumstances?"

She did not reply.

"Tell me where Tommy is," he said, "and I'll look into those circumstances."

"I can't!" she said, and stepped away two paces.

Gideon heard stubbornness in her voice, and he knew

can't meant won't. She possessed a steely and unyielding trait that matched, he thought, the temperament of the mules hitched to that ore wagon.

"Well, I can see I ain't welcome here," Ruth said, and moved to the steps of the verandah. "Mister Coopersmith, all I aimed to do was return that pony to your Annie. Now, if you'll just give my animals water, I'll haul outta here."

Maggs swiftly moved toward her, reaching out in a feminine gesture. "Ruth, come in where it's warm. You are welcome to stay. Extra bed's made and ready for you." With another glance at Gideon, she added: "Stay as long as you like."

Gideon saw the big woman's eyes range from Maggs to him and back again, as though measuring the sincerity in the invitation. At the same time he felt his wife's gaze, felt it like a magnet's invisible power. He nodded once. In the next moment cries came from the house.

"My, oh, my!" Ruth exclaimed. "You never told me you had a baby, too! A dear, sweet baby! My, oh, my! Boy or girl? Come on! I gotta see!"

Gideon watched the two women hurry to the door, one deer-like, the other buffalo-like.

"Oh, Mister Coopersmith, wouldja put those mules up and water 'em?" Ruth bellowed over her shoulder. "They could use a couple scoops of grain, too."

Sled stacked high with hay, Gideon guided his team of geldings across the field of snow. Patrocino rode on top, hunched against the cold. Their destination was a wide bend in French Creek, a geological formation marked by a curving line of willows and scattered cottonwood trees. Centuries of erosion had created a vast hollow, the bank enclosing some five hundred acres. This low expanse of terrain was lush with high grass in summer, protected from frigid winds in winter.

When he had first landed in North Park with a handful of cattle, a spare horse, and pack animals lugging panniers that bulged with gear and supplies, Gideon had come to this place. He had found horned buffalo skulls, bleached bones, flint arrowheads, and spear points among the tracks and leavings of large mammals—elk, moose, deer.

He had made camp and considered this spot for a building site until exploration had revealed soggy marshes. Not only were mosquitoes thick, but he had noted evidence of minor flooding. In the spring, he had judged, run-off from melting snow sent swift waters around this bend, cutting away the bank and churning soft soil.

Gideon had moved his camp several times in the following days, drawn at last to a south-facing slope covered with short grass and stubby sage. At the base of the slope he had found a miner's tunnel. Long abandoned, the digging was marked by an outcropping of quartz. White quartz often signaled the presence of gold, but clearly the miner had not found "color" and had given up after tunneling ninety-seven feet into the rocky slope.

Gideon knew the exact distance. For, instead of a failed mine, he had seen a ready-made cellar. After measuring the length, he had dug straight down, opening the back of the tunnel with a vertical shaft, and shored it. Later he had built his house directly over it, fashioning a steep and narrow staircase for access from a trap door in the kitchen. Then he had closed off the tunnel mouth with scrap lumber, and shoveled dirt and rocks over it.

Gideon was proud of this innovation. Rain or shine, hot or cold, all the meat, vegetables, and preserved foods in the root cellar were conveniently available without leaving the house.

During the first two winters he had discovered an important fact about the range land he had selected and formally claimed after registering his brand. Even though winter snows gathered within the curving bank of French Creek, domestic cattle instinctively bunched in the hollow, surviving the worst storms Old Man Winter threw at them. In unfenced range, cattle would naturally turn tail to cold winds, driven to hell-and-gone by blizzards. Water, a salt lick, and regular feedings of hay in this hollow kept them on home range all winter. It meant hard work, but the herd thrived on North Park hay. With eighteen steers to a cattle car at the Buckhorn railhead, Gideon measured his success every autumn by the increasing numbers of critters wearing the Double Circle C brand.

Now, when Gideon and Patrocino reached the hollow, cattle lifted their heads and bawled, following leaders toward the sled. Gideon guided the team in a wide circle while Patrocino forked hay to the snow-covered ground. All the while both men studied the livestock. Weak, sick, or injured beeves would be moved to a fenced pasture near the horse barn in an attempt to restore their health. Relentless sub-zero temperatures marked this winter of '94 as a severe one even by North Park standards, and Gideon was relieved to see every animal in good condition. Many were triple-wintered, big and strong, and would bring top dollar next fall.

Feeding completed, Gideon lugged a sledge-hammer to the frozen creek. He broke ice in several places along a fifty-yard stretch to create water holes.

"*Señor.*"

Gideon turned, looking at Patrocino on the back of the sled. The wrangler pointed to the east.

Bundled in heavy clothing, eight horsebackers moved

slowly through deep snow with breath clouds pluming from the nostrils of their mounts. Even from a distance Gideon knew these men were not neighbors. They rode stoop-shouldered and wore narrow-brimmed hats, some with heavy scarves wrapped over headgear and tied bulkily under their chins—townsmen, not cowhands.

Gideon moved to the sled and dropped the sledge-hammer on the plank bed. Hearing a shout, he turned and lifted a gloved hand in greeting.

"Name's Sam Whitlock," the lead rider called out when he drew closer. He reined up and gestured to the men behind him. "These deputies are riding with me."

Gideon introduced himself and Patrocino. "Welcome to the Double Circle C. How can I help you?"

Whitlock swung down. He was a short man with a full, black beard and mustache, small dark eyes buried in a serious face. He moved swiftly toward Gideon, hand extended.

The other men sat their saddles. All were armed, Gideon noted, with holstered revolvers and repeating rifles in saddle scabbards. Whitlock's was a sharpshooter's weapon, a custom made bolt-action, long-barreled rifle with a telescopic sight. Gideon shook his hand, seeing tiny icicles in the man's mustache now. At close range Whitlock smelled of whiskey—fortification against the cold, Gideon figured.

"I've heard of your brand, Coopersmith," he said, eyeing the livestock. "Good-looking animals."

Sam Whitlock turned and pulled the lapel of his coat open far enough to show a badge. "We're riding out of Laramie."

"How can I help you, Sheriff?" Gideon asked.

"Two jailbirds flew the coop," Whitlock replied. "Busted out of the Laramie pen, robbed a hardware store at knifepoint, and stole horses from Mike's livery barn." When he said Mike, he jerked his thumb at a red-bearded rider wearing a gray wool cap with earflaps.

"The bandits headed south," Whitlock went on. "Crossed your land, likely."

"Haven't seen any riders or sign," Gideon said.

"Any idea where they'd go in North Park?"

Gideon shook his head. "Buckhorn, maybe."

"I mean, friendly ranches in these parts."

"I don't follow you."

"Come now, Coopersmith. You know what I mean. Friendly to longriders."

Gideon shook his head.

"Lending aid and shelter to murderers and thieves is a crime," Whitlock said. He moved a step closer. "You know that much, don't you?"

Gideon felt hot anger well up. "What're you driving at, Sheriff?"

"Answer my question," he said.

"I damn' well take offense to it."

Red-bearded Mike spurred his mount and rode closer. "Sam," he said, as though quieting a bronc'. To Gideon, Mike added: "He doesn't mean anything. . . ."

Whitlock dragged a mittened hand through his mustache and full beard. "The hell I don't. Ranchers live by their own laws. You know that."

"We're worn down from a long, hard ride," Mike explained. "Up north . . . at the state line . . . we lost the trail. We angled down into Colorado on a long shot. Reckon all we can do now is head for home."

"We've come this far," Whitlock countered. "I say we keep riding. Quit now, Mike, and you'll never see your saddle stock again."

The horsebackers exchanged looks, but none ventured an opinion. No one wanted to buck Whitlock, Gideon figured.

"Don't know exactly what you're accusing me of," Gideon said to him, "but I'm law-abiding, like most folks. Tell you what. I've got an empty bunkhouse if you men could use a straw bed and hot meal while you make your plan."

Whitlock's belligerent expression turned sheepish. Along with the other riders, Mike grinned at the mention of a hot meal. "That's mighty decent of you. Mighty."

"Obliged," Whitlock said gruffly. Then he gestured toward Patrocino on the sled. "That Mex yours?"

"I don't own him."

"You know what I mean," he said. "Reason for my question is that the pair we're chasing were heard talking Mex. Maybe he's taking care of his own kind."

Gideon shook his head. "There's just my family and Patrocino here through the winter." He added: "Save a good word for him."

"What do you mean by that?"

"He's the one who will fix your supper," Gideon replied.

Gideon saw Maggs on the verandah, waving. Her urgent gestures told him something had happened. Tossing the lines to Patrocino as soon as the team reached the yard, he jumped off the big sled and jogged through boot-deep snow to the verandah steps.

"Brownie got out."

"Got out," Gideon repeated.

"Annie and Ruth went to the corral and opened the gate," Maggs said. "Brownie bounded out of there as though his tail was on fire. I heard both of them shriek and caught one glimpse of that pony, tail high, galloping over the hill." She took a deep breath. "Right now Annie's in her room crying because I won't let her chase after him."

Gideon turned toward the crest of the rise. "That jughead won't last the night. If the cold doesn't get him, wolves will."

She looked past him. "Gideon, who are those men?"

"Posse from Laramie," he said. "They're staying overnight in the bunkhouse. I'll help Patrocino rustle up grub to feed them."

"Don't you worry about that," Maggs said. "I'll give Patrocino a hand. You get going, so you can be home by dark."

In the barn the first stall was empty, a reminder that Tommy had stolen the best cutting horse of the string. In the next stall Gideon saddled and bridled his most promising horse, a paint mare he'd bought at auction in Denver last year—bought her cheap because no one else wanted her. Indian ponies were believed to be inferior, weak, and difficult to train, and Gideon violated conventional wisdom when he placed the sole bid on this one. She had size, and something about the way she carried herself hinted of intelligence and strength.

As a hit-and-miss judge of horseflesh, he had guessed right. Straight off the range and no doubt tracing her heritage back to the *conquistadores* of Hernan Cortés, this mare moved with a wild and ancient grace. With Patrocino's savvy, she was soon under saddle, learning to work cattle.

Gideon rode out now, the mare tossing her head in eagerness. In the corral, Whitlock and his posse tended their mounts while Patrocino stoked a fire in the bunkhouse and swept out wood chips and shavings as he readied the place for the unexpected guests.

Gideon picked up the trail of small, unshod tracks through deep snow. The colt's stride was short, and in places loose snow had been tossed left and right from twisting leaps, the exuberance of a young animal tasting freedom. What surprised him was the distance that pony put between himself the corral in a short time. Gideon pressed the paint for two hours without catching sight of the runaway.

"What the hell does that jughead think he's doing?" he muttered, knowing at once a young horse will run for the joy of running, and, like a toddler, gives no thought to the return trip.

Gideon was confident he would close the distance sooner or later. The greatest danger lay in headlong galloping through fields of snow. Terrain that looked soft and smooth was actually rough and uneven—and dangerous. The longer he searched, the more he feared the pony was down, leg busted, and reduced to wolf bait somewhere on this high white plain.

Then Gideon cut sign. He reined up. Tracks of shod horses in the snow led from north to south. Not one, but a pair. Two saddle horses had passed through here in the last day or so. The tracks led southward over a hill, coming from the direction of Laramie, the riders either lost or avoiding the wagon road. Gideon rode on, following Brownie's trail through the snow.

After another hour and a half of riding over hills under a darkening sky, he found fresh droppings—a brown mound steaming in the snow. "Brownie," he said aloud, "where are you?"

As if in answer, he heard a soft whicker. Topping the next rise, he came upon the forlorn colt—unhurt, head down, standing spread-legged in knee-deep snow.

"Well, Brownie," he said, loosening his lasso, "are you done for this day?"

Too played-out to duck or even make an effort to side-step the loop that settled over his neck, the colt gazed at his captor.

"Home," Gideon said. "That's where we're going . . . home to a nice, warm barn where you can plan your next escape."

After a late supper Gideon reclined on the cushioned chaise by the fireplace, boots off. Annie came to him. She had already kissed his beard-stubbled cheek and thanked him for rescuing Brownie. Now she snuggled close at his side.

Earlier Gideon had overheard her ask Ruth how she came to have the scar on her face. Ruth had launched into a long tale. In vivid detail she had described a fight in Miner's Delight, and her "damn-fool" decision to intervene when a miner drew a folding pocket knife on a barber wielding a straight-edge razor. One stabbed. The other sliced. Annie listened wide-eyed to the account of a night the saloon floor ran red with blood.

"In a fight," Ruth concluded, "it's the peacemaker who gets hurt. I got cut. Shoulda stayed behind the bar and let 'em kill each other. That's my policy now."

Barroom stabbings were not common topics of discussion in the Coopersmith household, and Annie was clearly fascinated. Gideon listened to his daughter's retelling of the tale. Then she talked about Brownie. Ruth was the one who had opened the corral gate, he learned, when Annie assured him she knew better than to pull a careless stunt like that.

"I know you do, darlin'," Gideon said, seeing her eyes growing heavy with sleep. "I know you do."

Ruth had insisted on cleaning up the kitchen to earn her keep, and, after a great clanging of pans and crashing of dishes mixed with curses, the job was done. The big woman trudged out of the kitchen through the great room with the announcement she was dog-tired, and went to bed. Minutes later, Maggs came tiptoeing out of the master bedroom, as lithe and quiet as Ruth had been heavy-footed and noisy.

The baby was fed, Maggs whispered, and now asleep in the crib next to their bed. She took sleepy-eyed Annie to her room and came back, settling in beside her husband.

"I'll mark this day on the calendar," she said.

"What are you going to call it?"

"The longest day of the winter of Eighteen Ninety-Four," she replied.

Gideon grinned. He asked if the men of the posse had been given enough firewood to last through the night.

Maggs nodded. "Ruth and I fed them. Patrocino took care of everything else." She added: "Gideon, about that posse. . . ."

He had turned his gaze to the warming fire, but, when her voice trailed off, he looked at her. "What about them?"

"Ruth helped me throw together supper for eight hungry men," she explained. "She's a trooper. I don't know how I could have managed without her." She paused, then added: "She confided something to me."

"What?"

"Her son Tommy," she said, "was arrested and jailed by the sheriff up in Laramie."

"That's not news," he said.

"I know," she said. "But Ruth went on to tell me that man with the badge in our bunkhouse, Sam Whitlock, is not the sheriff up there."

Gideon stared at her.

39

"She says the sheriff's portly, a balding man by the name of Tyler . . . Henry Tyler."

"Maybe there's been an election," Gideon said. "Or maybe a new lawman was appointed since she was there."

"Ruth's convinced Sam Whitlock is an impostor."

Gideon shook his head slowly. "Reckon I know what her middle name is."

Maggs looked at him questioningly.

"Trouble," he said. "Ruth Trouble Logan. That's her full name."

Chapter Four

In the morning, after breakfast, the men saddled and bridled their mounts in the corral by the barn. Gideon came out of the house, shouldering into his sheepskin. He heard shrill whistles and shouts as the riders worked the kinks out. Horses bucked and sun-fished, twisting and leaping until they decided to accept their riders and a cold bit on a sub-zero morning.

"Thanks for the hospitality," Mike said when he saw Gideon coming.

A rider, sporting a fresh shave, grinned and added: "I feel almost human after a hot meal and a night's rest in a warm bunkhouse."

Others agreed heartily, and Mike offered to pay for room and board.

Gideon shook his head. "The latchstring's out. You men stop by anytime for some Colorado hospitality."

Mike said: "And next time you ride to Laramie, look me up, so's I can return the favor. You'll find my livery barn on Second Street."

"Fair enough," Gideon said. He paused, his gaze sweeping past Sam Whitlock.

"Speaking of Laramie," Gideon said, "maybe you gents can answer a question that's come up. Any of you know a Wyoming lawman by the name of Henry Tyler?"

They looked at him in silence. Whitlock had not mounted yet, and now he kept the horse between himself and Gideon, head down as he fussed with the saddle cinch.

Mike was the first to speak. "What about him?"

"I hear he's sheriff up there," Gideon went on. "I figured you men knew him."

"We know him," Whitlock said, swinging up into the saddle. His horse bucked once and hopped sideways before calming enough to stand.

"Is he sheriff up there," Gideon asked, "or isn't he?"

"He is," Whitlock allowed.

"I thought you said you were the sheriff," Gideon said.

"You are mistaken," Whitlock said. "I never claimed to be a city marshal or a county sheriff, either one."

"Now, hold on," Gideon said. "You showed a badge yesterday, and you told me these men are deputies."

He acknowledged those facts with a nod.

"Well? What is the truth?"

Whitlock explained: "Any man who gathers a posse of citizens and rides in pursuit of lawbreakers is a sheriff . . . legal and above board."

Gideon stared at him. "By what authority?"

"Posse comitatus," Whitlock said, as though two Latin words explained everything.

"Posse what?" Gideon asked.

"Read your American history, sir," he replied as he urged his horse toward the gate, "and you will learn the right of law-abiding citizens to make arrests is guaranteed by law."

Gideon opened the corral gate. "Sounds to me like you got a notion to take the law into your own hands, Whitlock."

Anger flashed in his face as he reined up. "When you are besieged in your home, Coopersmith, and your family is threatened by armed outlaws, you will gladly exercise your right to gather friends and neighbors to repel the infidels. You'll be called sheriff, and your posse will follow you as long as you are fit to lead them. Justice will be done."

With a long beard black as coal and small dark eyes, the man spoke with the edgy fervor of a mad prophet. He looked like one, too, Gideon figured, watching him kick his horse and canter out of the corral. Mike followed, slowing as he leaned in the saddle toward Gideon.

"I'm just trying to get my two saddle horses back," he said. "That's all I'm trying to do."

Gideon heard a tone of uncertainty in the liveryman's voice. Whitlock must have overheard, for he suddenly reined his horse around.

"You know as well I do, Mike," Whitlock said, "thieves and killers have little to fear from Tyler." He turned to Gideon and added: "A while back a thieving kid sneaked out of custody. He stole food and shoved a lady to the floor at the Wyoming Mercantile . . . took her handbag. Tyler never even bothered to give chase."

Gideon saw the other men nod in agreement with this account. He said nothing, figuring the thieving kid in question was Tommy.

Whitlock concluded: "The law must be upheld to preserve life and liberty. That is our purpose, Mister Coopersmith . . . preserving life and liberty. Nothing less."

"Why didn't Sheriff Tyler deputize you?" Gideon asked. "Seems like he could use a little help."

"The man's a coward," Whitlock replied. "A sniveling coward."

He turned his horse and lifted a hand in a needless signal to the others. Shod hoofs tossed up clods of snow when he kicked his mount and rode away with the other riders following. Mike looked back and raised his hand in a parting gesture.

Gideon waved. He closed the gate and stood there for a long moment, squinting against the sun glare on the crystalline landscape. He had considered telling Whitlock about the tracks he had seen in the snow last evening, but decided against it, just as he had not said anything about Tommy Logan. He disliked Whitlock. Why hand the man an excuse to accuse him of protecting longriders?

Doctoring livestock, never easy or safe for man and beast, was a year-'round job, and as every rancher knew, if it wasn't one thing with critters, it was another. The only known treatment for mange, for example, was to swab down the infested cows with spirit of turpentine. Whenever possible, this task was given to the greenest hand on the place.

Gideon had heard of the Bar T L and a kid there named Robby Streamer, said to be a runaway from Albany, New York. Eager to prove himself to the foreman and the stone-faced cowhands looking on, the kid took to it with diligence. He doctored twelve steers, suffering from the mighty itch, but, when he swabbed turpentine on the thirteenth, the horned critter busted loose, tried to jump a nearby branding fire, and halfway succeeded. The other half caught fire.

Ablaze, the animal staggered away to join the herd. Robby Streamer and the cowhands followed in a mad, boot-pounding pursuit, only to see the fire spread from cow to cow. In a sudden conflagration the thirteen doctored animals—burning, leaping, bellowing—bloated and blew up, scalding the Bar T L men with boiling blood and exploding guts.

True or not, Gideon had heard varied accounts of a youngster's introduction to the cowhand's life—a bunkhouse tale told and retold, bellished and embellished. Details changed with the retelling, but the number thirteen was in every version, and so was the name of the kid and the ranch brand. It was said Bar T L stood for Tough Luck, but no one knew that for certain, any more than the exact location of the storied ranch was known. "Robby Streamer" became a catch phrase in bunkhouses throughout the West, and the greenhorn who did not know its significance was the butt of practical jokes until he caught on.

On the Double Circle C, Gideon faced problems other than mange, most weather-related, from blue northers freezing water holes to summer sun-burned udders. Even a mother's love has its limits, and a sore-teated cow often would not allow her bawling calf near her. Lashing mama to a pair of sturdy posts kept her still—and allowed the youngster to suckle without getting kicked senseless. It was a job and a half, but Gideon had mastered it and was just as glad he had never faced the danger of exploding livestock.

"Hell, I'm leaving."

Overhearing Ruth's words drift out of the kitchen, Gideon recalled a line from Ben Franklin's POOR RICHARD'S ALMANAC: "Fish and visitors stink in three days." Now his jaw clenched when he heard Maggs insist Ruth stay longer.

"Thank you anyways, Missus Coopersmith, but you've been kind to me . . . more kinder than anyone could ask . . . come morning, I'll start back for Columbine . . . and find out if my place of business is still standing. Oh, let me think . . . would you pack a lunch or two for me . . . and tell your mister to have them mules in harness at dawn . . . and ask him, please, if he'd throw in a couple nosebags of feed, too, if you wouldn't mind. Sorry to be a bother."

That night in the darkness of their bedroom, Gideon felt his wife's touch and heard her soft voice: "Ruth tells me you're warm-blooded."

Gideon turned to her, making out her vague shape beside him.

"Well?" Maggs said.

"Well, what?" he asked.

"You know."

"I'll know when you get around to telling me. . . ."

"Sh-h-h-h. You'll awaken Andrew."

Gideon tried to whisper: "When you get around to telling me, I'll know what you're talking about."

"I've heard men do this."

"Do what?"

"Exactly what you're doing."

"Just what am I doing?"

"Sh-h-h-h."

"If you won't let me talk, let me sleep."

"Playing dumb."

"Huh?"

"I've been told men will play dumb . . . every time."

"Huh?"

"Husbands play dumb when they're asked about other women."

"Oh?"

"That's what you're doing . . . playing dumb and muttering questions. You're fishing to find out how much I know. Then you'll know how much you have to admit to. That's it, isn't it?"

"Maggs. . . ."

"Sh-h-h-h."

Irritated, he rolled over. "I can't talk so danged low like you can."

"Ruth told me."

"Told you what?"

"She took you to her bed and held you close. You never said anything about that adventure."

"I never told you her breath would peel paint off a wall,

either . . . ," he said, interrupted by her muffled laughter.

"Don't worry . . . Ruth claims you're a perfect gentleman . . . perfectly dull."

When he turned to her, she slipped into his arms, her supple body quaking with laughter. "I love you, Gideon Coopersmith, my perfectly dull gentleman."

Gideon was not prepared for Annie's reaction to Ruth's departure. With Whitlock's posse gone and now with Ruth waving good bye as she drove the clattering ore wagon along snow-covered wheel ruts leading away from the home place, he was ready for their lives to get back to normal. Surprised to see tears in his daughter's eyes, he asked what was wrong. Annie turned abruptly and strode into the house.

Gideon stared after her. Then he saw Maggs smiling at him.

"Our daughter's arrived at that age," she said, slipping her arm through his as they mounted the steps to the verandah and entered the house.

Gideon closed the door Annie had left standing open. "Age? What age?"

"The age when she needs more than a pony to train," Maggs replied, "and dolls to play with . . . and Mommy and Daddy to talk to."

"What're you driving at?" he asked. "Annie's fixing to run away?"

"Gideon, Annie needs friends."

"Friends."

Maggs nodded. "With no close neighbors, she gets lonely. She wonders what the outside world is like. Think about it, Gideon. She doesn't even know what it's like to sit in a classroom full of boys and girls."

"Well, neither did I when I was a youngster," he said.

"Growing up in the sand hills of Nebraska, I never even saw a stranger until I was seven or eight."

"And look how you turned out," she said.

"Good, huh?"

She smiled. "You turned out to be a man who thinks he can handle every problem by himself."

"All men figure that way, more or less," he said, but saw a look in her eye that told him he had not followed her line of thought.

"Girls are different," Maggs said softly.

Gideon did not pursue the subject. He knew where this discussion was headed.

Maggs's mother, Lucretia Margaret Stearns, was a forceful personality. She had lobbied for the last two years to have Annie enrolled in Mrs. Dowd's Academy, a private school for girls in Denver. Living with her grandmother, as this plan went, Annie would "blossom," and "develop into a fine young modern woman with the proper guidance of a social and academic regimen."

Gideon was not sure what it all meant, but her highfalutin tone never failed to light his fuse. Proper guidance, hell. Annie received guidance. She learned plenty from her parents, book-learning and otherwise. Every return trip from Denver included a box of books as well as art supplies. Maggs was well educated, having attended the University of Colorado in Boulder for two years, and she taught school lessons to Annie.

On most winter evenings the three of them read aloud from the hefty leather-bound volumes of RIDPATH WORLD HISTORY. By lamplight they studied drawings and daguerreotypes of famous people and landmarks—from Marco Polo to Francis Parkman, from the pyramids of ancient Egypt to Big Ben of modern England—and world leaders. Last winter they had studied the history of France. Annie concluded Napoléon was skinny. Her mother corrected her. The famous man was short, barely five feet in height.

"But he must have been skinny," Annie said.

"What makes you think that?" Maggs asked.

"His name."

"His name?"

"Yes . . . 'Boneyparts.' "

Winters were long, and, in addition to studies, Annie was kept busy with chores from cow shed to chicken coop. In summertime she helped her mother prepare meals for the hands. Gideon knew she was learning the value of hard work. And she had always liked ranch life. . . .

His thoughts returned to the look on her face. There was no mistaking the depth of her anguish. Ruth had befriended her and fascinated her. In truth Gideon had been surprised by the gentle side of a rough-hewn woman, and figured in some way Ruth was seeing Annie as her own daughter. Now the separation of even a brief acquaintanceship was painful.

Two days passed, and, while Gideon was not ready to say so aloud, he knew Maggs was right. Annie was changing before his eyes. She had always been a healthy, growing girl. She loved to play, loved to tease, loved to laugh. Now she was changing in ways he did not understand.

He had expected the day of Ruth's departure to be an occasion to mark on the calendar—the day his burden was relieved, the day of repayment of his debt to her, a day to celebrate. During her stay they had been courteous to one another. Courteous and uncomfortable. Other than mealtime, Ruth avoided him.

Gideon figured she craved feminine companionship. She enjoyed the baby. She regaled Annie with tales of violence.

And, Gideon supposed, she was distant to him because she did not want to be questioned about Tommy.

Now Ruth was gone. At last. Her foot-stomping, pan-clanging, cussing presence was gone. Life on the Double Circle C would return to a familiar rhythm. So Gideon had thought. But life never stands still, and, after his conversation with Maggs, he sensed the next crisis coming over the horizon—the decision to send Annie away to school in Denver.

The thought of it alone tightened his gut. But after mulling over limited possibilities, he decided to negotiate.

"I've been thinking," he said, when he and Maggs were alone in the great room the next evening.

Maggs looked up from her needlework. She was working on a cross-stitch panel for a cushion cover, the tiny X-shaped stitches slowly revealing red roses against a maroon background.

"Maybe we ought to send Annie to the schoolhouse in Buckhorn," Gideon went on. "She can board there with Ollie Moore and his wife. They have a spare room, a couple kids, and live close to the school. . . ."

"Gideon, remember? Last year the school closed. The county could not pay a teacher."

"Maybe this year," he said.

"Perhaps," she said without enthusiasm. She placed her sewing in her lap. "Gideon, I've been thinking, too."

Here it comes, he thought. Aloud he said: "Thinking what?"

"Taking her to Denver myself."

He stared at her. "Maggs, I've been pounding my head against the wall over the notion of losing my girl. Now you're telling me I'll lose my wife and son out of the deal, too?"

"You're not losing us," she said. "It's the dead of winter. This is the time of year when you and Patrocino can manage without us. You could even come to Denver for visits while Patrocino handles the chores."

Gideon started to protest, but fell silent when he saw tears well in her eyes.

"Oh, Gideon, I know . . . I know how hard this is. It's not what I want, either. I want things to be the way they always were. . . ." She cleared her throat. "We have to think about what is best for Annie. I have no illusions about my mother. Give her half a chance, and she'll take over Annie's life. But Missus Dowd's Academy is a very good school. Annie will enjoy making new friends. That's why I thought of wintering in Denver while she's enrolled there."

Chapter Five

In dry whispers the sleigh rails sliced through fine, white powder. Gideon held a long-handled whip aloft in one gloved hand, lines in the other. Sharing a lap robe, Annie sat close to him on the tufted seat. She was bundled against the cold with only her eyes and part of her cheeks and nose exposed.

Gideon smiled as they exchanged glances. Ahead Deadman loomed high in the cloudless sky of mid-morning, the granite peak reaching far above timberline at eleven thousand and six hundred feet above sea level. A forested slope below the bare rocky summit, Annie had once observed, resembled a long, green skirt.

In the distance today that skirt was dark green, almost black. Left and right, rolling snowfields stretched out as far as the eye could see. French Creek was marked by willows on either bank, the bare branches orange this time of year. Except for the blue sky and a curving slash of orange color along the frozen creek, the world was black and white, like an illustration from RIDPATH.

And cold. The thermometer registered minus-fourteen degrees this morning when Patrocino helped Gideon ready the sleigh. The rising sun, although bright in a clear sky, raised the mercury barely half an inch to six degrees below zero. How can the sun be so bright, Annie had asked several times, and the air be so cold?

Ham sandwiches, hard-boiled eggs, and oatmeal cookies baked last night were now packed into an empty horseshoe nail keg, along with a sealed quart jar of coffee. Tucked under the seat with paper and firewood were extra socks, mufflers, skates, and paraffin wax from Maggs's canning supplies. Their destination lay due north—a beaver pond at the base of Deadman.

An hour later Annie pointed to a pair of dugouts, side by side, on the southern exposure of a hillside. Carved into the earth like twin burrows, the dugouts had log fronts, each with a hand-hewn door mounted on leather straps for hinges and each with one small window pane.

Those mirror-image dwellings were home sweet home to the Blake brothers. Middle-aged bachelors, Clarence and Charles lived fifty yards apart. They existed separately, not from sibling love/hate as an outsider might guess, but as a way to satisfy the letter of the law—in this case the Homestead Act signed thirty years ago by President Lincoln. After proving up adjoining claims, the brothers would combine holdings, move, and repeat the process to acquire two more claims.

Hailing from Davenport, Iowa, the brothers ran only a few head of cattle. They were farmers at heart. Life began and ended in the soil, they believed, and man was meant to plow and plant even with an early freeze and late thaw at North Park's high elevation. Every summer the brothers rooted out more sage and rabbitbrush, and increased their network of ditches from French Creek. They plowed soil undisturbed since the Ice Age.

Clarence and Charles enjoyed their triumphs in an unforgiving climate. They raised lettuce from seedlings nurtured in south-facing cold frames—a first for North Park. Word spread. The crop was quickly sold to local buyers, Maggs chief among them, along with peas and carrots and potatoes. Fresh lettuce was a luxury in the Coopersmith house. With dandelion greens, spinach, and hard-boiled eggs, Maggs prepared large salads all summer.

The road forked. One branch angled toward Laramie, the other, rarely traveled, headed straight to Deadman.

"There it is, Daddy!"

Gideon peered ahead as the sleigh topped a rise, the frozen pond coming into view through a stand of aspens. With white-barked trunks gnawed by elk, the trees looked delicate and frail. In summer the branches bore small, pale green leaves; in autumn those leaves turned gold and fell to the ground like coins; in winter bare, spindly aspen branches looked as lifeless as wire. But far from lifeless, far from frail, the trees not only survived deadly winters, but grew quickly in summer, sending up new shoots during a short growing season.

The pond was flanked by pointed stumps. In summers, busy beavers chewed the trunks to topple the aspens, and then dragged branches to water's edge. Using mud and sticks, the animals dammed the creek rushing from the slopes of Deadman. Here, in this aspen grove, beavers backed water into an oval pond some seventy yards long and fifty yards across.

A rounded mound of mud and sticks in the middle marked the deepest water. It was the roof of a half-submerged dwelling. With only an underwater entrance, the beaver was safe from predators in that mud lodge. Fattened in autumn, the lord of the pond was prepared to hibernate in winter darkness, sleeping until stirred by sun-warmed water bearing rich scents of spring.

Gideon halted the sleigh at the edge of the pond. He built a fire while Annie waxed skate blades. He had brought a straw broom and swept snow off the ice while the fire crackled on the bank. Near the dam he paused, hearing water gurgle under milky ice like a secretive voice of nature.

He swept his way from the dam to the shoreline, stomping to test thickness. Diamond-hard, the ice did not yield or crack. Thickness was six or eight inches, he estimated, easily strong enough to hold the weight of two skaters.

Two skaters? One skater and one stumblebum, he decided after falling a third time. The surface of the ice was hardly glass-smooth, and, when his skates hit washboard ridges, he swung his arms out for balance, leaned forward, and bent his legs—and went down, hard.

"Oh, Daddy, you're so funny!" Annie called out, her skates hissing as she made a wide sweep around the pond.

He sat on the ice and watched, his gaze caught by an elegance of motion that came naturally to her. Uneven ice did not trip her or send her sprawling. She skated past again, and Gideon remembered previous winters when he and Maggs brought their little girl here for their annual "winter picnic." Not so long ago Annie was an unsteady child, trying her hardest to keep up with Mommy and Daddy. The first time she was able to skate on her own, she stretched her arms out, arched her back, and shouted: "I'm flying! Look at me! I'm flying!"

Time flies, Gideon thought now, *too fast . . . with no turning back.*

Changes in life seemed tumultuous to him: Annie marching into womanhood; Maggs staying at home with the baby, missing their winter picnic for the first time; his own sore backside as a reminder of legs stiffened and bowed by too many years in the saddle. *Hell of a deal,* he thought, *when I can't keep up with my daughter on a pair of danged skates.* He unstrapped them and walked gingerly to the fire. Opening the jar, he poured coffee into a tin cup. The coffee was cold now, and he placed the cup on red hot coals. Soon steaming, he lifted it with gloved fingers, and sipped the brew.

Presently Annie joined him, cheeks flushed. They sat together on a blanket spread on the snow and looked past the blazing fire to the beaver pond. In years past, Annie had been full of questions about the unseen beaver, the fate of trout under the ice, where the white goes when the snow melts, what happens to stars in the daytime, on and on in her questioning chatter. Now she was pensive, quiet. Soon rested, she got up, walked to the pond, and, with a smile at her father, she skated gracefully away.

After their lunch of sandwiches and hard-boiled eggs, Gideon gave her a cookie and a sip of hot coffee.

"Annie, I've been wanting to talk to you."

"I know," she said, making a face as she swallowed coffee.

"You do?"

She nodded seriously and looked into his eyes. "Daddy, will I go away to school? To Denver?"

"How did you know . . . ?"

"Oh, Daddy, I hear you and Mommy talking," she said, taking a bite of the cookie. Around it, she asked: "What's going to happen?"

"Reckon I should be asking you," he said.

"Oh, Daddy."

"Annie, what do you want to happen?"

"Well," she said slowly, "I don't want to leave the ranch. I have to train Brownie. But I want to go to school. I want to learn things. Lots of different things. And friends. I want lots and lots of friends."

Gideon put his arm around her. "You pretty well summed it all up, darlin'."

Their eyes met and held. Then the moment passed.

"Come on, Daddy!" Annie said, scrambling to her feet. "Skate with me. Come on, I'll hold you up!"

"Howdy, Gideon. Howdy, Miss Coopersmith."
"Howdy, Gideon. Howdy, Miss Coopersmith."
Greetings from Clarence Blake were echoed by Charles Blake. Hearing their distant shouts, Gideon had drawn rein and waited while the brothers caught up with the sleigh on foot. Lean and gaunt, they were skinny copies of one another, like mosquitoes wearing several layers of clothes.

Gideon had known the brothers long enough to be aware both men let their graying beards grow long in winter and rarely changed their clothing. Only in a semi-annual bath in French Creek did their long handle underwear come off. So did the beards. The brothers held with those traditionalists who believed too many baths were harmful to human hide, and twice a year they lunged, splashing and blowing, into the frigid creek, naked, shivering and white-skinned like shorn sheep.

Now Clarence reported they had seen campfire smoke from the aspen grove and figured it was the Coopersmiths on their annual winter trek to the pond. When asked about "the missus," Gideon cleared up that mystery for them.

"Say, do ye know anything about, uh . . . uh . . . ?" Clarence started his question, but stammered and ran out of steam.

"Some kinda posse?" Charles said.

Gideon eyed them. "Whitlock and his posse?"

The brothers nodded in unison. Clarence said: "Packing enough uh . . . uh . . . uh. . . ."

Charles finished the thought: "Packing enough firepower to start a war."

"Asked iffen we was uh . . . uh . . . hiding outlaws?"

Charles added: "Or iffen we knew anybody who is?"

"Whitlock said law-breakers gonna be run clean outa North Park," Clarence said.

"Or strung up," Charles said. "Hanged by the neck, he said."

"We told him . . . to uh . . . go to hell. . . ."

Charles cast an apologetic glance at Annie. "We told him to go hunt somewheres else for his outlaws."

Gideon felt Annie lean against him. "Daddy, I'm cold."

"Reckon we'd better move on," he said, putting his arm around her shoulders. He added: "Been a while since you gents paid a visit to the Double Circle C. Hike down our way for supper one of these days. Stay the night."

"Obliged, Gideon. Uh . . . good bye, Miss Coopersmith."

"Good bye, Miss Coopersmith."

Annie giggled as she waved to the brothers. Gideon popped the whip over the horse's back and pulled away. Annie snuggled against him, smiling up at him.

Thoughts of a rogue posse ranging through North Park in search of outlaws turned to another unpleasant prospect—a winter season without his family. Ever since he had completed the house, Gideon had pictured his life on the home place with a wife and children. Now he could not imagine even one day without them.

One more unpleasantry lay ahead, he discovered, when he drove the sleigh into the yard. He saw Patrocino standing in the doorway of the bunkhouse. The wrangler beckoned to Gideon in a swift motion of his arm.

At the corral Gideon tied the lines and sent Annie into the house. With her safely inside, he jogged through the snow to the bunkhouse.

Gideon stepped past Patrocino. A hatless young man sat on the bunk closest to the stove. His hair short-cropped and his clothes soiled, the youngster turned at the sound of boot steps on the plank floor.

Gideon halted. "What are you doing here, Tommy?"

"Mister Coopersmith, Ma told me to make things right with you," Tommy said.

"She did, huh?"

"Yes, sir. Make things right, she told me, or you'd hunt me down and hand me a whipping like you'd whip an egg-sucking dog. Ma said I won't have no peace until I made things right by you."

"You'll have peace," Gideon said, moving closer to the stove, "when you return my property."

"Mister Coopersmith, I'm sure sorry. . . ."

"Did you bring my horse and gear, or didn't you?"

The youthful face was marked by scabbed pimples. Flat cheekbones and heavy features again reminded Gideon of the resemblance between mother and son. Even the cadence of their voices was similar, he noticed now.

"Mister Coopersmith," Tommy said, "that horse, well, it ran off. Flat ran off. Then I sold that unbranded pony. And everything else. Then I done lost all the money to a gambling man. I . . . I'm sorry."

Gideon heard self-pity in the kid's voice, not remorse. "Your mother returned the pony."

"Which she paid to a crooked trader outta her own pocket," Tommy answered with indignation. "She paid twice what I got for him. Now I gotta pay her back, too. Twelve dollars. Where am I gonna get twelve dollars?" He cast a tentative look at Gideon and added: "Reckon I could ride for you."

"No *caballero, Señor* Gideon," Patrocino said, pronouncing the name: "Gee-dee-own."

Gideon nodded agreement: This kid was no cowhand.

He cast a lingering glance at Patrocino, aware the wrangler understood enough English words to follow this conversation.

Truth was, Gideon did not want Tommy on the place. He had given up any notion of recovering his horse and gear. Tommy apparently had some notion of working off the debt. Supervising the kid would take more time than the effort was worth. Worse, Gideon did not trust him. The kid might put up a good front for a while, but after that first paycheck . . . ?

"Ride out," Gideon said, motioning toward the bunkhouse door. "You leave now, and we'll call it even."

Tommy cast a pleading look at him.

Gideon assured: "I won't hunt you down or send the sheriff after you."

"If you don't," Tommy said, "Ma will."

"Sounds like you've got more to fear from your ma than from me."

"Yes, sir, Mister Coopersmith," he said seriously.

Gideon had intended the remark as a joke, but clearly the youngster found no humor in it.

Tommy Logan answered Gideon's questions. He had not hiked or ridden horseback to the ranch house. His mother had driven him from Columbine to Buckhorn in the ore wagon, and taken him north to the French Creek crossing. According to Tommy, she had practically shoved him off the wagon seat and hollered at him.

" 'Go on, go on!' " he said, mimicking her voice. " 'Make things right with Mister Coopersmith! Go on!' "

Funny and sad at once, Gideon thought as he looked at Tommy. This kid was trying to act the part of a man while ruled by his mother. Maybe that was why he had turned to thieving. With money, he had some wild hope of freeing himself from his mother's apron strings. As much as he would have liked to, Gideon could not push Tommy out of the bunkhouse, afoot, into the sub-zero temperatures of winter. He felt annoyed with Ruth for dropping her son in his lap like this. When it came to Tommy, she had a knack for expecting others to solve his problems. At last count Gideon had enough of his own.

After supper he expressed his frustration to Maggs. They discussed the situation, finally deciding to make a family trip to town out of the occasion. Gideon would leave the kid in Buckhorn to catch a ride to Columbine in a freight wagon—if he ever got up the nerve to face his ma.

Two days later Gideon was caught up on the essential ranch chores, caught up enough that he felt he could leave the home place in the care of Patrocino. Departing two hours before dawn, he drove the buckboard along the frozen southbound road with Maggs at his side and a footwarmer at her feet. She wore a full-length, hooded coat of thick wool, and held the baby in blankets under it. Annie and Tommy sat in the wagon bed, sharing quilts—closer together than Gideon liked. *All the more reason,* he thought now, *to get Tommy pointed in a direction away from the Double Circle C.*

Mid-morning brought them in sight of a local landmark, an abandoned log cabin known simply as Dutchman's. Among the bits and pieces of local history Gideon had learned during his years in North Park was the account of a Civil War veteran with a withered leg who arrived in the spring of '66.

Said to hail from Holland, this homesteader was a man who had assured his citizenship by volunteering for service in the 13th New York Heavy Artillery. He still wore the regiment's blue uniform and forage cap, folks said, when he rode into North Park on the back of a big, black-nosed mule. That much was known. That, and the fact he had been crippled by a sharpshooter's bullet on April 3, 1865.

April 3 in that last year of civil war was a day marked on Union calendars. That was the day Captain Loomis L. Langdon raised the stars and stripes over the Confederate capital. Langdon was an instant hero, lauded by newspapers throughout the Northern states. Forgotten was the name of the Dutchman at the captain's side, the private who took a sniper's bullet intended for Loomis. Severely wounded in the upper leg, the man's name went unrecorded then just as it was unknown later when he built his cabin in North Park. Distant neighbors heard a thick accent, and called him Dutchman.

Well-constructed, the cabin still stood straight and square twenty-nine years later. A way station for travelers, it had served as a shelter, a stop-off for anyone who needed it. The cabin stood empty because the Dutchman and other homesteaders failed to prove up. For in this section summer was paradise, winter hell. The lay of the land worked against even the most diligent homesteader, a unique topography channeling northerly winds like death's army. Domestic cattle, unable to withstand the extreme conditions, either galloped south or bunched and froze in their tracks.

Gideon had bought the claim from the state. In the summers he ran cattle in lush grasslands fed by a tributary to French Creek. After fall roundup, he would either sell the fattened cattle, or move those critters into the protected hollow that curved along French Creek on Double Circle C range.

Now the gurgling brook was dead silent, a narrow, wind-polished ribbon of ice. The creek was marked by cotton-woods, standing like skeletal sentinels. Gideon always marveled at the squat cabin in the shadows of those trees. Whatever his name, that Dutchman was a craftsman. Pine logs had been cut, shaved, and fitted together like pieces of a square puzzle. After all these years the hand-cut shakes were still in place on the roof, the ridgepole arrow straight.

The cabin loomed a hundred yards away when Gideon turned the team toward it with both animals plowing through deep snow. A rest stop was planned here. Gideon would build a fire to melt snow for water and to replenish coals in Maggs's foot warmer.

"Oh!" Maggs exclaimed. "Oh, Gideon!"

She was not a woman to shriek without cause, and Gideon abruptly hauled back on the lines, jerking the buckboard to a halt.

He followed her gaze to the stand of cottonwood trees beyond the cabin. A lower limb of the nearest tree bore the corpses of two men, bare feet off the ground, both hanged by the neck.

Chapter Six

"Mommy, what's wrong . . . ?" Annie began, her voice rising in alarm.

"Sh-h-h-h," Maggs said. She looked urgently at Gideon.

He backed the team until the cabin stood between them and the hanged men. Setting the brake, he swung down.

"Stay here," he said. "All of you."

Opening his sheepskin, he drew his Colt. Snow crunched under his boots as he eased around the front of the cabin. He pushed the weathered door open and leaned in, gun at the ready.

The one-room cabin was empty, bare except for an old stove, rusted cans scattered on the dirt floor, a box of firewood. Gideon backed out. He turned, his gaze scanning the ground as he moved to the corpses. With no fresh tracks visible, it was obvious no one had been here since the last snowfall two nights ago. He holstered his gun.

Frozen and lifeless, the corpses were dusted with snow, heads twisted grotesquely away from slipknots. They wore tattered clothes, no boots.

"Never seen a hanged man before."

Startled, Gideon jumped when he heard Tommy's voice close behind him. His first thought was to reprimand the kid for disobeying his instructions. Then came the second thought. "You know them?" he asked.

Tommy shook his head while staring up at the ashen faces. "Ain't never seen them Mexicans before."

Gideon knew Mexican nationals sometimes worked for

the railroad. If this pair had gotten in trouble in Laramie, they could have busted jail and headed for home.

Tommy pointed at the hanged man on their left. "What's that paper?"

Now Gideon saw a folded sheet of paper sticking out of the trouser pocket of the corpse on his left. He stepped closer, pulled it out, and opened it. Seven words were printed in large block letters:

TREE OF JUSTICE
BEARS FRUIT
POSSE COMITATUS

★ ★ ★ ★ ★

Buckhorn was dying at the edges. Empty shacks and abandoned cabins ringed the perimeter of the town site, many leaning away from high winds, others with roofs caved in under the weight of spring and winter snows. Built of cast-off boards and scraps of tar paper, these shelters had been occupied by men employed at the largest crushing mill, the Buckhorn Gold & Silver Mill, as well as smaller operations nearby. Most were gone now, laborers and skilled milling men driven out in '93, when the government announced an end to bimetallism. From that day forward gold would be the standard for U.S. currency. The price of silver nose-dived, and took Buckhorn down with it. Plenty of silver remained in the Columbine district, according to every miner in the land, rich ore ready to be extracted. But at $.57 an ounce it would stay in the ground.

The Denver & Rio Grande Railroad made twice-weekly Denver-Buckhorn runs, instead of the twice-daily runs of more prosperous times. Townspeople tried to hang on, grasping at rumors while drowning in facts. Rumors ranged from new gold strikes in Columbine Gulch to hopeful talk of the federal government reversing its position on silver.

True, new gold deposits had been found. True, the largest mines were not played out. And, true, hard-rock mining was unpredictable. The lure and the fascination of it came from that very unpredictability, a miner's belief that the next charge exploded deep underground could expose a new vein, a deposit of gold that would make the claim holder rich in an instant . . . igniting a new rush to Columbine Gulch . . . bringing a new wave of prosperity to Buckhorn.

Wild rumors and cautious hopes aside, sober folks in the Columbine district found no cause for celebration. They sensed a dark winter of decline, a slow, cold slide into oblivion. Such a fate had befallen dozens of other camps in the Colorado Rockies, camps once raucous and rolling in bullion, now standing empty in ghostly silence. It was happening here, folks said. Yet most held on.

Gideon drove the buckboard past milling operations now cast in the white light of a full moon. The huge, timbered structures were built on a steep hillside, and seemed to cling there. When the mills were up and running, the air was filled with dust, smoke, and noise. Mined ore was delivered by teamsters to the top level of the mill. Gravity did the work of classifying, and steam power crushed the material tumbling downward in chutes. At the bottom, concentrate was loaded into ore wagons for delivery to the railhead. From there it was taken in open rail cars to a Denver refinery where the ore from Columbine Gulch was melted into ingots. Gold bricks were then shipped to mints in Denver or San Francisco, or back East to Fort Knox.

Even though mill owners lived in luxury in mansions as

close as Denver and as distant as Chicago, they served as absentee commissioners, wielding mighty influence in this mountain county—not only with their tax base, but with heavy-handed political clout. Owners and supervisors were Republicans, most employees Democrats. Vastly outnumbered, Republican candidates still won every election.

A mill policy lay behind this numerical miracle. On election day mill bosses gave their employees the day off to vote. This generous offer was followed by an announcement: men who worked the twelve-hour shift on election day would be paid double-time. Nearly every man worked instead of voting, tipping the balance to the minority party.

Sheriff Nate Clarke was a Republican, his politics shaped by the men in power. Hand-picked by mill owners, Clarke had served Buckhorn, Columbine, and the outlying county for a decade. In richer days a red brick building had been constructed, the prominent structure housing the lawman's office and a modern concrete cell block. This "bar hotel" stood directly across the street from the Colorado Hotel, red brick, too, but elegantly styled with curtained bay windows and brass-trimmed turrets at the corners.

Buckhorn benefited from more planning than other Western towns. Most had sprung up willy-nilly, usually close to a water source—the shore of a lake, the bank of a river, a spring. Here D & R G railroad tracks ended at the mouth of the valley narrowing into Columbine Gulch. Crushing mills were built on steep hillsides, and this was where Buckhorn came into being.

The town site was surveyed and designed on a grid of streets. In 1876, the nation's centennial year and the year of statehood for Colorado, brick buildings with native sandstone trim were built on granite foundations in Buckhorn—schools, banks, hotels and rooming houses, liveries, dry goods and groceries, barbershops, drug stores, steepled churches—and on the opposite end of town, saloons, gambling parlors, and dance halls.

Graded streets were lined with residences, clapboard or brick, with gingerbread decoration following the steep angles of roofs designed to shed heavy snows. Front porches sported lattice trim, screened gazeboes graced back yards, and a number of houses used south-facing glass solariums to turn winter sunlight to heat. Buckhorn quickly took on a look of permanence, and held it for nearly twenty years.

Gideon halted the team in front of the four-story Colorado Hotel. He carried the luggage in while Maggs and the baby waited with Annie in the lobby. After warming his numbed hands at the nickel-plated stove, Gideon signed the guest register, accepted a key, and carried luggage upstairs to their second-floor room. When he came back, he found Tommy standing by the stove. An awkward moment passed when their eyes met.

"What am I gonna do now?" Tommy asked.

Gideon glimpsed uncertainty and, perhaps, fear in the boy's expression. *No know-it-all cockiness in him now,* Gideon thought, as he moved to the stove and held his hands out to the heat. At Tommy's age, Gideon had been on his own long enough to look out for himself. Seeing this scrawny kid on the edge of manhood brought a surge of memories. . . .

Reginald James Coopersmith was a poor farmer with pretensions, a "remittance man" who subsisted on false pride and a small inheritance doled out by a solicitor in London. A favored older brother had received the bulk of the Coopersmith fortune, and in lifelong anger over this favoritism "R.J." ruled his family in America with a kingly hand—and a belt.

Two sisters to Gideon had died in infancy—died of

weakness inherited from their mother, according to R.J. Gideon had survived, but bore scars from his childhood. At age fourteen, a year after the suicide of his mother, he had made up his mind. He would no longer endure the cursings and the lashings. He had left in the night, on foot.

Young Gideon had worked in a Red Cliff, Nebraska livery for a drunken employer. Leo Lewis, the liveryman, had blamed him when anything went wrong, from rat-infested feed to a runaway horse, and finally a hay fire. Gideon had saved the animals from the raging flames that night, and, for his trouble, Lewis accused him of knocking over the lantern that had ignited the fire. Worse, Lewis withheld pay.

Gideon had had his fill, and with $8.46 in his pocket he had started out in the general direction of somewhere, still on foot. He had ended up at a cattle ranch across the line in Wyoming, and had hired on. The work had been hard. Summer and autumn hours on a ranch started early and ended late, with cowhands working the shift known as "dark to dark." But he had been treated well by the rancher, even had received a bonus when fattened and healthy cattle were delivered to the stockyards. With that bonus, Gideon had bought his first horse and saddle. He liked the work. He reveled in the pride unique to a man on horseback, but soon had determined the only way to be free was to become his own boss. At age sixteen he had made three promises to himself. He would own a ranch someday, a home place. He would marry and raise a family. And he would be a good husband and father. How to accomplish such lofty goals, he had not been certain. But one private promise loomed above all others: He would not repeat the errors of his father.

A coin here, a paper dollar there, the years had slid past

with Gideon banking money saved from cowhand wages, the thirty-a-month-and-grub and occasional bonuses he had earned on ranches throughout southern Wyoming and northern Colorado. Of the three cowboy vices—wild women, smooth whiskey, and draw poker—he gave up two.

Then it had happened. While accompanying a rancher on a buying trip to Denver, Gideon had tripped over his own spurs when he saw a young woman step out of an elegant, red-wheeled carriage on Larimer Street. He had not been able to take his eyes off her, and in a vivid moment never to leave his memory she had met his gaze. She had turned away only after someone had called her name—twice.

Gideon had thought Maggs was the strangest name he'd ever heard, but more than anything he had wanted her to know his name. From a discreet distance that day he had followed her home to a columned house on Capitol Hill.

He had contrived to meet her again. And again. They had become engaged, much to the ill-concealed horror of Lucretia Margaret Stearns. Finally the day had come when Gideon, a landowner at last, rode into North Park, trailing pack horses and herding a handful of steers. Overlooked by most ranchers, this natural park at high altitude was noted for vast grasslands and deadly winters. Wild animals survived here, but domestic cattle were high-risk at best.

Most folks predicted failure for Gideon, including a hopeful Mrs. Stearns. The notion of her daughter marrying "that shiftless cowboy" was more than she could bear, and she had insisted their continued relationship depended on his success in North Park. Gideon had set out to prove her wrong, had nurtured his herd, and had built a fine house.

Now in the lobby of the Colorado Hotel, Gideon reached into his trouser pocket, pulled out a dollar, and handed the silver coin to Tommy Logan.

"Drive my rig to the Buckhorn livery," he said, "and tell Silas I'll be along in the morning to settle up. This dollar will get you a hot meal and a room for the night. In the morning head for Columbine. Tell your mother we're square. . . ."

"Gideon, hello!"

Before Tommy could protest or even reply, the hotel door was flung open. Nate Clarke stepped into the lamplit shadows of the entryway.

"Sheriff," Gideon greeted him.

"I was making rounds," the lawman said, closing the door, "and saw you in here. What brings you to our fair city this time?"

A dapper man of fifty-two, Clarke took pride in a waxed handlebar mustache, kept his graying hair cut short in the modern style, and usually wore a light brown or gray suit with laced shoes on his feet instead of riding boots—the fashion of city men who rode trolleys, not horses.

Gideon saw Tommy slowly circle the stove, moving behind the lawman. The kid turned, hurried to the door, and let himself out.

"I was just now headed for your office," Gideon answered.

"Reckon you want to find out if we've recovered your belongings," he said. "Well, I may have. . . ."

Gideon shook his head.

"What is it?"

"Nate, I found two corpses on my property . . . both hanged."

"Hanged," Clarke repeated. "You mean . . . lynched?"

Gideon nodded.

"Lynched," he repeated in disbelief. "Where?"

71

"Dutchman's," he replied. "You know where that is?"

"Sure, I do," he said. "In the summer I camp there on my way to fish French Creek." He stared at Gideon and said again: "Lynched?"

Gideon started to tell him about Sam Whitlock and the Wyoming riders, when the sheriff raised a hand.

"Hold on. I'd better get this in writing. Come on over to my office, so I can take your statement."

They crossed the snow-packed street. At this lower altitude the surface of the snow melted during the day and froze at night, leaving a crust of ice that broke underfoot like cheap glass. They crunched through it to the sheriff's office. Inside, Clarke waved Gideon to a captain's chair. After stoking the fire, he sat in a swivel armchair at a massive rolltop desk. Gideon watched him pull a form out of a pigeon hole, open an ink bottle, and take up a pen.

He described the macabre scene at Dutchman's and answered Clarke's questions. He told the lawman about his encounter with the so-called posse, speaking while the point of the ink pen made dry, scratching sounds on the crime report.

"Never heard of this Whitlock joker," the sheriff said, setting the pen down, when Gideon finished. "But I can tell you Tyler's a good man. Like most of us wearing the badge these days, he's overworked." He leaned back in the chair. "Folks claim they want more officers of the law, but, when the tax man comes around, they run and hide."

Gideon handed Clarke the sheet of paper he had pulled from the trouser pocket of one of the dead men. He repeated Whitlock's comments about *posse comitatus*.

"Vigilantes by another name," Clarke said, shaking his head. "Damned if things don't have a way of coming back on a man."

"How so?"

"My dad ran cattle in Montana. Neighbored with Granville Stuart. You've heard of him?"

Gideon nodded. "Every cowhand worth his salt knows the name of Granville Stuart."

"In those days of wide open ranges," Clarke went on, "ranchers lost livestock to rustlers by the dozens. Same as cash draining out of a bank account. They had to put a stop to the thievery, but there was no law, not even a detachment of bluecoat troopers closer than a four, five day ride."

The swivel chair creaked when Clarke leaned forward. He filled a meerschaum pipe from a tin of tobacco bearing the portrait of an Indian wearing a feather headdress. After firing it, he exhaled a cloud of smoke.

"So the ranchers banded together and quietly hanged nineteen men . . . some were outlaws, some homesteaders. All of them were running unbranded cattle, or stock that didn't belong to them. Dad never talked much about that time in his life until he lay on his deathbed and figured to set things straight before he crossed the divide. Of the nineteen, he believed most were guilty of rustling. Most. Some were innocent. He remembered fathers and husbands begging for their lives as nooses were tightened. Terrified cries of men about to die lingered in Dad's dreams, and, even years later, wide awake, he sometimes thought he heard a man cry. 'A damnable curse,' Dad called those voices echoing in his mind."

They sat in silence for a long moment. "Well, those wild days are gone, aren't they, Gideon? We're all cooped up like chickens these days. We climb aboard a train or trolley car whenever we get the urge to go somewhere. Even a backwater town like Buckhorn is connected to the outside world by steam engines and telegraph wires. We live by laws, not by the gun and the rope. No room for vigilantes, not in this modern world." He drew on the pipe and added: "Maybe there never was."

Gideon listened while the sheriff spoke of rounding up a volunteer first thing in the morning, and driving a buckboard to Dutchman's to recover the bodies.

"As far as an investigation goes," Clarke said, "I'll do what I can. You know that, Gideon. But the fact is I don't have the budget or the manpower to make a sweep through North Park. To tell you the level truth, down here we just hope Wyoming and Nebraska outlaws stay on their side of the state line." He set his pipe down. "Speaking of outlaws, weren't you jawing with the Logan kid over there in the hotel lobby?"

Gideon nodded. "He lit out when he saw you."

"With good reason," Clarke said, and stood.

Gideon watched the sheriff cross the room to a locked cabinet.

"Tommy Logan," Clarke said, skeleton keys clinking as he opened the cabinet, "was sneaking into saloons, caging drinks and free food. My night deputy caught up with him in the Crystal Pistol. The kid was making a pest of himself in that gentleman's club by selling guns, ammunition, a pocket knife . . . various items, stolen, likely. My deputy took a pair of saddlebags off him, used his blackjack to take the fight out of him, and ran him out of Buckhorn. Here, take a look."

Clarke pulled saddlebags out of the cabinet and brought them to his desk. Turning them upside down, he dumped out the contents.

"Speak up, if any of these items belong to you. . . ."

"For starters," Gideon interrupted, "those saddlebags are mine." He got to his feet and picked up the wallet that had tumbled out with his Remington hand gun and holster.

"When this was in my pocket," he said as he opened the empty wallet, "cash was inside. That pistol's mine. The cartridge belt and holster, too."

"So it was the Logan kid who robbed you in Columbine," Clarke said.

"Robbed me," Gideon repeated. "Hell, he clubbed me and left me for dead."

Chapter Seven

No salary, no teacher. No teacher, no school session.

That was the second message Gideon brought to Maggs when he returned to the hotel room. The first message darkened her face. Annie and the baby were asleep in the other bed when Maggs spoke in angry disgust: "Tommy Logan's the one who attacked you?"

Gideon nodded.

"And then he had the temerity to ask you for a job!"

Gideon eyed her. "Reckon so. What's temerity?"

"Effrontery," she replied.

"Oh."

"Will Sheriff Clarke arrest him?" she demanded.

"If he can find him," he said. "We checked rooming houses and saloons here in town, but couldn't run him down. We'll ride to Columbine in the morning."

"We?" she repeated. "You and Nate?"

He nodded.

"Gideon," she said, "let the sheriff handle this. It's his job."

"Nate's short-handed," Gideon replied. "Besides, I want to see that kid behind bars."

She pursed her lips as she gazed at him. "You've got that look in your eye, Gideon Coopersmith."

"Maggs," he said, "if we have to stay in Buckhorn until the circuit judge gets here, I'll do it. That kid needs to be put away before he kills someone."

She cast a doubtful look at him, but said nothing. In

their married life, her husband had never been away from the ranch for more than a few days.

Gideon went on to recount the sheriff's tale of woe. The teacher's wage had been eliminated from this year's budget because there was not one dime to pay the salary. Clarke had confided he did not know how much longer the county could pay the salaries of his deputies. In winter two lawmen could manage, barely, but warm weather brought wagons and passenger train coaches loaded with men bound for Buckhorn and Columbine—honest laborers and trouble-makers alike—and Sheriff Nate Clarke would need more manpower to keep the peace.

"You can't squeeze blood out of a turnip," the lawman had conceded to Gideon, "and you can't tax folks who run from you."

In the morning Gideon was up before dawn, long before the hotel dining room opened. Restless and with nothing to do, he bundled up and walked the snow-packed streets of Buckhorn. *Townsfolk start late,* he thought, slapping gloved hands together as the sky over the eastern horizon brightened.

He came back to the hotel for breakfast with Maggs, Annie, and the baby. Taking meals together as a family was their ritual, an important one to Gideon. But despite Annie's chatter and Maggs's good cheer now, he felt frustrated and restless. Afterward, he paced the lobby, waiting for Nate Clarke. A good chunk of the morning had been wasted by the time he saw the sheriff heading for the livery on Front Street.

Gideon grabbed his coat and left the hotel. Crossing Front Street, he fell into step at Clarke's side. At the livery barn they were greeted by Silas, a lanky man with the hands of a blacksmith. Long ago Silas had posted a sign on the door to answer the most frequently asked question of his profession:

Stoppage of Bowels Cure-all—2 qts soft, fresh manure
Add 1 qt boiling water
Strain & give 1 pint as a drench
This will not fail for man or beast
Dose for a man—1 tbspn per hour
Until it acts
It will act.

Clarke saddled his smoke-gray horse while Gideon rented a bay mare. Riding out, they followed the wagon road to Columbine, slow-going in snow that deepened as they drew closer to the Never Summer range. The sun was high in the sky when they came in sight of the mining camp. A few blackened stovepipes spouted smoke, and a number of snow-covered roofs bore icicles like gaudy jewelry. Miner's Delight was one of them, the icicles breaking sunlight into tiny rainbows.

Tying their horses at the rail, they entered the narrow saloon. The place was empty now, ripe with the odors of stale tobacco and spilled liquor. Ruth Logan greeted the two men with a look as cold as outdoors.

Clarke moved to the bar, pulling off his hat and gloves. "Where's Tommy?"

She waved a hand at Gideon. "Ask him, Sheriff."

"I'm asking you," he replied.

"Hell, I dunno where he is ever' minute!" she exclaimed. "Last I seen, he was hiking through knee-deep snow to Mister Coopersmith's ranch house." She turned to Gideon. "What'd you do with my son?"

"Gave him a free ride to Buckhorn," he replied.

"What'd you do that for?" she demanded. "I brung him your way so's he could work off his debt to you."

"Ruth, I don't have time to train a cowhand," Gideon said. "Tommy apologized, and I told him we were square."

"Then what the hell are you doing now?" she said. "Bringing the law down on him?"

Clarke said: "Tommy's wanted for questioning in a crime."

"Crime? What crime?"

"Robbery and assault," he said.

Attempted murder, Gideon thought, jaw clenched.

"Oh, hell," Ruth said in disgust. "Ever' time something happens, you lawdogs chase after my Tommy. Why cain't you just leave him be?"

"When he answers my questions," Clarke said, "I will. Now, where is he?"

"Told you," she said, "I ain't seen him since I brung him to Mister Coopersmith's place." She suddenly turned to Gideon. "Say, how's that daughter of yours . . . Annie? And the baby?"

Gideon acknowledged the question with a nod, but said nothing.

"Your daughter's a beauty," Ruth said, a smile creasing her scarred face. "Yes, sir, a beautiful girl, Annie is. And that baby . . . oh, he's a precious one."

Surprised by her abrupt change of mood, Gideon kept an uncomfortable silence. He heard Sheriff Clarke clear his throat.

"Mind if we take a look in your house, Missus Logan?"

Her smile faded as she snapped: "How in hell can I stop you? Go ahead! Go on! You ain't gonna find him."

She was right about that, and this time she seemed to be

telling the truth about her son. The door to Ruth's cabin was unlocked. They found the place empty, stove ice cold. A single set of shoe tracks in last night's snow led to the outhouse, doubled back, and angled downslope to the back door of Miner's Delight. Ruth was alone.

On their way out of camp Clarke interviewed the one liveryman still in business there, and then questioned half a dozen men passing on the street that twisted between boulders. They all knew Tommy Logan. None had seen him in Columbine in the last day or so.

"I sent a wire to Mama."

Back in their hotel room Gideon received this news from Maggs in silence. He sat on the bed and tugged off boots stiffened by the cold.

"Thought I'd better find out if Missus Dowd's Academy has any openings," she went on, "before we made a decision."

Gideon nodded. He already knew what his end of the decision would be: Maggs and the children would not leave the ranch. Yet at once he knew he could not intervene if she was set on taking Annie to Denver to further her education. He'd just have to grit his teeth and figure out how he could live with it.

He stretched out on the bed, watching Maggs cross-stitch blood-red roses. Idle time did not suit him. With no chores, he felt aimless. He closed his eyes, but could not sleep. He felt a strange sensation, as though the walls of the hotel room were closing in, the space growing smaller with every passing minute.

Gideon sat up and put on his boots. He left Maggs with Annie and the sleeping Andrew, and descended the stairs. From the dining room he took a cup of coffee into the lobby, sat in a wicker armchair, and read newspapers for an hour. Of more than casual interest was an account of the trial and sentencing of Henry R. Rathbone, a man driven mad by his anguish.

Twenty-nine years ago, in 1865, Rathbone was a major in the Union Army. He was betrothed to Clara Harris, the daughter of the senator from New York, Ira Harris. Mrs. Lincoln had invited the couple to share a box seat at Ford's Theater with her and the President. The play, "Our American Cousin," was said to be amusing.

Gideon read the all-too-familiar account: **The assassin had timed his pistol shot with a scene that always brought hearty laughter from the audience. When the well-known actor, John Wilkes Booth, leaped from the box down to the stage, most people believed the stunt was part of the play. They laughed at the limping actor until Rathbone leaned over the railing and shouted: "Stop that man! Stop him!"**

Only then, Gideon read, **in the hushed silence of that horrifying moment in the history of our Republic, did theater-goers hear the screams of Mary Lincoln.**

Rathbone and Clara Harris were wed two years later, but, according to the article, the man never forgave himself for failing to protect the President. Worse, rumors surfaced—none true—of his involvement in the conspiracy to slay Lincoln. His judgment and reason twisted by anguish, Rathbone murdered Clara last month, three decades after the assassination. There was no question of his guilt, the horrible crime of a confused man. Rathbone was declared to be mentally deranged, and the judge committed him to an asylum for life.

Gideon put the paper down and stood. He moved to the frosty window and looked outside. He thought of President

Lincoln, and wondered how the course of history might have changed, if he had lived. Countless lives had been altered by that assassination—even Gideon's.

He had not thought about this for a long time. The homestead claim of R.J. Coopersmith was isolated in the Nebraska sandhills south of Red Cliff, and word of the assassination did not reach them until four weeks later, when a drummer had brought a newspaper. Gideon had been shocked to learn of the President's death, and had wept. R.J. had scoffed and pronounced the assassination to be insignificant. The history of Britain was more important, he had said, searching the newspaper for news from a country he called home.

When R.J. had pressed the issue and announced—"The memory of that Lincoln bloke shall be lost to history."—a father-son debate had flared into an argument. It had earned Gideon a whipping for "disrespect." That was the day he had resolved to leave—even though he had only a vague notion of life beyond the Coopersmith homestead and the bustling town of Red Cliff. His father had often told him that he would fail, if he ever struck out on his own.

Gideon pushed sod-house memories away. If the father's repeated threats of failure had driven the son to succeed later in life, this son would not thank that father for applying the spur. Never. For he knew R.J. wanted only to defeat him.

Crossing the hotel lobby now, Gideon took the stairs two at a time to the second floor. In the room he put on his sheepskin, kissed Maggs, and left the hotel.

Gideon walked the rutted, snow-covered streets of Buckhorn. Other than Front Street, numbered streets ran east and west with avenues named for states running north and south. He figured he might cross trails with Tommy—

or find someone who had seen the kid. But in this cold weather few people were about. After poking his head into saloons—the Crystal Pistol Gentleman's Club, Nugget, Three Aces, Bimetallic—and three livery stables, he decided this hunt was futile.

Tommy must have guessed Sheriff Clarke would show Gideon the saddlebags and their contents, and had fled. Right now he could be hiding in any one of those tumble-down shacks on the edge of town, or he could be holed up in an empty mill building. From that hillside he would see anyone coming in time to slip away.

Gideon walked in that direction. At the far end of Front Street he came to the peak-roofed train station and telegraph office. Inside, he found the waiting area of the dépôt warm and empty. He sat on a high-backed bench there, as uncomfortable as any church pew. Turning sideways, he stretched his legs out and dozed until awakened by the ticket agent.

"What?"

"I said, may I help you, sir?"

Gideon rubbed his eyes. He had slept, but did not feel rested. If boredom could be deadly, he thought, he should be shopping for a casket. "Reckon not," he said. Then he corrected himself and stood, crossing the room to the agent's cage. "When does the next passenger train roll in?"

The agent was a slender man, wearing a dark vest and sleeve garters, thin hair slicked back on his head like a coat of paint. He did not have to consult a timetable to answer that question.

"Tomorrow morning, early."

"What do you mean by early?" Gideon asked.

"Eight," the agent replied.

Gideon scowled. "Eight."

"You'll hear three whistles at eight sharp," the agent went on, "unless the train's been delayed by a snowslide." He explained: "The D and R G runs a freight train with one passenger car up here every Monday and Thursday. She leaves Denver at one in the morning, drops freight cars here in Buckhorn, takes on empties, and pulls out for the return trip by nine in the a.m."

Gideon turned to a tall, narrow window and looked outside at the tracks. The thought crossed his mind that Tommy might hop a train—a sure way to put some distance between himself and the law in Buckhorn.

"Anything else I can help you with?" the agent asked.

"My name's Coopersmith," he said, turning to him, "Gideon Coopersmith. My wife's expecting a telegraph message. Has anything come in for Missus Margaret Stearns Coopersmith?"

The agent checked a board with slips of paper clipped to it, each one folded in half. "No, sir. Nothing here for Coopersmith."

"Obliged," Gideon said. He left the dépôt and walked back to town. Angling across Front Street, he found Sheriff Clarke in his office, feet up, pipe clenched in his teeth, and kept him company for a while. Clarke had found a volunteer, Royal Ellersby, owner of the Crystal Pistol. With a wagon from the livery, they would accompany Gideon to Dutchman's tomorrow.

In their hotel room, Gideon and Maggs played hearts, and then included Annie in games of dominoes. Later, in the hotel dining room, they ate a leisurely meal until the baby fussed. Maggs carried Andrew upstairs while Gideon and Annie split a piece of apple pie. Sipping coffee, Annie made a face.

"Why do you like coffee? It's bitter."

"Bad habit, I reckon."

"Like liquor and tobacco?"

"Something like that, darlin'."

"Are coffee and tobacco your only bad habits?"

He nodded, deciding not to mention the fortifying properties of sour mash whiskey from Tennessee. "Was a time when I chewed. Learned it from cowhands. Men in the saddle would rather chew than roll a smoke and run the risk of setting off a grass fire." He added: "I quit because of your mother."

"She told you to quit?"

"Not exactly."

"What exactly?"

"Your mother said she'd never kiss a man with chaw in his mouth."

"Oh, Daddy," Annie said in mock embarrassment. She paused. "Tommy has a bad habit, doesn't he? He steals."

"He stole from me. I know that much."

"Will he come to the ranch again?"

"Nope," Gideon said.

Time dragged in town, as though some strange, invisible force slowed the clocks. Worse, night was longer than day.

Gideon lay awake in the darkness, the room cold as a crypt. He relieved some of his misery by deciding to abandon his search for Tommy. He'd had enough. Now he just wanted to get back to the ranch—the sooner, the better. Double Circle C was his place in the world. His life's work, from dawn to dark, was to raise his family and keep the ranch going. The more time wasted in a place where eight was early in the morning, the more behind he got.

The day finally dawned, but his confinement to this town was not over. He would have to wait here until Maggs received an answer to her wire. *Might as well keep an eye out for Tommy,* he thought, *as long as I'm stuck here like a danged cow in a frozen bog.* To keep himself occupied, he hiked to the train station. The high-ceilinged building was empty, doors locked. He returned to the hotel and was the first customer for breakfast. Then he went back to the dépôt, open now.

Three shrill whistles sounded at eight. The ground shook with the great locomotive's arrival, white steam hissed, and black smoke belched into the air. Gideon stood in the covered dépôt entry, hunched against the cold, watching for Tommy.

Brass bell ringing, the steam engine passed him, slowing to a noisy halt at the water tower beyond the dépôt. The conductor swung down from the passenger coach. Gideon saw him place a step on the ground for his sole passenger, a city man wearing a derby. The gent buttoned his navy topcoat over a slate-gray vested suit and a white shirt with a starched collar. His black shoes were polished to a gleam. Not only well-dressed, the heavy artillery slung over this man's shoulder caught Gideon's attention—a Sharps .50 caliber rifle.

The city man came off the step plate and gazed upward at the mountain peaks. He breathed deeply, inhaling the frigid air of morning, and exhaled a white cloud as he moved away from the passenger coach. In addition to the large-bore rifle, he lugged two outsize carpetbags, one in each hand. Leaving the dépôt, the man strode purposefully toward town.

If this gent had landed in Buckhorn in the autumn, Gideon would have spotted him for a hunter. A city man arriving to meet a guide was not uncommon here. But the season was winter, too late to go after big game.

With the water tank topped off and the gondola loaded with coal, the locomotive dropped loaded cars and then hooked up empty rolling stock, leaving on schedule, when the conductor swung up and signaled the engineer. Gideon had poked his head into empty boxcars on a siding as well as checking the open cars. Now he watched carefully while the departing locomotive hissed steam and sent up a column of smoke, cinders drifting down like black snowflakes. The train built speed, and the engineer let out one long whistle as the caboose rounded a bend.

No sign of Tommy. Convinced this search was as futile as the hunt yesterday, Gideon turned away and crossed the platform. When the ticket agent spotted him, he beckoned. Gideon went to the outside window of his cage.

"Message arrived for your missus," the agent said. He added: "The lady will have to sign for it."

Gideon thanked him. Hurrying along Front Street to the hotel, he heard his name called. He halted on the boardwalk near the hotel entrance. Across the street Deputy Oliver Moore leaned out of the sheriff's office.

"Got a gentleman here!" Moore shouted. "Asking after your wife!"

Loud of voice, Ollie Moore was the perfect foil to the soft-spoken Nate Clarke. Clarke was tall and lean, handy with a sidearm; Moore was heavy, slow moving, and so nearsighted that he squinted. The deputy was more likely to stop a bar fight with the weighted sap he carried in his hip pocket than the short-barreled .38 pistol holstered at his ample waist. In the close quarters of a crowded saloon, a swift blow from that leather blackjack generally crossed a trouble-maker's eyes and dropped him, no matter how big and strong he was.

Gideon hesitated. He was in a rush. He figured the "gentleman" was a drummer intent on selling kitchenware and home goods to every rancher and homesteader in northern Colorado. But then in the doorway behind Moore he spotted the man who had arrived on the train, the Sharps still slung over his shoulder. Edging past Moore, he raised a hand to the brim of his derby.

Curious, Gideon stepped off the boardwalk and crossed the snowy street.

"Mister Coopersmith?" the gentleman asked.

"Guilty."

"Pleased to meet you, sir," he said with a smile, "very pleased, indeed. My name is Mills Pillow."

Chapter Eight

Clean-shaven, chubby, and his round cheeks reddened from the cold, Mills Pillow looked almost cherubic. Yet something in this man's gaze—and his firm handshake—hinted of more steel than innocence. Gideon trusted first impressions, and he recognized a quality of determination the moment they met on the boardwalk in front of the sheriff's office.

A wagon approached as they crossed Front Street, and they stepped aside to let it pass.

"Sir, I was impressed by your wife's letter," Pillow said when Gideon led the way to the entrance of the Colorado Hotel. "Very impressed, indeed. She makes a keen argument in favor of re-naming Deadman."

"Reckon Maggs will be glad to hear your opinion," Gideon said when they reached the door. He well remembered her reaction to the terse letter from this government cartographer. The wording implied "Deadman" was stamped on the official U.S. map permanently, like a brand in a steer's hide.

Pillow added now: "When I learned others in the government had received letters from Missus Coopersmith on the subject of re-naming Deadman, I conducted some research. North Park caught my interest, so much so that I decided to come West and see it for myself . . . and see that mountain named by Monsieur LeDuc fifty years ago."

Gideon opened the hotel door and followed Pillow into the lobby.

"I must emphasize I am not here in any official capacity,"

he said. "I have traveled to Colorado on my own time and at my own expense, eager to leave my office duties behind." He paused. "As a private citizen, though, I can tell you I am sympathetic to Missus Coopersmith's point of view."

Gideon closed the door and gestured to a wicker armchair close to the stove. "If you'll wait here, Mister Pillow, I'll take your message to Maggs. Official or unofficial, I'm sure she'll want to see you."

A quizzical look crossed the man's round face. "Maggs? Is that how you refer to Missus Coopersmith?"

"She's Maggs to her friends," Gideon replied with a grin. "Short for Margaret."

Mills Pillow thought about that. "Perhaps we shall be friends one day, but for now, with your permission, I shall address her as Missus Coopersmith."

Upstairs Gideon saw surprise light Maggs's face when he told her who was waiting for her in the hotel lobby.

"Mills Pillow!" she exclaimed. "Mills Pillow!"

"Who's he?" Annie said.

"Your letter impressed him so much," Gideon went on, "that he decided to come out here and look at that old mountain himself."

"Who *is* he?" Annie repeated, louder.

Maggs was not easily flustered, but now her cheeks were flushed. She spoke in a hushed voice as though she could be overheard.

"Oh, Gideon, what . . . what shall I say to him? And why is he here in the winter?"

"Says he's on holiday," Gideon said.

"Holiday," she repeated, mystified.

"Who . . . who . . . *who?*" Annie said like a sing-songing owl. She would not be ignored a moment longer.

"The man's a cartographer, darlin'," Gideon told her. To

Maggs he added: "He's a citified dandy in a derby hat all the way from Washington, D.C., but something about him tells me he's tougher than a square nail."

"Oh, my," Maggs whispered. "I never expected anyone from Washington, D.C. to come all the way out here. . . ."

"There's more," Gideon said, and told her the telegrapher had a message with her name on it.

"Oh, that's Mama!" she said. "Gideon, I have to get her message. But that man's waiting for me. . . ."

"What's a car-tog-raffer?" Annie asked.

Gideon turned to his daughter. "We'll go downstairs and ask him." He said to Maggs: "Annie and I will baby-sit and entertain Mister Pillow while you hike to the dépôt."

Maggs drew a deep breath. "All right."

In the lobby Gideon introduced his wife and daughter and sleeping son to Mills Pillow. The man shook their hands and cast an admiring look at Andrew as Maggs passed the blanket-wrapped baby to Gideon.

"Maggs is headed for the telegraph office to fetch a message we've all been waiting for," Gideon explained. "If you don't mind, we'll wait for her here."

"I do not mind at all, sir," Pillow replied.

"Besides," Gideon said as Maggs departed, "my daughter has a question for you."

Annie asked immediately: "What's a car-tog-raffer?"

Pillow smiled at her and posed a serious question: "How much Latin do you know, young lady?"

At first bold in the presence of a stranger, Annie shrugged. She shyly took a step closer to her father.

"How much Greek?"

Annie shrugged again and leaned against Gideon's leg.

"Well, in Latin," Pillow explained, "*carta* means chart or map. In the Greek language *graphia* means writing or drawing. Put those words together, Miss Coopersmith, and you will know the work I do for a living."

"Map drawing!" Annie said.

"Correct," he said.

Annie asked: "Mister Pillow, did you come all the way from Washington, D.C. to draw a map of our ranch?"

"No," he said, "but, someday, I may include your ranch on a newly revised map of North Park. The region interests me. Surrounded by mountains, this park is a significant geographic and geological feature . . . one that is unknown to most outsiders." He added: "And did you know, Annie, long before Europeans set foot here, Arapaho and Ute tribes camped in North Park. French trappers came much later, and took it upon themselves to name that peak."

"My mother wants Deadman changed on your map," Annie said.

"I am aware of her wish," he replied. "I wonder if any Indian tribes had a name for that mountain."

"I don't know," Annie said.

"I hope to find out," Pillow said. "Do you know, Mister Coopersmith?"

Gideon shook his head. "The Arapahoes got pushed onto the Wind River reservation in Wyoming about twenty-five years ago."

"Wind River," Pillow repeated. "What a wonderful name!"

"Utes were forcibly moved to the southwestern part of the state," Gideon went on. He added: "I sometimes find teepee rings and arrowheads left by their ancestors."

"Ancestors, indeed," Pillow said. "Indigenous tribes traveled this land for centuries before our forebears sailed to North America in their rickety ships."

"You mean our land, too?" Annie asked.

"Yes," he replied. "Not so long ago, it was their land."

Annie paused as she thought about that. Then she asked: "What's indigenous?"

"The Latin root word is native," he replied. "It means native peoples." His hand came to rest under his chin as he looked at her. "You possess great curiosity, Annie. That's a fine quality. A fine quality, indeed."

Annie ducked her head with another attack of shyness. She looked up at her father. "Will I get to study Latin and Greek in the Dowd Academy?"

"Reckon so," he replied.

"What is this academy?" Pillow asked.

"A private school in Denver," Gideon explained. "We're thinking of sending Annie there."

"I see," Pillow said seriously, his gaze moving from father to daughter. "So you will be leaving home?"

Annie nodded.

"And I suppose that telegraph message to your mother has some bearing on this, doesn't it?"

"Yes, sir."

"I can see it in your faces," Pillow said. "This is not an easy decision, is it?"

Annie shook her head again.

Gideon was surprised by this insight from a stranger. Pillow had quickly sensed the gravity of a family decision looming large in their lives.

Minutes later, Maggs entered the lobby, a stricken look on her face. Gideon stood, Andrew in his arms. At first he thought her pained expression meant the school would not accept Annie. He was wrong.

"Mama reserved an opening to enroll Annie in the Dowd Academy," Maggs said, her voice tight. "She wants us to come to Denver for the remainder of the winter term. Right away."

Gideon realized the look on his wife's face meant the opposite of what he had thought. The day was at hand. *The* day. Lucretia Stearns awaited their answer. Now Gideon understood. With the telegraphed message clutched in her hand, the reality of it hit Maggs. Hit her hard.

When Mills Pillow accepted Gideon's invitation to visit the Double Circle C, he asked for directions to the nearest livery barn in Buckhorn.

"I'm headed that way," Gideon said, "to fetch my team and wagon."

"Excellent. I shall walk with you, then."

They made their way along the boardwalk, passing the First National Bank, Will Highfield's Hardware & Mining Supply, Johnny Ferree's New & Used Guns, and Mrs. Baity's Millinery, the latter boarded up due to a lack of business. As they walked, Gideon remembered Pillow's plan to see Deadman for himself.

"Something I'd better tell you, Mister Pillow."

"Yes?"

"My ranch is twenty miles from nowhere. In wintertime, if a saddle horse goes down, the rider will have to hike to safety . . . or he'll die from exposure."

"Sir, I'm no horseman."

Gideon slowed his pace, eyeing the city man.

"I use donkeys," he said, and added: "Two, as a precaution in case one is injured or runs away."

"Donkeys?"

"Why, yes," Pillow said. "Buckhorn's a mining supply town, isn't it?"

Gideon nodded.

"And the local liveryman has donkeys for hire?"

"Yeah," Gideon allowed. "Silas does, up the street here."

"Yet you seem a bit taken aback by my plan."

"Figured you'd rent a saddle horse. I've never heard of anybody riding a donkey in these parts."

"Oh, I won't ride the beasts. I'll lead them."

"On foot?" Gideon asked.

"Yes, of course," he said, and chuckled with amusement at their misunderstanding. "Perhaps I should explain, Mister Coopersmith. . . ."

"Call me Gideon," he broke in. "Folks are informal in these parts."

"Yes, of course. Gideon. As I was saying, Gideon, I've traveled a bit, here and abroad. In the last decade I have explored rugged terrain . . . on foot . . . from the Yukon to Yucatán, from the Adirondacks to the Alps, from Kilamanjaro to Katmandu."

Gideon's eyes narrowed. "Cat did what?"

"Katmandu," Pillow repeated. "It's the capital of Nepal. In the shadow of the mighty Himalayas, the city was built in the Seven Hundreds. It's home to the Gurkhas."

Gideon repeated: "Gurkhas?"

"They belong to the Rajput ethnic group," he said. "It's an ancient culture, pre-dating Christianity by centuries. Wonderful people, the Gurkhas. Simply wonderful."

They walked on to the livery barn. Gideon made a mental note to look up Gurkha and Nepal in the RIDPATH volumes. In truth, he had never been around a man as well traveled and knowledgeable as Mills Pillow. Aside from Maggs's schooling, he now had an inkling of the benefits of a formal education for Annie.

From Buckhorn north to Dutchman's, Gideon drove the ranch wagon with Maggs and the baby at his side. Behind him in the wagon box, Annie talked nonstop to Mills Pillow until her mother suggested she be quiet for one mile.

"It's all right, Missus Coopersmith," he said, smiling against the cold. "Your daughter has a keen mind. I thoroughly enjoy hearing what she has to say."

Gideon glanced back at them sitting under quilts. They faced one another as Pillow reclined against his carpetbags with the big Sharps at his side. Lead ropes to a pair of long-eared, gray donkeys were lashed to the tailgate. The animals followed meekly. Sure-footed donkeys were accustomed to steep terrain as they lugged food, cooking gear, picks, shovels, sluice boxes, and all manner of mining equipment through the mountains for prospectors in search of their fortunes. Following a wagon across a snowy flat was easy duty.

Gideon felt numbed, not so much from the cold, but from the enormity of the decision they had made in Buckhorn. In the privacy of their room in the Colorado Hotel, the three of them had talked it out. Annie had expressed her divided feelings. While she did not want to leave the ranch and be away from her father and her pony and her room, she did want an education—and friends her own age.

In the days since skating on French Creek, Gideon had given much thought to their dilemma. In time, he knew what he must do, difficult as it was. He had seen a flicker of surprise cross Maggs's face when he had spoken in favor of the Dowd Academy. Then she had stepped into his embrace, crying as he held her.

"Mama, don't cry," Annie had said. "This is a sad time and a happy time, but happy is bigger."

The decision made, their answer had been sent by wire. Next came travel plans. Gideon would take his family to Denver. To Lucretia.

Gideon turned in the wagon seat. Half a mile behind

them came a buckboard driven by Nate Clarke. Roy Ellersby occupied the seat beside Clarke. The saloonman wore a drooping mustache that gave him a sorrowful expression. Perhaps he was sorrowful. Closed mines had forced the sale of his house at auction, and now he lived in a back room of the Crystal Pistol.

Early in the afternoon they drew in sight of the lone cabin. Gideon tugged at his hat brim, squinting against the white expanse. In the distance he made out the two dark shapes suspended from a limb of the nearest cottonwood tree.

Gideon swung the wagon in a wide curve to the far side of the cabin, blocking view of the ghastly sight. He set the brake. Telling his daughter to stay in the wagon for now, he jumped down. Mills Pillow climbed out and followed him to the hanging tree.

Gideon saw tracks in the snow—too large to be coyotes. Wolves had discovered food and marked their territory here. The predators had shredded trouser legs in their clawing and gnawing, exposing the white bones in the feet and lower legs of the hanged men.

Gideon had advised the city man what to expect here, and wondered how he would react to the actual sight of death in a cruel form. Pillow stood at his side now, studying the ashen corpses mutilated by wolves until the sounds of the approaching buckboard drew his attention away from them.

Nate Clarke arrived, uttering a curse, when he saw the wolves' footprints and patches of yellow snow. "Rest in peace, huh, gentlemen?"

The lawman swore again, and pointed to small, round holes in the upper body of each corpse. "Wasn't enough to string up these men. No, the hangman shot them, too, and left the poor devils for the wolves."

Clarke turned the wagon and backed the team up until the tailgate was close to the corpses. He set the brake and stepped over the seat into the wagon box, followed by Roy Ellersby. Unbuttoning his heavy coat, Clarke pulled a folding knife out of his trouser pocket. "Give me a hand," he said, opening the blade.

Gideon and Mills Pillow steadied one frozen body while Clarke cut the rope. The sheriff and barkeep helped them lower the corpse to the wagon bed. It came to rest with a heavy *clunk,* head still twisted to one side. After the second corpse was lowered into the wagon, Clarke covered them with a tarp.

In the cabin a fire in the old stove warmed them while snow melted in a rusted bucket for the horses and donkeys. After saying their good byes, they parted, Clarke swinging south to Buckhorn while Gideon drove north toward the Double Circle C. Iron-tired wagon wheels made soft sounds as the wagon rolled through the deep snow. For several miles a silence settled over them as though ghosts of the dead had joined them. The quietude was broken by Annie.

"Donkeys have big, friendly eyes."

Pillow nodded in agreement as he looked at the pair walking along behind the wagon. "The beasts are known for being patient. Some people mistake patience for stupidity. I believe them to be intelligent."

Annie asked: "What will you do with those donkeys, Mister Pillow . . . ride them?"

"These beasts of burden will carry my food and gear, Annie." He added with a quick smile: "Your father informed me that men do not ride donkeys in this part of the world."

"Where in the world do folks ride them?" Annie asked.

Pillow thought about that. "Well, according to Scripture, on the first Palm Sunday, Jesus declined the horse in favor of a donkey. The multitudes spread their garments and palm leaves before the donkey on the road to Jerusalem." He pointed to one of the donkeys following the wagon. "See that black line running down the middle of his back?"

Annie raised up. She pointed to his withers. "Look! Another black line crosses the shoulders."

"And so goes the story," Pillow said.

"What story?" she asked.

"The story that Jesus rewarded the humble donkey with the image of a cross," Pillow said.

Annie's eyes widened.

"Those long ears have a long history," Pillow went on. "The Old Testament tells us the father of the Hebrew people, Abraham, journeyed from place to place on the back of a donkey. So did his son, Isaac. And his grandson, Jacob, rode a donkey, too." He paused. "The Bible says Jacob's twelve sons were progenitors of the twelve tribes of Israel. Some people nowadays contend the American Indians are the lost tribe of Israel. For myself, I don't believe that's true."

"Why?" Annie asked.

"Spaniards brought donkeys to the Americas in the Fifteen Hundreds," he replied. "If Indians were a lost tribe from across the sea, wouldn't they have their own donkeys?"

"Daddy, I've learned a lot from Mister Pillow!"

Gideon cast a smile at her. He had learned a great deal, too, but he was starting to wonder if the man ever had a short answer to a question.

Maggs said over her shoulder: "I wish the county would hire you to teach school, Mister Pillow."

Pillow laughed. "I'm no teacher. I'm a wanderer at heart,

99

a wanderer chained to a desk in Washington."

"Real chains?" Annie asked.

"Invisible chains," he replied with a smile. "The worst kind."

"What do you mean?" she asked.

"I work for the government until I can bear it no longer," Pillow explained. "Who can look at maps all day without being overcome by an urge to travel? Maps lead me out of Foggy Bottom, Annie, and rescue me from my workaday routine."

Annie gazed at him, trying to absorb the meaning of his words.

Pillow continued: "I'm a bit like the narrator of that book by Herman Melville, MOBY DICK. Have you read it? No? Well, someday you will. The main character is named Ishmael, the wanderer. Remember Abraham rode a donkey? Well, in the Biblical account, Ishmael was cast out after the birth of Isaac . . . and he is said to be the father of Arabs.

"Anyway, the Ishmael in MOBY DICK is a man who is sometimes overcome by wanderlust. When a foul mood settles over him, his appetite for trouble can only be satiated by a sea journey. Whenever he's upset and feels like knocking the hats off passersby, he knows he must travel. He says . . . 'It is a way I have of driving off the spleen, and regulating the circulation.' "

"Satiated," Annie repeated slowly. "What does that mean?"

Gideon built a fire in the great room, fanned it with bellows, and then carried a scoop of hot coals to the stove in the kitchen. That chore done, he left Maggs to tend the cooking fire and prepare supper.

After carrying in the luggage, he walked out of the house

with a spring in his step. In the barn he checked the horses, walking the length of the runway with a lantern in hand. The donkeys occupied two of the stalls now.

Gideon found the paint and his string of saddle horses currycombed and tended. Grain and water and everything else were in order. He'd expected as much from Patrocino, but he was relieved to see for himself that all was well.

In the morning they would load the sled with hay. Gideon wanted to see his herd and make a count of healthy critters. Unlike Mills Pillow who craved escape from the routines of his life in the city, Gideon was eager for his daily chores on the Double Circle C. Wanderlust held no appeal for him. He had wandered in his youth as he moved from ranch to ranch, from one cowboying job to another, carrying everything he owned in a canvas war bag behind his saddle.

To Gideon, wandering meant homelessness. Failure. Poverty. The home place had fulfilled his life's dream, and daily chores reaffirmed the security of his family. He craved those endless tasks, now more than ever as he faced a lonely winter.

Chapter Nine

"A beautiful sight, alpenglow," Mills Pillow said. "The poet calls it 'the sweet, delicate caress of Mother Nature's gaze, at once endless and fleeting.'"

The early morning sun cast a pink glow on the slopes of Deadman, the peak framed in white frost on kitchen window panes. The moment Mills Pillow had set foot out of the spare bedroom this morning, Maggs called to him. Gideon joined them in the kitchen as Pillow peered out the window.

"Missus Coopersmith, you did not exaggerate in your written description of this majestic sight. Not one iota, to borrow a letter from the Greek alphabet. This is a stunning example of Mother Nature's artistry . . . stunning, indeed." He turned to her. "I agree completely. That mountain deserves better than Deadman."

Over breakfast Pillow cautioned Maggs that an act of Congress was required to change the name of the peak—a difficult task under the best of circumstances.

"But to this day my father's reputation is well known to influential Congressmen," she said.

"Yes," he agreed, "the memory of Ezra Allan Stearns is respected in all quarters. That fact certainly works in your favor. I won't deny that. Not for a moment."

Gideon smiled at Maggs. She was energized by the prospect of attaining her goal at last, and now she had an ally in Mills Pillow—officially or not.

After breakfast Pillow bundled up in the heaviest long

underwear and the warmest outer clothing he had brought in his carpetbags. The sled was ready. Following Gideon to the barn, Pillow grabbed a pitchfork and climbed aboard with Patrocino for the ride to the French Creek hollow.

With cattle bawling, the city man observed the proper technique for pitching hay. Then he attacked this chore with enthusiasm that made up for his lack of experience. North Park hay was heavy and thick, and Pillow wondered aloud if cold temperatures and a short growing season at this high altitude made the species heartier than its counterpart back East.

"Scientists who study nature believe the toughest of the species not only survive," he said, "but propagate for the purpose of domination . . . plants and animals alike. Humans, too, some say. The weak die off, making room for the strongest and smartest. Do you share that opinion, Gideon?"

Gideon thought about that. "I've known some highly stupid men in my time."

Mills Pillow grinned. He caught Gideon by surprise when he turned to Patrocino and spoke to him in Spanish, gesturing to the hay to make his point about survival of the fittest. After Patrocino replied, Pillow turned to Gideon and asked: "Do you understand Spanish?"

He shook his head.

"You may be interested to know your wrangler agrees with you. He says stupid *hombres* sometimes come out on top."

On the return trip to the home place, Gideon said: "I didn't know you talked Patrocino's language."

"I know enough Spanish to get by," Pillow said. "French and Italian, too. Anyone who goes through the agony of memorizing that dead language . . . Latin . . . at an early age can pick up those languages rather easily. The French, Spaniards, and Italians are more alike than they'll ever admit."

Gideon glanced back at Patrocino on the rear of the horse-drawn sled. "What were you talking to him about?"

"I asked him where he's from."

"What'd he say?"

"Mexico," Pillow replied. "He says he made a trek, due north, on foot. Says he wove sandals from yucca leaves along the way. Does yucca grow around here?"

Gideon shook his head. "Not this far north."

"Well, that explains it," Pillow said.

"Explains what?"

"Patrocino says he walked until his sandals wore out," Pillow said. "He looked ahead and saw your ranch house on the horizon."

Gideon remembered Patrocino's first purchase in Buckhorn had been a pair of boots. He had caressed the leather as though admiring treasure.

"I don't know why he left his home," Pillow said, "but Patrocino says you're a good *padrone*. *Muy bueno*."

"What's that mean?"

"It's the Spanish equivalent of strawboss. He says you do not merely give orders, but you work hard, too."

In late afternoon unannounced guests arrived—the Blake brothers. Body odor and body lice came with them, and Maggs reminded Gideon that she did not want Annie or the baby close to them.

Clarence and Charles were not offended when Gideon told them dinner would be served in the bunkhouse. They assumed their proper places as guests on the Double Circle C were the bunkhouse and the barn. Their habit, when they came calling, was to first tour the barn and admire the

Double Circle C saddle stock. Then they retired to the bunkhouse to smoke Gideon's Prince Albert tobacco in their corncob pipes and rummage through the *Police Gazette*s and other racy publications left behind by cowhands last fall.

Now, after asking where the asses came from and why Gideon's best cutting horse was not in his stall, the brothers wondered aloud if the paint mare was good for anything other than processing grain. Clarence and Charles were happy to eat with Patrocino, waiting with great anticipation for Maggs to bring the two-layer, lemon-iced cake she always prepared for them, along with a jug of sweetened coffee. These were rare treats, gifts to be amply repaid in the summer with fresh lettuce and garden vegetables.

During this visit Clarence and Charles were soon engaged in conversation with Mills Pillow. He was clearly interested in the brothers and their account of trapping a three-legged coyote last summer. The creature had chewed a paw off to free himself from a leg-hold trap. Trapped again in the autumn, he chewed off another leg. The third time was a charm. The Blake brothers found him before he could chew off leg number three, and they let Mister Coyote hobble off into the pines instead of killing him for his pelt.

"Not . . . uh . . . uh . . . not the smartest coyote," Clarence said, "but . . . but. . . ."

Charles finished for him: "But danged iffen he ain't the almighty toughest!"

"Uh . . . uh, luckiest, too," Clarence said, for once getting in the last word.

"Lucky, yes," Pillow said thoughtfully, "when one considers skinning the creature was the alternative."

Those three ate together in the bunkhouse with Patrocino while Gideon had supper with Maggs and Annie in the dining room of the house. Even though oil lamps burned late in the bunkhouse that night, Clarence and Charles awakened at first light. With the remains of the cake wrapped in newspaper, they shouted good bye to anyone in earshot, and hiked back to their dugouts.

That morning Gideon winced when their shouting stirred the donkeys. The critters brayed from the barn, a jarring, discordant noise. Over breakfast Mills Pillow cited a legend claiming the donkey's soul was expressed in braying.

Gideon doubted that story. Watching the beasts swell up and bray was a disturbing sight. The donkeys raised their heads skyward, jaws opening as nostrils flared, and out came a horrible wheezing and rasping *hee-haw, hee-haw, hee-haw,* pained and strained cries that tore up their innards for all Gideon knew. No worse for wear, though, the donkeys did it all over again the next morning, like roosters performing their duty.

For Maggs and Annie, packing clothes and personal items occupied the day and evening hours while Gideon got caught up with ranch chores. Time passed quickly. All too soon came the day to circle on the Coopersmith calendar. A red-letter day? Or black for sorrow?

Both Gideon and Maggs fought back tears when Annie hugged Patrocino, with Brownie looking on from the corral. He saw his daughter's shoulders quake as she sobbed in the wrangler's arms.

"If this is the right decision," Maggs whispered, "then why does it hurt so much?"

In an unexpected way they benefited from the presence of Mills Pillow. Even though Patrocino always nodded politely when spoken to, Gideon was never certain the wrangler understood every word and shade of meaning. Now

Pillow explained in Spanish why the Coopersmiths were leaving, and when Gideon expected to return. Conflicting emotions ran through Patrocino, too, as tears welled in his eyes.

Later Pillow said to Gideon: "I must say, the West is every bit as adventuresome and raw as I'd been told it was."

"How's that?" Gideon asked.

"Think of it, man," Pillow said. "The sight of that great mountain peak at dawn, two men hanged in the shadow of a ghostly cabin, the eccentric Blake brothers, the bottom falling out of the mercury every morning, and that wonderful North Park hay." He added: "Out West the full range of experiences stimulates body and soul."

"Reckon so," Gideon replied. "Around here a man works hard, sleeps hard, and tries hard to keep up."

Pillow asked permission to stay on the ranch for a few days. He needed time to acclimate himself to the thin air at this altitude and adjust to minus-zero temperatures. He offered to lend Patrocino a hand with chores as a way to earn his keep.

Gideon took him up on his offer. Even though Pillow was a city man with no experience in ranch life, he was ever the student, energetic and eager to learn. For his part, Patrocino seemed to enjoy the opportunity to speak his native tongue. And he was clearly pleased when Pillow admired his sculptures in the bunkhouse.

"Wonderfully expressive works of art," Pillow said, his arm sweeping past the carved faces showing heavy brows, bold noses, and thick lips. "Examples of this uniquely American artistry should be on exhibit in the National Museum of Art." Pillow repeated that in Spanish, and added: "I'm acquainted with the curator. I hope to take one or two of these carvings back to Washington."

In heritage and background, they could hardly be more different, Gideon thought of these two men, no more alike than night and day. Yet they got along well. Pillow did not shy away from mucking out stalls, and he deferred to Patrocino's knowledge of horses. Showing such respect and good sense were enough to convince Gideon. This talkative, round-cheeked city man was welcome to stay on the Double Circle C.

Cold and stiff from long hours on the seat of the Studebaker ranch wagon, the last thing Gideon wanted in Buckhorn was a fight. He halted the wagon in front of the Colorado Hotel. In a pool of light cast by kerosene lamps flanking the hotel door, he saw three horses tied at the rail. One looked familiar. Gideon knew he had seen that mount somewhere, but he came up blank until the hotel door swung open. The man who came out and paused on the boardwalk to light a thick cigar was Sam Whitlock.

Gideon tossed the lines to Maggs and jumped down. In long strides he rounded the wagon and stepped up onto the boardwalk in front of the man.

"Whitlock."

He puffed on his stogie and tossed the match aside. In the glow of lamplight, he gazed at Gideon without recognition.

"Do I know you, mister?"

"Gideon Coopersmith. Double Circle C."

"Yes, now I remember. . . ."

Gideon stepped closer and thrust out his arm, thumping Whitlock in the chest with the heel of his hand.

Whitlock swore. "What the hell . . . ?"

"Shut up and listen," he said, and thumped him again.

"What the hell's wrong with you, Coopersmith?"

"Lynch another man on my land," Gideon said, "and I'll come after you."

He did not reply for a long moment. "Don't threaten me."

"No threats, Whitlock. I'm telling you and your damned posse. Stay off Double Circle C range."

"The law of the land will be served," Whitlock said, "regardless of time or place. You cannot deny justice. . . ."

"Justice," Gideon broke in. "Did you hang those men before you shot them, or after?"

Whitlock said: "I won't take insults from you."

"Cross my land," Gideon said, hitting him again with the heel of his hand, "and you'll get more than insults."

Rocked back, Whitlock caught his balance. His anger flaring into rage, he drew back his fist.

"Don't get reckless now," Gideon said. He ducked an awkward punch, sidestepped Whitlock, and let go with a right cross to his jaw. The blow sent his cigar sailing into the night with a fiery trail like a miniature comet. Dazed, Whitlock sank to his knees.

The hotel door opened. Two men came out, one buttoning his coat, the other pulling on gloves. Gideon remembered them from Whitlock's posse, and in that moment he noticed the second man was missing half a thumb on his left hand—a steer roper's injury. Both drew up when they saw what was happening.

Whitlock said hoarsely: "Take him, boys."

Gideon faced them, raising his fists as the pair came for him. From the wagon seat Maggs gasped.

The man with half a thumb was wiry with a trimmed beard, the other thick-bodied and ponderous, bull-like. Gideon made a quick decision. He went after the wiry man on his right, feinting, and then landing a blow to his temple.

Staggered, the man was driven against the wall of the hotel by the force of the punch.

In the next instant Gideon was hit hard. He went down with a roaring in his ears. From a great distance, it seemed, he heard Maggs: "Annie, take the baby!"

Gideon raised his head. Vision blurred, he saw Maggs leap down from the wagon seat. She yanked the pry bar out of the wagon box. The tool was hickory, longer than a shovel handle and thicker, normally used as a lever to pry against an axle or wheel to free a stuck wagon.

Neither of Gideon's assailants saw her when she moved behind them, cocking the length of hickory over her shoulder like a baseball bat. Her first blow hit the back of the neck of the big man who was busily kicking Gideon in the ribs. Knees buckling, he dropped to the boardwalk like a pole-axed steer. The second swing of the pry bar struck the wiry man in the middle of his back. When he half turned, raising his arms to ward off the next blow, she swung lower and hit him in the mid-section. He stumbled back, crying out in pain.

Whitlock was on his feet now. "Damn you, she-bitch, back away."

Maggs gazed at him in the glow of lamplight. "What did you call me?"

He drew his gun. "I'll cripple you, bitch."

"Get your hirelings off my husband," she said, advancing a pace, "or you'll have to shoot me."

Whitlock stared at her in disbelief. He cocked the gun and took aim at the boardwalk between her feet. He pulled the trigger.

The gunshot was loud in the quiet night. A tongue of red flame flared out of the barrel, the bullet plowing into a plank inches from the toes of her buttontop shoes.

Maggs did not retreat or flinch. And she did not lower

110

the pry bar. "Missed," she said.

"Mama!" Annie called out in fear from the wagon.

"I'm all right, Annie," she said over her shoulder.

Nate Clarke came running across snow-rutted Front Street, revolver held high. "Drop that gun! Drop it!"

Whitlock holstered his pistol. "Sheriff, we were accosted and assaulted by these people."

Clarke halted. "Looks to me like it was the other way around. You took a shot at Missus Coopersmith, didn't you?"

Head clearing, Gideon managed to stand. Maggs tossed the pry bar into the wagon and came to her husband's side, slipping her arm around him.

"Sheriff," Whitlock said, "they attacked us without warning. . . ."

Clarke asked: "You all right, Gideon?"

"Yeah."

Whitlock said: "Mister Ben Anderson and Mister Tom Griffith, here, and myself, were attacked without provocation. The clerk in the hotel lobby may have seen it, too. Ask him."

Clarke studied him. "You aim to press charges?"

"Or fit a noose around my neck?" Gideon demanded.

Whitlock paused, stroking his beard as he gazed at the two men. "I see how it is."

"How what is?" Clarke asked.

"A lawman extending favors to friends," Whitlock replied. "No room for justice in this town, is there?"

"Press charges, mister," Clarke said, "or move on."

Whitlock glared at him. "You have no authority to run law-abiding citizens out of town."

"Sir, I'm inviting you to move on," Clarke said, "before charges are lodged against you."

"Charges," Whitlock said. "Such as?"

"Endangerment, for starters," Clarke replied. "I can add discharging a firearm in town, if you wish."

Whitlock stared at him long enough to show defiance. Then he and Griffith grasped the arms of the heavier man, Ben Anderson, lifted him to his feet, and steadied him until he could walk. The three made their way to their horses tied at the rail, mounted, and rode away.

"Friends of yours?" Clarke asked.

"The one with the full beard and mustache," Gideon replied, "is Sam Whitlock."

"Whitlock," Clarke said. He looked down the street at the departing riders. "Did he admit to the lynchings?"

"Nope."

"But you figure he's the hangman?"

"Nate, as sure as we're standing here, I know Whitlock and his posse committee . . . or whatever he calls his gang . . . hanged those men. . . ."

"Daddy! Mama! I'm tired of holding Andrew!"

Maggs called out: "I'm coming, Annie, I'm coming."

In the darkness of their hotel room, Gideon lay in bed beside his wife. Maggs reached out, her hand feeling for his face. Her fingers found his beard-stubbled jaw. In a whisper she asked again if he were injured.

"I already told you," Gideon said. "I'm not hurt."

"The reason I keep asking," she said, "is that you're not a man to admit to injuries. You're sure you're not hurt, not in any way?"

"If you want to know the truth, I'm embarrassed."

"Gideon, why?"

"It's danged embarrassing for a woman to horn into a man's fight."

"It is?"

Join the Western Book Club and GET 4 FREE* BOOKS NOW!
A $19.96 VALUE!

Yes! I want to subscribe to the Western Book Club.

Please send me my **4 FREE* BOOKS**. I have enclosed $2.00 for shipping/handling. Each month I'll receive the four newest Leisure Western selections to preview for 10 days. If I decide to keep them, I will pay the Special Members Only discounted price of just $3.36 each, a total of $13.44, plus $2.00 shipping/handling ($22.30 US in Canada). This is a **SAVINGS OF AT LEAST $6.00** off the bookstore price. There is no minimum number of books I must buy, and I may cancel the program at any time. In any case, the **4 FREE* BOOKS** are mine to keep.

*In Canada, add $5.00 shipping/handling per order for the first shipment. For all future shipments to Canada, the cost of membership is $22.30 US, which includes shipping and handling.
(All payments must be made in US dollars.)

NAME: _____	
ADDRESS: _____	
CITY: _____	**STATE:** _____
COUNTRY: _____	**ZIP:** _____
TELEPHONE: _____	
E-MAIL: _____	
SIGNATURE: _____	

"By now Clarke's probably told everybody in Buckhorn who wants a good laugh. . . ."

"Gideon, three against one isn't a fair fight."

"I admit I didn't see those other two coming," he conceded. "But I had a plan."

"A plan! One man punched you in the face so hard you were knocked off your feet. The other tried to kick you to death."

"I had them right where I wanted them."

"Oh, you did?"

"With that big sheepskin I was wearing," he said, "the kicks didn't hurt me hardly a-tall. I was letting that big one get over-confident."

"Over-confident!"

"I was fixing to pound the living hell out of him," he went on, "as soon as he wore himself down. Then I was going to hand that skinny one a beating he'd never forget."

"Gideon Coopersmith!" she said in exasperation. When Annie stirred in the next bed, Maggs moved her hand from his jaw to his throat and tightened her grip as though to strangle him. She whispered: "Gideon Coopersmith."

Chapter Ten

Long before his stellar political career, Ezra Allan Stearns was a timber man. He hiked the great forests of Michigan in his work as an estimator for lumber companies. Virgin timber in that region, he told his daughter years later, grew so thick that a squirrel could leap from pine branch to pine branch all the way across the northern reaches of the Lower Peninsula without ever touching the ground.

Stearns possessed an uncanny talent for eyeballing a stand of trees while making his calculations on a scrap of paper with a gnawed pencil stub to estimate correctly how many board feet of usable lumber the forest would yield. It was not unusual for the young Stearns to be out in the timber of the old Northwest for two or three weeks at a time, alone, without seeing another human.

Also remarkable for this youth was his foresight in declining a lump sum payment for his services. Instead, he negotiated a fee of two percent of the gross profits for each contract. By twenty-five he was wealthy. By thirty-two he was married to a woman half his age. With Lucretia, he moved to Denver where he invested in mining properties, built his white-columned mansion, and launched a political career that led to Washington.

Although the exterior was brick and stone, Gideon thought of the mansion as a house of wood. The sitting room was sycamore, the oval library curly birch, the dining room paneled in a pattern of white oak and black walnut, the staircase golden oak, the bedrooms maple—all selected by a lumberman who never again slept on pine boughs in a great, silent forest.

A hired coach met the Coopersmiths at Union Station. Dodging electric trolley cars, wagon traffic, speeding two-horse carriages, and scurrying pedestrians, the coach carried them and their luggage to the Stearns mansion on Capitol Hill. This hillside commanded a view of Denver with a panoramic mountain backdrop from Long's Peak to the north, Pikes Peak far to the south. Closer at hand was the confluence of Cherry Creek with the South Platte River. Half a mile wide and half an inch deep, this branch of the Platte, folks said, was too muddy to drink and too thin to plow.

As fine and stately as the Stearns mansion was, the stark contrast to Gideon's upbringing always reminded him of poverty. Unlike the soddy, rooms here were large, high-ceilinged, and elegantly furnished from thick Persian carpets underfoot to crystal chandeliers overhead. Stained glass windows illuminated floral-patterned wallpaper and filled interior spaces with gem-like colors at certain hours of the day. Fireplaces in every room were framed by rectangles of Colorado marble streaked with gold, in winter the flames tended by maids.

It was Lucretia's domain, and she enforced her rules. The back staircase was for hired help only. Gideon was required to "dress" for supper. All three meals were prepared by a chef and served by silent servants, and only Lucretia could directly address them. At mealtimes the atmosphere was strained, falsely quiet. Lucretia clearly did not speak her mind in Gideon's presence, and always seemed to be waiting for him to leave the room.

Room. Gideon had grown up in a cramped sod house where his mother had gone mad and killed herself, dying in agony after swallowing a mouthful of strychnine. The few objects inside the soddy and a small root cellar—oil lamps, buckets, rusted cooking utensils, tattered quilts, two broken-down ladderback chairs, a dozen books from England, most water-damaged or mouse-chewed, and a table made of pine boards—were all he knew, those utilitarian objects hauled across the plains in a covered wagon to Red Cliff and then on to a dry and desolate site for a homestead.

If a man's life span is a journey, his own had taken him from a low soddy on the prairie through a succession of bunkhouses to the house he had built in North Park, built with his sweat and hard-earned cash. He sometimes found himself wishing he could bring his father to the home place, proving him wrong once and for all.

It was a daydream that quickly passed. Gideon never set out to locate his father, to discover if he was still living, and where. Maybe it was no more than a closely held conceit, a false pride, but he figured R.J. Coopersmith, always more of a talker than a worker, had been unable to keep up with the chores. He well might have abandoned the place and returned to England, a frequent threat shouted to the gods during Nebraska dust storms of summer or howling blizzards of winter. Whether he lost the homestead claim and went "home" to Lord of This and Earl of That rarely occupied Gideon's thoughts.

Room. No matter how much pride Gideon took in the Double Circle C, the house of wood in Denver was a reminder his journey had reached Comfortable, but he had not made it to Prosperity. Worse, to keep her son-in-law in his place, when Lucretia spoke to him at all, she trumpeted her inherited fortune as though she had earned it, claiming the sum was too vast to be spent in a mere lifetime or two, that someday Annie and Andrew would have it. In truth, the benevolent grandmother had never forgiven Gideon Coopersmith. He had stolen her precious daughter, her only child. In the guise of love a shiftless cowboy with manured boots and patched clothes had lured Maggs away, taken her from a life of ease and high social standing to an isolated existence in that snowbound icebox far from Denver.

After nodding a terse greeting to Gideon, Lucretia embraced her daughter and granddaughter in tearful reunion. She was a buxom woman with a booming voice to match her girth, her salt-and-pepper hair pinned up in a style that added elevation to her towering presence. She clucked over a fussing Andrew like a hen, sing-songing about Maggs's own baby clothes stored in a trunk upstairs, neatly folded and ready for the next generation. After all, she added with an accusing glance at Gideon, "Grammy" had never had a chance to dress Annie when she was a baby.

Gideon turned away, jaw clenched. No son of his would ever be dressed as a girl. That was the thought in his head, but he did not challenge Lucretia by allowing the words to fly out of his mouth. He knew Maggs would draw the line. If he had gained any wisdom at all in ten years of marriage, he had learned to keep his trap shut when his mother-in-law carried on.

"Daddy always said Mama has to blow her steam," Maggs once confided to Gideon. "Give her time to blow, and she's harmless enough."

Helping the coachman carry in luggage, Gideon overheard the proud grandmother rave about her granddaughter's unsurpassed beauty and intelligence: "The Dowd Academy awaits you! The star pupil! A star burning bright! Oh, this will be such fun!"

Gideon stepped into the hallway in time to see Annie staring up at her grammy, mouth open in amazement.

This was a day of victory for Lucretia. At last her daughter and grandchildren had been pried out of Colorado's version of the Yukon. At last they would live a proper life in the centermost orbit of Denver's social circle.

"During school holidays we will travel by train to Boston, New York, and Washington, D.C.," Lucretia said, "and in the summer to Europe by steamship we shall go!" She cast a sidelong glance at Gideon and added: "All for the benefit of Annie's education. And soon Andrew will be learning, too. . . ."

"Mama," Maggs said before this flight of fancy took wing, "Annie's formal education will be at the Dowd Academy. In the spring we'll return home." She put her arm around her mother's shoulders. "To the ranch."

"Grammy!" Annie said excitedly. "Come to our ranch in the summer. I'll show you my pony. Patrocino's helping me train him. Brownie's beautiful . . . and very fast. You should see him run!"

Lucretia nodded with a tight smile. "Of course, my dear. Of course."

Gideon went upstairs to the guest bedroom. Over the washstand, framed needlework bore a message in an elaborate heart entwined with a leafy vine, a gift long ago from daughter to mother:

**A Merry Heart
Maketh A Cheerful
Countenance**

Peering into the beveled mirror over the basin, he gave himself a toothy grin.

118

Cold Wind

This bedroom on the second floor of the mansion opened out to a widow's walk. The view from the railed porch overlooking the city and snow-covered mountains, was spectacular, day or night.

On the eve of his return to the Double Circle C, Gideon stepped out onto the widow's walk to smoke. Before him, a grid of street lamps marked city blocks like a map come to life, bright lights under stars scattered across the black and endless sky.

In his shirt sleeves, Gideon lit a cigar from the late senator's humidor. No snow on the ground here. He felt like he had traveled from winter to summer. The night air at this lower altitude was balmy compared to North Park. And noisy. The whine and clatter of trolley cars, shrill train whistles, whinnying horses, barking dogs—all these sounds ran together in a cacophony that carried through the night. Life in Denver was rushed, loud, foul, the air rank with coal and kerosene fumes. And even from this distance muddy riverbanks reeked with sewage.

Gideon would take the midnight train to Buckhorn. He and Maggs had talked about this. She knew he was uncomfortable in her mother's house, and there was no need for him to stay longer than the three-day interval between trains. He had passed the time by walking the streets of Denver, sitting in on horse auctions at the Elephant Livery Stable, and renting saddle mounts to take Annie for a ride on the prairie, east of town. He smiled when he heard his daughter talk happily about school. She had taken to it right away, clearly enjoying her teachers. Difficult as it was, he knew they had made the right decision by coming here.

Sitting at his daughter's bedside that night, Gideon stroked her face and promised to return for a visit next month. After the baby was down and Annie was asleep, Gideon and Maggs said their good byes in the bedroom.

"This is the moment I've dreaded," Maggs said, her voice muffled in their embrace.

Gideon kissed her. He pulled back and looked into her eyes. She held his gaze, unblinking. He remembered the first time their eyes had met, the moment he knew he loved her, as if he had always loved her. That feeling of recognition had never left him. He tried to speak now, to say good bye to her, but the words caught in his throat as though he had swallowed logs.

"Maggs," he whispered, "I love you."

"Forever, Gideon Coopersmith, forever," she whispered as she held him. "We've never been apart more than a few days at a time. This is . . . this is so hard." Maggs reached up, her fingertips brushing a tear from his cheek. "See, Gideon Coopersmith, you are sentimental."

As the train rolled into Buckhorn, Gideon looked out the frosted window of the passenger car, his gaze drawn to a strange sight. Townsmen were gathered at a street-level door to the Buckhorn Gold & Silver Mill. The mill was not operating this time of year, yet the door stood open, and a crowd of men were clustered there.

Eight in the morning, Gideon thought, *was an early hour for all those townsfolk to be up and around.*

Bag in hand, he moved along the aisle of the empty coach to the door. He opened it, stepped over the coupling, and swung down while the train rolled slowly into the station with its bell ringing. He crossed the platform to the ticket agent's cage.

"What's going on down there at the mill?" he asked.

The agent pushed his green visor higher on his forehead

and looked up from his paperwork. "Somebody found a man down there. Dead."

Gideon rounded the steep-roofed dépôt to Front Street and looked toward the mill building. Fresh footprints had been left in the snow by the townsmen. Standing in the open doorway of the mill was Nate Clarke. A head taller than the others, he wore the low-crowned, cream-colored hat of a city man. When he spotted Gideon, he lifted his hand and beckoned.

Gideon left his grip on the loading dock. Buttoning his sheepskin against the cold, he walked to the mill. When he drew near, hushed conversations halted. Townsmen watched him as he made his way to the sheriff.

Clarke pointed to the hasp above the door handle. The wood was splintered, split where it had been pried open. With no word of explanation, he led him into the building and closed the door behind them.

Gideon looked around. This place was cold and dark, smelling vaguely of rock dust and chemicals.

"There's a corpse over here," Clarke said.

The lawman lifted a lantern. He adjusted the wick. The flame exposed a long, plank worktable with mortar and pestle, scales, clear glass test tubes, and other assay equipment. Gideon saw packing crates for ore samples and long chutes constructed of heavy lumber. When the crushing mill was operating, concentrate slid down those chutes to ore wagons outside. Overhead, thick timbers criss-crossed the top of this structure built on the side of a slope overlooking town and the valley narrowing into Columbine Gulch.

"Last night a drunk, looking for a place to sleep, found the door busted open. What he found sobered him up, *pronto.*"

Gideon peered into dim light. He saw only the dark form of a hanged man, hatless, the thin body suspended a few inches off the floor by a rope looped over one of the timbers.

"Who is it?" he asked.

Shadows swayed and darted away as Clarke raised the lantern. An arc of bright light crossed the lifeless face of Tommy Logan.

Gideon stared in disbelief. Hair rumpled, the boy's head twisted sharply away from the rope's slipknot. Gideon heard the rattle of paper.

"Found this on him," Clarke said, unfolding a single sheet.

Gideon looked at the paper. His vision blurred. He blinked when he read the words printed in bold letters:

JUSTICE WILL BE DONE . . .
POSSE COMITATUS

"We'll cut him down as soon as Ollie gets here with a wagon," Clarke said. "I looked around. No sign of a struggle. The kid took a hell of a blow to the head. I figure he was clubbed, dragged in here, and strung up. . . ." Clarke reached out and grasped his arm. "Gideon, are you all right?"

"Yeah," he said, but his face grew hot, then he chilled. Revulsion swept through him, a deep and sickening disgust mixed with sorrow.

Sorrow. Why? The kid had lied to him, stolen from him, slugged him from behind, and left him for dead in the snow. Yet, seeing the hanged corpse of Tommy Logan afforded no satisfaction. Gideon swayed as nausea overcame him. He tried to take a deep breath, fought for air, but had to turn away, his stomach heaving.

Cold Wind

In the Buckhorn County sheriff's office, Gideon nodded when Clarke offered him a drink for "what ails you." The lawman leaned down and opened a desk drawer, pulling out a pint of Old Overholt rye whiskey. He uncorked it, and handed it to him. Gideon tipped the flat-sided bottle to his mouth, took a long swallow, and passed it to Ollie. The deputy drank and returned it to Clarke. He took a pull and corked it.

Gideon said: "You've hunted for Whitlock?"

"He's not in Buckhorn," Clarke said, putting the bottle in the drawer. "Ollie searched for his horse in the liveries, and I checked the rooming houses."

"No sign of his hired toughs, Anderson and Griffith, either," Ollie added.

"Reckon they wouldn't hang the kid," Gideon allowed, "and then take a room here in town."

"They rode out of here hell-for-leather, likely," Clarke said. He added: "I keep wondering who sicced the hangman on Tommy Logan."

"A lot of folks were fed up with that kid," Moore said. "He was a thief, and everyone knew it."

"The kid busted jail in Laramie," Clarke mused. "Maybe Whitlock tracked him this far, and headed back to Wyoming last night. I sent a wire to Henry Tyler to keep an eye peeled for him."

A long silence followed. Gideon looked at Clarke. The lawman rubbed his jaw. He shook his head.

"Something else on your mind, Nate?" Gideon asked.

"Oh, I've got a hell of a job ahead of me," he said.

Gideon had not thought about it until that moment. "Somebody has to tell Ruth Logan."

Clarke nodded. He cast a glance at Ollie Moore.

"No, sir," the deputy said quickly. "No, sir. Nate, you know me. I'll risk my neck in a saloon fight or take any other law enforcement job you throw at me. But I don't get paid enough for this one."

"Neither do I," Clarke said.

Chapter Eleven

Due north, a storm was building over Deadman. From the wagon seat Gideon watched a gray cloudbank on the horizon ahead, hoping it would break up and veer off to the east in harmless clouds scudding across the sky. Three and a half hours later the cloudbank looked as solid as cement. Then cold winds hit him in the face like a slap.

The team of two horses tossed their heads and pranced. Gideon tried to calm them under a tight rein. In minutes wind-driven snow swirled about him. Horse sense told him to turn back, turn back and gallop south until banana trees came into sight. Winds sweeping off the high plains of Wyoming to northern Colorado this time of year sent temperatures plummeting.

Past noon now, Gideon knew he had traveled too far from Buckhorn to turn back. Horse sense or not, his best hope was to head into the wind and drive to Dutchman's. Tossing his hat under the seat, he looped a heavy wool scarf over his head, wrapped it around his face, and tied it snugly under his chin. He pulled the fabric away from his eyes so he could see, and then turned his coat collar up. Even so, cold air knifed through him as he drove northward.

Five hundred yards farther a trio of ghostly figures appeared in swirling snow off to his right. Gideon glimpsed the three horsemen the moment before they were swallowed by the storm. He halted. Cupping gloved hands to his mouth, he called out. The howling wind ripped away his voice.

He guided the team in that direction, searching for the riders. He saw no one. He shouted again, at once knowing his voice would not carry. He shielded his eyes and tried to peer through the wind-driven snow, but could barely see beyond the horses' ears. With the relentless winds quickly erasing any tracks, there was no sign, no trail to follow. He shouted one more time. Neither man nor beast without shelter could last long against this wintry onslaught. He turned the team back the way he had come.

Gideon pushed on, facing the frigid wind. He drove the horses without the aid of landmarks to guide him, trusting his instincts and simply hoping to hell the wind had not changed direction. Hunched against it, he felt numbed by the cold. Blood backs away from toes and fingers, from hands and feet when a man freezes to death, he had once been told, the limbs numbing as warm blood protects the heart until a last deathly chill stills it.

He heard a brittle sound—horseshoes clattering on ice. The horses had found the frozen tributary to French Creek. Gideon turned the team and followed it, and in the coldest two hours of his life, that ribbon of ice which led to the Dutchman's cabin. The grove of cottonwoods was no more than a dark and vague shape in the swirling snow.

Gideon jumped down from the wagon seat. He shoved the door open, unhooked the horses and yanked off harnesses, and led them inside. After closing the plank door against the howling winds, he pulled off his headgear and flung it across the cabin. He let out a shout, hollering with the elation of one who has escaped death. His triumphant call to the gods drew a blank look from the trembling horses.

He yanked off his gloves and unbuttoned his coat with numbed fingers. Shouldering out of the snow-caked sheepskin, he hung it from a peg on the door. The wind howled on the other side of it like a hungry beast, a sound reminding him of corpses gnawed by wolves.

Soon he had a fire crackling and popping in the old sheet-iron stove. He stood close to it, letting the warmth seep into him. His fingers stung as feeling returned, and he stomped to drive the numbness from his feet. After he melted water in a rusted bucket, he drank it hot like tea. For the horses, he cooled snow water and held the bucket for one to drink, then the other.

Over the years Gideon had supposed this cabin had saved lives as lost or stranded travelers came upon it. Now he knew for a fact it had saved him, and his horses. He wondered about those three riders, wondered if they had survived. Then he wondered what he had seen. Ghosts in the storm? Maybe his mind was numbed by frigid winds, too, and had played tricks. Or maybe he had barely missed an encounter with Sam Whitlock and the two men riding with him. . . . Gideon figured he would never know the answer.

The storm blew itself out before midnight. With no reason to wait for daybreak, he left Dutchman's and pressed on, his horses bucking snowdrifts by starlight. When he reached the home place, Patrocino and Mills Pillow met him in the barn, lanterns in hand. Pillow shook his head in answer to Gideon's question: No riders had sought refuge here. The chances of horsebackers surviving that storm were slim. Pillow launched into a tale of half a dozen hunters in Nepal caught in a violent winter storm. Their bodies were not discovered until spring, frozen and perfectly preserved in their final sleep.

The day dawned clear and still. As often happened in North Park, frigid winds dragged warm air in their wake. Temperatures shot up, topping off at +18°. Mills Pillow

commented on the sweltering heat wave as he said his good
byes. Gideon shook the man's hand. The big Sharps rifle
was slung over his shoulder, and his carpetbags were lashed
to the backs of the donkeys.

"As you likely noticed," Gideon said, "we get sudden
changes of weather in these parts."

Pillow wore layers of winter clothes and knee-high boots
of black leather, polished, of course. "I'll watch the sky. If I
get caught in one of those killer storms, I'll dig a snow cave
and wait it out." He gestured toward Deadman. "The Blake
brothers invited me to visit. I'll make my base camp there."

Patrocino drifted over from the bunkhouse. "*Vaya con
Dios, amigo.*"

"*Adiós, viejo,*" Pillow replied with a grin, and trudged
away in the deep snow, donkeys following.

Without knowing why, Gideon found himself thinking of
Tommy Logan in the following days. An omen, maybe. For
when he heard the racket of a heavy wagon pulling into the
yard one evening, he was not surprised to find Ruth outside. Bundled up under the ratty, buffalo robe, the big
woman was perched on the seat of the ore wagon with a
cigarillo clenched in her yellowed teeth. She awaited an invitation.

Gideon stepped out on the verandah. Greeting her, he
asked her to come in. He expressed his sympathies over her
loss as she mounted the steps, and ignited an explosion of
curses.

"Them Buckhorn lawdogs won't go after Tommy's
killers," she said in disgust as she tromped into the house.
"Tommy caused a mite of trouble in Buckhorn. Sheriff
Clarke didn't like him, not one bit."

"Clarke's short-handed . . . ," Gideon began.

Ruth cut him off. "Not enough deputies. Too much snow. No tax money in the coffers. Mister Coopersmith, I've heard all them damned excuses. Hell, Clarke won't do his job. That's all there is to it."

"He sent a wire to the sheriff in Laramie. . . ."

She broke in: "If one of Ollie Moore's sons got murdered, you can be certain-sure they wouldn't rest until the killer was brung in, dead or alive. You can be certain-sure of that."

Arguing with her was a pointless exercise. Gideon knew that much. Besides, he had to admit her words bore an ounce of truth. Clarke was a good lawman, and so was Ollie Moore. But, given the circumstances, they weren't likely to gallop after Tommy's killers—even if they had known where to gallop.

Gideon stood in the kitchen while Ruth fried slabs of bacon and scrambled six eggs for herself. After eating, she mopped grease out of the frying pan with a hard biscuit she had excavated from a back corner of the bread box.

"Denver, huh?" she said after Gideon explained where his family had gone.

He nodded.

Her cracked lips shiny with bacon grease, she chewed on the dried-out bread while she spoke: "Denver's a booming town. Booming into a city, Denver is. A barkeep can make a pile of money on Market Street . . . a big, heaping pile. Not that saloon owners would ever let a woman do the job. No, they won't. Men only. That's the policy, and it can't be busted. I know. I tried. One saloonman down there said I had a figure like a busted bale of hay. Hell, I know I ain't never going to be no dance-hall chippie, Mister Coopersmith, but why'd he have to say that to me?" She swallowed. "So I took what I could get . . . which left me stranded up in Columbine, trying to get through winters drink by drink, coin by coin, in a mining camp damned near emptied out by the silver crash." She added with finality: "Well, I'm done, done with all that."

Before Gideon could ask what she meant, her jaw quivered and she sobbed suddenly. He stood by helplessly while she covered her mouth with both hands. After a moment she pulled her hands away, eyes downcast as though weeping revealed weakness.

"Mister Coopersmith," Ruth said in a trembling voice, "my boy's buried in the Buckhorn cemetery. Clarke and his deputy, they lowered him into the ground. Shoveled dirt over the box. Ever heard clods of dirt and rocks hitting a pine casket? A hollow drumbeat if there ever was one. Well, when them lawmen left, it was just me. Just me and my dead son. Not even a marker for his grave. . . ." She wiped tears from her face and lifted her gaze. "I always figured Tommy would get hisself straightened out, and . . . uh . . . outgrow his wildness. Boys are like that, ain't they? Boys don't cause trouble when they's older. Ain't that a fact? My Tommy, he never . . . he never had that chance."

Gideon filled his pipe. He avoided talking about Tommy first by tamping the tobacco with his thumb, and then by inviting her into the great room.

Ruth Logan lowered herself into Maggs's platform rocker, the wood joints creaking under her weight. She gazed at him for a long moment.

"I'm hunting for Sam Whitlock," she said. "Reckon you guessed that much."

"Yeah," Gideon said, moving to the fireplace.

"I knowed Whitlock was lying when he called hisself sheriff. Done told your missus, I did, soon as I seen him. Ask Missus Coopersmith. That lovely lady'll tell you the Lord's truth."

Gideon knelt and stoked the fire. "She told me."

"I seen the sheet of paper found in my boy's trouser pocket," Ruth went on. "I didn't make sense of them words till Clarke told me. Said you found two men lynched on your land with words printed on a sheet of paper . . . posse something-or-other, huh?"

Gideon nodded.

The rocker creaked in a loud protest when Ruth leaned forward and spoke with urgency: "Mister Coopersmith, you figure Whitlock lynched my boy, don't you? He strung Tommy up in the mill, shoved that piece of paper in his pocket, and slunk away. Don't you figure it that way?"

"Yeah," Gideon said, not mentioning the blow to the head Clarke had discovered. He pulled a firebrand from the flames and touched it to tobacco packed in the blackened bowl of the pipe. He drew smoke and tossed the flaring stick back into the fire.

"Well, I'm here to ask you, Mister Coopersmith . . . where's Whitlock now?"

"I don't know."

"You figure he's in Wyoming? He calls Laramie home, don't he?"

"Ruth, I don't know where he lives," Gideon replied. He stood, adding: "I don't even know if he's alive."

"Alive? What in hell do you mean by that?"

He told her about seeing three riders caught in the storm. "Either they died, or found a place to fort up."

Her gaze moved to the window. "So Whitlock could be dead? He could be laying out there somewhere, froze solid in some damned snow bank that won't melt till June?"

Gideon drew on the pipe, and nodded.

Ruth Logan leaned back in the rocker, the scar pulling one eye shut. "Well, I have to know," she said. "I have to know."

* * * * *

At dawn Gideon fixed breakfast for himself and Patrocino. He did not have to open the door to the spare room to know Ruth was still asleep. Her rip-saw snoring and steam-engine snorting blasted through the bedroom door as though she had opened a lumber mill in there.

In the barn Gideon climbed the ladder to the mow. He forked hay down to the sled where Patrocino spread it out. With a full load and the team in harness, they were on their way out of the yard when Ruth came lunging out of the house. She stepped onto the verandah, still in her night-clothes. Stringy hair spilled around her face, and her breath plumed into a white cloud when she cupped her hands to her mouth.

"I'll have dinner ready when you boys get back!" she shouted with more volume than necessary. "Dinner will be ready! And . . . uh . . . Mister Coopersmith! I'll be leaving in the morning! First thing! Thought you'd wanna know! I ain't staying long enough to be a bother to you!"

Ruth was a bother, but she was a woman of her word. Dinner was prepared as promised, and in the morning she was up and stomping before dawn. Patrocino hooked the mules to the ore wagon, and Gideon handed her up to the high seat. She took the lines in one mittened hand, a long-handled whip in the other.

Gideon offered a sack of grain for the mules, but Ruth shook her head. She motioned to the wagon box where a tarp half covered the old trunk Gideon had seen in her cabin, and some crates.

"Got ever'thing I need for travel, Mister Coopersmith. Food, bedding, firewood, you name it. Includin' this here man-tamer."

Gideon watched her lean down and reach under the seat.

She yanked out the sawed-off shotgun she'd pointed at him in Miner's Delight.

"I'm lugging ever' damned thing I own," she said, "in this-here big ol' wagon."

"Everything you own," Gideon repeated.

"Didn't I tell you?" she demanded.

"Tell me what?"

"I done cashed out," she said. "Sold Miner's Delight, and bought this-here vehicle and team of jacks."

"What do you aim to do?"

"By damn, Mister Coopersmith," she said, "ain't you been listening? Ain't you heard one thing I've said?"

Jaw clenched, Gideon eyed her.

"I'm hunting for Sam Whitlock," she said with exaggerated patience. "Don't you understand? There ain't nobody else to bring my son's killer to justice. Nobody on this earth but me." She slid the shotgun under the seat. "Mister Coopersmith, if Whitlock's alive, I'll see him take that last walk to the gallows. Won't rest till I do." She added: "Or I'll put him on the short road to hell with my twenty gauge."

Gideon stepped back as she cracked the whip over the backs of the mules. The ore wagon lurched forward. She drove out of the yard, retracing wheel ruts etched in the snow.

If Whitlock's alive, he thought, *she's driving to her death.*

He well remembered the man was ready to shoot Maggs when she confronted him outside the Colorado Hotel in Buckhorn. If Ruth stomped after Sam Whitlock in Laramie, bellowing her threats, he would kill her in the name of self-defense.

"Damn," Gideon whispered.

He knew what he had to do. He knew, and at once hated the prospect of it. He kicked a clump of snow, sending up a small explosion of white powder. Swore again for good measure.

Chapter Twelve

Fields of white stretched out as far as Gideon's squinting, earthbound eyes could see. Off the east shoulder of Deadman, soft undulations of North Park terrain were marked by stands of pines and clumps of brush, and here and there an eroded cut in the land made a dark crease across the endless blanket of snow. For mile after mile, though, most of the land was white under a blue sky, pure white and pure blue. And purely cold.

At the home place Gideon had saddled the paint and ridden out after noon, knowing he would easily track and overtake the team of mules pulling a heavy wagon. Those animals were strong and steady of pace, but not fast. The mare, on the other hand, was eager and ready to run the moment her rein loosened. Gideon held her to a canter.

As best he could, Gideon had explained to Patrocino that he was leaving on a journey of four days, maybe five. Patrocino's expression revealed that he understood the length of the trip, but not the reason. Gideon had enough trouble trying to explain that one to himself, much less find words to say to Patrocino. All he knew was that he had to do the right thing—or at least try. Ruth Logan needed help whether she knew it or not. He suspected she would not welcome his company. Late that afternoon he found out he was right.

Crossing over the pass out of North Park, Gideon left Deadman behind. Presently he saw the ore wagon on the flat ahead, a dark rectangle on the snow-covered road.

Drawing closer, he heard Ruth's voice and realized she was talking a blue streak to the mules. The animals sensed the presence of a horse and rider, and tossed their heads nervously. Ruth abruptly stopped talking and looked back. Surprise registered on her scarred face. She hauled back on the lines.

"Mister Coopersmith!" she exclaimed.

Gideon closed the distance and reined up beside the ore wagon.

"What're you doin' here?" she asked.

"Figured you might need a hand," he said, "bringing in Sam Whitlock."

She squared her shoulders. "You might as well turn back. I can handle him."

"You're out-numbered," Gideon said. "Last time I saw Whitlock two men were working for him."

Ruth gazed at him. Her expression softened. "I appreciate your kindness, Mister Coopersmith. I know how you felt about Tommy. But I'm asking you to turn back. You've got a family depending on you, a ranch to run, critters to feed. You sure as hell got no business making this-here ride to Laramie."

"If Whitlock's alive," Gideon said, "I want him brought in, too." He added: "I believe I can locate him."

She leaned toward him with sudden interest. "How?"

"One of the men riding in the posse," he replied, "owns a business in Laramie. Reckon he can take us to Whitlock . . . or point us toward him."

"What's this feller's name?"

"I don't know his full name," Gideon said. "He goes by Mike. I know where his place of business is."

"You do?" she said. "Tell me."

Gideon shook his head. "I'll take you to him."

She tried to stare him down, but gave it up. "First time we met, Mister Coopersmith, you done told me you had no quit in you. You ain't planning to quit now, are you? You'll ride to Laramie with me or without me."

"Faster without you," he replied with a grin.

"Hell's bells," she said. She drew a deep breath and exhaled a plume into the cold air. "Oh, I'll go along . . . for now. But, when I cross trails with Whitlock, you stay outta my way. Hear? Stand back and stay outta my way."

"I'm not making any promises, Ruth."

She grabbed the whip, swung it, and popped the end over the mules' backs, sending the big animals on their way. Gideon touched spurs to the paint.

At dark they made camp by a frozen water hole ringed by trees and brush. While Ruth warmed tins of food over a fire, Gideon found a stone heavy enough to break the ice. After the water hole was open, he let the animals drink their fill. Then he led them into the cover of the trees and fed them from nosebags full of grain.

Rather than sit in the snow, Gideon joined Ruth on the tailgate of the wagon. The campfire burned a few feet away, the embers glowing red-orange. Normally Gideon would roll out his blanket and sleep on the ground, but when Ruth unloaded the wagon box and spread out bedding and the buffalo robe there, he did not decline her invitation to a warm and dry bed.

"I done told your missus," Ruth said, holding the blankets open for him.

"Told her what?"

"About us sleeping in the same bed," Ruth said. "Here we are, doing it again. Onliest thing is . . . this time your eyes are open. Now, take off them pointy-toed boots. I won't have you kicking me in the night."

Cold Wind

★ ★ ★ ★ ★

From 1868 onward, the lifeblood of Laramie pumped into the heart of town on the transcontinental railroad. The growing freight business of the Union Pacific line kept the town in good health even after statehood in 1890, when Cheyenne was named the capital. A poor second cousin, Laramie was awarded the state university and penitentiary—Ivory Tower for graduation, Stoney Lonely for incarceration. Those two institutions, along with the roaring trains of the U.P. day and night, assured jobs and cash for the windswept town on the high plains of North America.

From first light until noon, Gideon rode behind the ore wagon at a slow and tedious pace. Every so often he dismounted and walked two hundred yards, as much to break the monotony as to rest the horse. The sun was past its zenith when the faint cry of a train whistle reached his ears. Mounting, he stood in the stirrups and looked ahead. Over the snow-covered horizon a smudge of smoke sullied the sky. An hour later, he saw water towers, coal bins, corrals, and U.P. section houses.

Steel rails led to the business district of Laramie. Whistle sounding again, the locomotive departed eastward, sending a column of black smoke into the still sky. Gideon was close enough now to see that the train was composed of flat cars and boxcars, and half a dozen passenger coaches. The procession was long gone by the time he and Ruth reached the shiny tracks.

In town, he let the paint trot ahead of the team of jacks. Passing the stone U.P. dépôt on Main Street, he led the way through horse and wagon traffic, with a few pedestrians crossing here and there. Streets were snow-packed and deeply rutted. Unlike Denver, the pace was slow with no clanging trolleys or the fast, high-wheeled carriages of the

137

rich racing through the hordes of the unwashed with shouts from a uniformed driver.

Gideon spotted a sign marking First Street. At the next intersection he reined to the right. Three blocks away, on Second, he saw the wide, sloping roof of a livery barn. Set back from the street by a stout corral, a sign was painted over double doors in black, frontier-style lettering:

Livery Stable
Michael O'Connor, Prop.
Blacksmith

Gideon reined up. He turned in the saddle and signaled for Ruth to halt. "Wait here."

"Is that the place?" she asked, looking past him. "That livery?"

Gideon nodded.

"I'm coming with you, Mister Coopersmith."

"Ruth, I thought we settled this."

Gideon saw her scarred face stiffen as they gazed at one another in a silent battle of wills.

"I'll hear what that murdering bastard has to say for hisself," Ruth said at last.

"He won't say anything," Gideon said, "if you light into him. Let me handle this."

"So you two gents can talk over this-here weather?" she demanded. "Or will you be cussing over politics or women or horses or. . . ."

"Ruth, just wait here a spell. If I can't get any information out of the man, I'll stand aside."

She made no reply. In an odd, turtle-like move, she pulled her wool hat down lower on her head, hunched her shoulders, and glowered some more.

Gideon turned the paint and rode down the street to the livery. He followed tracks and horse droppings in the snow around the perimeter of the empty corral. Inside the barn, horses whinnied, and the newcomer—the paint—answered. As Gideon rounded the stock pen, a weathered plank door to a tack room swung open. A wide-shouldered man, hatless, with bushy hair the color of carrots stepped outside. Mike O'Connor studied the mount for a long moment, and then lifted his gaze to the rider.

"Welcome to Laramie!" he said. With a grin he asked: "Are you the feller who owns the Double Circle C down in Colorado, or are you the thief who stole his Indian horse?"

Gideon dismounted. "Howdy, Mike. Name's Gideon Coopersmith."

"Now I recollect your name," he said, and vigorously shook Gideon's hand. He motioned to the doorway. "Coffee's on the stove, thick enough to grease an axle and strong enough to warp a horseshoe. Come in outta the cold for some Wyoming hospitality."

The tack room smelled of tanned leather and woodsmoke. Gideon surveyed a scarred workbench, clamps and jacks, and the usual assortment of hand tools—wrenches, flat files, half-rounded rasps, hammers, pliers, screwdrivers, pry bars, saws—all neatly hanging from pegs on the wall.

Mike poured coffee and handed a steaming cup to Gideon. "Business or pleasure?"

Gideon shrugged. "Little of both."

"I remember seeing that pony in your barn," he said. "Don't believe I've ever laid eyes on a paint showing that kind of bunched musculature. Strong, isn't she?"

Gideon nodded. "She'll go all day."

"I believe it," Mike said. "Want to swap her out? Maybe

two or three of mine? I've got some pretty good horses for the type of range work you need them for."

"Nope," Gideon said.

"Can't say I blame you," he said. "That paint is one unusual horse. I'm thinking . . . breed her to a good quarterhorse stud, and you might get speed and power in the same animal."

Gideon considered that notion. Then he said: "Speaking of horses, Mike, did you ever recover those stolen saddle mounts?"

A pained expression crossed Mike's face. "Yeah."

"What about the thieves?"

Mike's gaze darted away.

Gideon set the coffee cup down on the workbench. "I found the hanged men, Mike."

"I wouldn't know about that," he said.

"I think you do," Gideon said. "Sam Whitlock and his posse hanged those two men from a cottonwood limb by an old cabin. You were there, weren't you?" When he did not reply, Gideon went on: "Mike, I've got you spotted for a straight-shooter. Lies don't come easy to an honest man."

"Now, don't call me a liar," Mike said.

"I figure you were truth-telling until you got hooked up with Whitlock," Gideon said. "Now you have to lie to save your neck. Am I right?"

The liveryman knotted a fist. "I ain't gonna tell you again. . . ."

"Here's what I came to find out," Gideon said. "Where is Whitlock?"

"I don't know," he said.

"Sheriff Clarke down in Buckhorn wants to talk to him," Gideon said. He added: "Fact is, he's looking for all the men who rode in that posse."

"Mister, if you don't have livery business or smithing work, you'll have to leave."

"Mike, I can help you."

The big man eyed him, both fists clenched now.

"Tell me where Whitlock is," Gideon went on, "and Clarke won't hear your name from me. . . ."

Startled, both men jumped when the outside door was flung open with enough force to bang against the wall. Ruth charged in, one hand thrust under her coat.

"That lawdog will hear it from me!" she exclaimed, "if I have to drag you to Buckhorn myself."

Mike retreated through an open doorway leading into the barn. He quickly reached out, grabbing a pitchfork leaning against the wall inside.

"Get off my property," he said, thrusting the tines toward them in a jabbing motion. "Both of you."

"Oh, put that thing down before you get hurt," Ruth said in disgust as she drew out the sawed-off shotgun from under her coat. Pointing it straight up, she pulled one trigger, the gun recoiling as she fired a load of buckshot into the rafters. The blast seemed to shake the whole barn with horses squealing and banging against their stalls.

"Next one's for you," she said, bringing the weapon to bear on Mike. "Murdering bastard."

Ears ringing, Gideon saw Mike drop the pitchfork as though the handle was suddenly red-hot. Color drained from the liveryman's face as he peered down the twin barrels of the weapon, powder smoke drifting out of one.

"Tell me the names of the men who murdered my son. Ever' damned soul."

Mike slowly shook his head.

"You wanna be the first man in that cockamamie posse to die?" Ruth shouted, her face beading with sweat now.

"When you hanged my son in the Buckhorn Gold and Silver crushing mill, you wrote your own death sentence."

"Mill," Mike repeated dully. "Mill?"

"Don't lie about it!" she shouted.

Mike said in a thin whisper: "I don't know anything about hanging a man in Buckhorn."

Gideon lifted his hand while Ruth was aiming at the liveryman.

"You stay outta this, Mister Coopersmith," she said, without looking at him. "You promised."

"You didn't exactly keep your end of the bargain."

"I ain't gonna stand here and argue," she said, her eyes still on Mike. "I'm fixing to send this lying bastard to hell."

"Please . . . please . . . ," Mike said, holding his hands up as though he could ward off buckshot.

"Mike," Gideon said, "you saw Whitlock hang those two men who broke out of the pen. Didn't you?"

"Yeah. He . . . he shot them out of their saddles . . . then he strung 'em up. . . . I didn't take a hand in it."

"From there, you went home with your horses?"

"Yeah," he replied.

"Were you with Whitlock when he hanged a kid in Buckhorn?"

"Hanged a kid?" Mike repeated. "No, I never knew nothing about that. I swear."

Gideon turned to Ruth. "Sounds to me like he's telling the truth."

"Oh, hell, you gonna let him weasel out?"

Hands sinking to his sides, Mike said: "I just . . . I just wanted my horses back. I never killed anybody. . . ."

"What's going on here?"

Gideon heard a gasping voice. He turned and saw a pear-shaped man, badge on his coat, revolver drawn.

"Lady, put that Greener down."

Ruth lowered it. "Howdy, Sheriff Tyler."

"Put the gun down," he said again.

Tyler was breathing raggedly. Gideon figured he had come running when he heard the blast of a shotgun.

Ruth set the gun on the workbench. She turned and pointed at Mike. "Sheriff, this man murdered my son down in Buckhorn. A fifteen-year-old boy! Him and Sam Whitlock, they lynched him."

"I had nothing to do with it . . . ," Mike began until he was interrupted by shouted accusations from Ruth.

"Lady, stop your caterwauling," Sheriff Henry Tyler said, "so I can get this thing figured out."

"There's nothing to figure out, you flea-bit lawdog. . . ."

"Lady!" Tyler broke in loudly in another attempt to silence her. "You are a lady, aren't you?"

"Hell, no," Ruth replied. "I'm a mother."

Tyler stared helplessly at her, his attempt to appeal to feminine sensibilities at a standstill.

"Don't you understand?" Ruth demanded. "My son's been murdered. Ain't nothing more fiercer than a mother on the trail of her child's killer."

"All right, all right," Tyler said. "I understand when you put it that way."

"About damned time," she said. "Now, put this murderer in jail so he can hang, legal-like."

"Nobody's going anywhere until I understand what's going on," Tyler said. He turned to Gideon. "How do you fit into this, mister?"

Gideon introduced himself, explaining where he was from and why he was here.

"I heard from Nate Clarke about that lynching in Buckhorn," Tyler said. "He wanted to know Sam Whitlock's whereabouts. Nate suspected Whitlock was involved in the boy's murder."

"That's right," Gideon said, wondering why he stated it in the past tense.

"Sheriff," Mike asked suddenly, "what was the date of that lynching?"

Tyler paused as he tried to recall it.

Gideon remembered his train ticket that day. "January Twenty One."

Tyler nodded slowly. "That'd be right. The Twenty First."

Mike brightened. "I was here, Sheriff, here in Laramie."

"You have witnesses?" Tyler asked.

"I believe that was the day I repaired a wheel hub on Hiram Reed's spring wagon. Yeah, it was. And that afternoon Joe Warner brought his gelding for shoeing. Sheriff, Hiram and Joe will tell you. I was here."

Ruth cursed again. "He'll take the truth and turn it upside down, Sheriff, if you let him."

"Miz Logan," Tyler said, "you know Buckhorn's a three, four day ride from here, don't you? Now, if two good men under oath place Mike in Laramie, then a reasonable person would say he was here the day your son was hanged. Will you agree to that much?"

Gideon spoke over Ruth's loud protestations: "Sheriff, give us time to think on it. Right now, we're looking for Sam Whitlock."

Tyler turned to him. "I answered Nate's wire, Mister Coopersmith. Didn't he tell you?"

"My ranch is a hard day's ride from Buckhorn. I haven't seen him since the Logan boy was found."

"Well, I already told him," Tyler said. "Whitlock's dead."

Chapter Thirteen

Gideon stared at Sheriff Henry Tyler. For once Ruth was silent, her mouth hanging open as though she'd been stomach-punched.

"You're sure?" Gideon asked.

"Sure as I can be," Tyler replied. "Saw the body myself when our Laramie undertaker lifted it into a casket and nailed the box shut."

"What happened?" Ruth whispered.

Tyler said: "Whitlock's partner . . . a man by the name of Ben Anderson . . . brought in the body. They got caught in a blizzard down in Colorado. Anderson was frost-bit and damned lucky to be alive. He said Whitlock was thrown and dragged by his horse over the edge of a bluff. The corpse was battered and scraped up . . . terrible sight."

"How do you know it was him?" Ruth demanded.

"It was Whitlock, all right," Tyler said. "I saw his black hair and a growth of beard on what was left of his face. His initials were stamped into his gun belt, too."

Gideon looked at Ruth. Her shoulders sagged. Then she snatched up her sawed-off shotgun from the workbench, and, with a last whispered curse, she strode out of the tack room.

"Can you figure that woman?" Tyler said, turning to Gideon. "First, she wants Whitlock dead. Now she can't stand the idea that he is."

Gideon said: "Ruth's been on a crusade ever since her son's body was found. That blizzard cheated her out of the revenge she was counting on."

"You think Sam Whitlock's the killer she makes him out to be?"

Gideon nodded. "Whitlock and his gunmen lynched two men and a boy. All three busted jail here in Laramie."

"You seem sure of that."

Gideon told the lawman of his first encounter with Whitlock. He described the hanged men at Dutchman's and the printed note he had found on one of the corpses. Then he repeated Clarke's account of the hanging of Tommy Logan and the second message from *posse comitatus*.

"I don't doubt what you're saying," Tyler said. "I heard the saloon talk. Whitlock blamed me for failing to bring in some escapees, even though it was out of my jurisdiction. I'm not a federal marshal." He continued: "But Whitlock never committed any violent acts around here that I know of."

"He was smart enough not to foul his own yard."

"Maybe so," Tyler conceded.

"What about his background? What did he do for a living?"

Tyler shrugged. "According to rumor, Whitlock was a man of means. He was always well dressed, and he came to Laramie on the westbound train."

"From where?" Gideon asked.

"Folks said he hailed from Omaha," Tyler replied. "Don't know if that's true. All I know is . . . Ben Anderson told me he was taking the casket to Red Cliff for burial. That surprised me because there's not much left of that windswept town."

Gideon repeated: "Red Cliff?"

"You know the place?"

He nodded once. "It's across the state line in Nebraska."

Gideon turned and looked for Mike. The liveryman had slipped into the barn. Clearly, Tyler knew nothing about Mike's participation in Whitlock's posse. Gideon figured Mike did not want to be the one to tell him, probably fearing prosecution in Colorado.

Gideon headed for the outside door of the tack room. He paused there. "Sheriff, I saw Whitlock in Buckhorn with two men. One was the big, rangy gent, Anderson. The other went by the name of Griffith . . . dark hair, trimmed beard, medium build. Know him?"

"No," Tyler said, "can't say I do. But a lot of men fit that description."

Gideon left the livery barn. Leading the paint, he caught up with Ruth at her wagon.

"I didn't get a chance to drink that hot coffee Mike poured for me," Gideon said to her. "You barged in before I could get my mouth around it."

She leaned against the front wheel, a combative look flaring in her eyes. "What else you gonna blame me for, Mister Coopersmith?"

"I spotted a couple cafés on the main drag. A hot meal in a warm café sounds good, doesn't it? On me."

"I ain't hungry, and I don't need your charity." She turned away and started to climb up to the wagon seat.

"Ruth, I talk better when my stomach's being fed."

She stopped in mid-climb and eyed him. "Talk? About what?"

"I'll tell you when there's a platter of grub setting in front of me. And a mug of hot coffee."

"Just tell me what's on your mind, will you?"

He shook his head. "Nope."

"Mister Coopersmith," she said, stepping down and turning to face him, "you're a good and decent man, but there's times when you angrify me."

He was thinking about Griffith. Tyler did not know the man. In the frigid storm that day, Gideon had glimpsed three horsebackers in the swirling snow, not two.

Ruth slammed a hand down on the white tablecloth, knocking over a cut-glass salt shaker. She quickly righted it and brushed away spilled salt. "Mister Coopersmith, what the hell are you getting at?"

Gideon had just told her of the riders in the storm. Her eyes widened when he described Griffith, a man about the size and build of Sam Whitlock. Then came her booming voice. Aware of startled looks from other patrons in the Cattleman's Café, Gideon lifted his hand, signaling her to crank her voice down.

She leaned forward. "You're saying Sam Whitlock's alive?"

"I'm saying," Gideon replied, "that we need to ask a few more questions than Sheriff Tyler did."

"That lawdog's in-grunt."

"He's what?"

"In-grunt. Don't know nothin'."

"Oh. Ignorant."

"Whatever the fancy word is," she said, leaning back as she squinted across the table at him. "You know my meaning."

"Tyler's not the man to talk to," Gideon said. "He figures the case is closed."

"Then who?"

"Mike."

"Mike!" she repeated. "You couldn't get nothing outta him before. What makes you think . . . ?"

While she rattled on, Gideon plunged a fork into two

inches of medium-rare sirloin fresh off Wyoming range. Bone-handled steak knife in hand, he sliced off a bite-size piece and put it in his mouth. He chewed, a contented man with an appetite honed by the mouth-watering odors of fried steak, baked potato, carrots and peas, a buttered roll twice the size of his fist, and freshly ground Arbuckle coffee. Across the table Ruth had calmed down enough to pick at her baked chicken.

"You blame me for a showdown that went bust at the livery barn, don't you?" she said in a muted voice.

"You're the one who fired off a cannon to bring that lawman running."

She lowered her gaze to her plate.

"Ruth, let me handle Mike," Gideon went on. "Will you do that?"

She pursed her lips. After a long moment she nodded without looking at him. "Oh, all right. I just don't see what good it's gonna do. . . ."

"That's why you need to stand clear," he broke in.

She looked at him now. "Well, what do you figure happened in that blizzard?"

"I don't know," Gideon replied. "I don't think Mike knows, either."

"Then why . . . ?"

He lifted his hand again. "One step at a time, Ruth. I've got a plan."

She snorted. "You're gonna talk to a liveryman who don't know what we're trying to find out? Some plan."

"A work of art, huh?" Gideon said as he dug into the steak.

After custard pie and more coffee, they parted on the boardwalk in front of the Cattleman's Café. For shelter against the frigid air of the high plains, Ruth agreed to wait in the Union Pacific dépôt while Gideon returned to Mike O'Connor's livery barn.

Gideon swung up and rode back to Second Street. He left the paint tied at a rail one block away. He had a feeling Mike would duck him, if he had a chance. Circling the block, he eased into the barn through the rear entrance. A door hinge squealed. Stabled horses snorted and stamped their hoofs.

His instinct had been right. At the far end of the runway he glimpsed a broad-shouldered man moving into the deep shadows of an empty stall.

"Mike."

When no answer came, Gideon called to him again as he closed the distance. "I'm not here to make trouble for you, Mike. I figure you've got a family. You want no trouble with the law. Am I right?"

His question was met with silence.

"Mike, you got nothing to fear from me. I want information. Soon as I get it, I'll leave."

A long moment passed before a shadow moved out of the stall. Hatless, Mike stepped into the runway. "What, uh, what kind of information?"

"About the men in Whitlock's posse," Gideon replied. "I want to know who they are. And where I can find them."

Mike shook his head. "I don't know. They weren't local men. I was the only one from these parts."

"None of them are in Laramie now?"

"I haven't seen any of them."

"Any idea where they went . . . or where they came from?"

Mike shook his head again. "From what I gathered, Whitlock hired half a dozen men in Nebraska. He outfitted them with guns and winter clothing and saddle mounts, and then he took them to Red Cliff for training."

"Training," Gideon repeated. "What kind of training?"

"I don't know exactly," Mike replied. "They talked about sighting in new rifles, swearing loyalty to the flag of the United States, demanding justice from lawmen, and I don't know what-all. Whitlock heard about the prison breakout and came to Laramie on the train. He offered to help get my horses back. Tyler's a town man, not much for giving chase. 'Strike a blow for justice' . . . was what Whitlock said at the time. I figured it was my only chance to get those horses back."

"Sounds like a bunch of hungry bounty hunters."

"Whitlock has something bigger in mind than collecting a reward or two."

"What?"

"From what I overheard, when I camped with him and his deputies," Mike said, "I gather he has some scheme for staking out a new territory somewhere in the West. Sort of like the Mormons did in Utah."

"A new territory?" Gideon repeated, amazed.

Mike nodded. "A place where folks respect law and order, where they can live in peace, without fearing thieves and murderers. That's what he said."

Gideon remembered the image of a mad prophet the first time he met Sam Whitlock. "Can you board my mare?"

"Sure," Mike said. "What you got in mind?"

"I'll grab the next passenger coach to Red Cliff."

"That prairie town went bust," Mike said.

"Maybe it's the place Whitlock was looking for."

Mike studied him. "If you run up against him, be careful. Damned careful. He's the most ruthless man I ever met. I wish I'd never crossed trails with him."

Gideon did not ask what prompted him to say that. He

figured he knew, having spotted Mike as a man of good conscience. The liveryman had witnessed the deaths of those two prison escapees, and the murders troubled him, even if he had not taken an active rôle. Gideon remembered Clarke's account of his father riding with Montana vigilantes, and figured Mike was haunted by the experience, too, unable to rid his mind of cries from doomed men—"a damnable curse."

At the dépôt, Gideon told Ruth to wait in Laramie. He would make this trip alone, and report back to her.

"You figure Whitlock's in Red Cliff, don't you?" she said, yanking a *cigarillo* from her mouth. "The bastard's sitting in front of his fireplace, safe and toasty warm, because folks think he's dead. That's how he aims to get away with killing three men in Colorado, ain't it?"

"Reckon that could be his thinking."

"Hell, I'm coming with you," she said.

They stared at one another as a Union Pacific mantel clock audibly ticked the seconds away. Gideon knew he could argue, reason, and threaten, but decided to save his breath. He'd spent enough time with Ruth Logan to know a lost cause when he saw one.

"That cut-down shotgun lands you in trouble, Ruth," Gideon said. "Leave it here with your wagon."

She punched the *cigarillo* back into her mouth. "Tell me something, Mister Coopersmith."

"What?"

"You aim to leave your Colt revolver here?"

"No."

"There's your answer," she said.

They bought tickets on the two a.m. eastbound coach, and then drove the mule team and ore wagon to Mike's livery. After returning to the dépôt, Gideon dozed on a hard, high-backed bench close to the stove, awakened by the shrill whistle of the train. He got up and walked, stiff-legged, to the window, seeing the steam engine's light stabbing into the darkness.

He and Ruth boarded a half-filled passenger coach. They sat across the aisle from one another. Gideon pushed his hat over his eyes, leaned back, and slept. The monotonous clicking of steel wheels on the rails crept into his dreams. The clock was ticking again, but, in his dream, time suddenly sped up, ticking faster and faster with no force to stop it beyond death itself—until the mournful whistle sounded and the huffing locomotive slowed.

Gideon opened his eyes. Shaking off the troubling dream, he straightened up. He cupped his hands to the window. The lights of Cheyenne slid into view. The train stopped here for an hour before resuming its eastward course through the night. The next stop announced by the uniformed conductor was Red Cliff, Nebraska.

So named for the reddish sandstone formation rising above the bank of the Platte River, the red cliffs had attracted pioneers bound for Oregon and California in the rush of '49, and then again a decade later when gold was discovered in Colorado. They had camped here, resting man and beast while Conestoga wagons underwent repairs. In rare moments of leisure on a westward trek that must have seemed endless, they had carved their names and dates of passage into the stone.

After daybreak the train slowed to a stop at an empty dépôt. During Gideon's childhood Red Cliff was a supply center for distant ranches and sandhill homesteads. He'd heard this town had lost business over the years to the Wyoming towns of Cheyenne and Laramie down the U.P. line, but had not expected to find it abandoned.

With Ruth at his side, he walked down the main street. It was empty and windblown. Unlike Laramie, no snow was on the ground here other than dirty drifts in the shade of northern exposures. Gideon looked left and right. Store buildings were run down, doors and windows missing or broken, the board-and-batten long unpainted and weathered to ashen gray. Ruth carried her Greener, a weapon unneeded here.

They walked the length of the street to the site of Leo Lewis's livery. Gideon had last seen this spot on the night of a hay fire that had changed his life. Now it was a vacant lot, overgrown with weeds. Tugging his hat brim against the gusting prairie breeze, he looked at the dozen or fifteen buildings and three dozen residences clustered around them, all empty, a sawn-pine skeleton of a town.

He marveled at how much larger this place loomed in his memory. Red Cliff had seemed like a hustling, bustling city to a boy fresh off the homestead, all the more exotic and exciting with the Union Pacific trains stopping daily to bring freight and passengers. Silent now, this place was stilled except for a dust devil spiraling fine dirt into the air and tumbleweeds rolling down the main drag.

Two houses near the end of the street showed signs of recent use. With Ruth trailing behind him, Gideon walked around them, and then peered in through openings where windows had once hung. The floors were strewn with discarded tins and open crates. Outside, the ground was littered with shiny brass shell casings. Gideon picked one up amid boot prints in a crust of snow by the porch. It was .30-30 caliber.

"Some plan of yours," Ruth said as she surveyed the weathered buildings of the town. "Nobody's home. Not one living soul. Say, where're you headed? Mister Coopersmith! Mister Coopersmith!"

Boothill was on a rise outside of town. Gideon remembered it well from his childhood. His mother was buried there. Now he ignored Ruth's shouted questions and strode to the cactus and sage-covered hill. By the time she caught up with him, he was walking among the grave markers. Few were stone. Most were planks stood on end, half buried, with names and dates etched into the wood. Harsh summer sun and sub-zero winters had cooked and frozen the pine markers to a dull gray, obliterating many of the names. Gideon halted at the foot of a fresh grave with a new marker, the only new one here: **Samuel A. Whitlock**.

Ruth moved to his side. She stood there in silence, breathing heavily as she stared at the marker.

Gideon strode past it to the crest of the rise. Ruth lunged after him. She demanded to know what he was doing now, her voice shrill against his silence. She halted suddenly, her gaze caught by a pair of weathered markers bearing the name of Coopersmith. Gideon knelt there. He reached out, his fingertips touching dry and warped wood. Barely visible now, the carved letters spelled **Emily Owens Coopersmith**. Gideon pulled off his hat. He bowed his head. Then he withdrew his hand and touched the other marker. It bore the name **Reginald James Coopersmith**.

In the town of whispering breezes Gideon found a discarded spade. Rusted and pointless, handle broken, just enough of the tool was left to move loose dirt. The rocky soil of the new grave on boothill was loose, and under Ruth's watchful eyes Gideon uncovered the raw pine box in minutes. Nails squeaked when he used the edge of the shovel to pry apart the boards. The moment he opened the coffin, a stench of death sent him reeling.

The body was wrapped in a shroud. Gideon managed to

lean over the box and pull apart the white fabric. No clothing, boots, gun belt. Rotting flesh clung to bone and sinew and strands of black hair. Sheriff Tyler had been right. The ruined face of the corpse could hardly have been more damaged if it had been shoved through a meat grinder.

"Well, he's dead," Ruth said. "Deader'n a coffin nail."

Gideon glanced at her. "This isn't Sam Whitlock."

She lunged and grabbed his coat sleeve, shouting over the prairie breeze: "That ain't him? You're certain-sure?"

He pointed to half a thumb on the corpse's right hand. "I saw this gent with Whitlock in Buckhorn. He went by the name of Griffith."

"The bastard's alive! Sam Whitlock's alive!"

After the gravesite was restored, the distant whistle of the westbound sent them hurrying from boothill to the dilapidated train dépôt. The locomotive halted there, but with no need to take on water or coal, it was soon under way with a shrill blast of the whistle. The passenger coach was nearly empty. Ruth followed Gideon to the far end and sat heavily in the upholstered seat across the aisle from him.

"You know more than you're telling me," she said. When he did not reply, she pressed him: "Mister Coopersmith, what're you holding back?"

He repeated everything Mike had told him.

She studied him, the scar on her cheek pulling one eye shut. "What do you figure Whitlock's up to, playing dead like he done?"

"The only reason for a man to do that," Gideon replied, "is to disappear off the face of the map."

"So he won't hang for murdering my son," she said. "Well, I aim to find Sam Whitlock. He can't hide forever."

After a long moment measured by the clicking wheels of the

train car, she turned to him and asked: "How can we locate him?"

"Ruth, as I recollect, you lack high regard for any plan of mine."

She stiffened and seemed ready to argue, but then her expression softened. "Mister Coopersmith, I'm sorry if I was hard-nosed. You proved your point about Sam Whitlock. I'm grateful to you." She paused. "You never told me your folks was buried on that windblown hillside. If I'd known, well, my folks, they're gone, and with my Annie gone and my boy dead and buried, I know. . . ."

Gideon heard her sob, and turned to her.

"I've done wrong things in my life, plenty of them," she went on. "I never knew who Tommy's father was. In those days I needed food to get us through the day. The cries of a hungry child tears at the soul. Men paid me, and, well, I done what I had to. Tommy, he used to ask about his daddy, so I made one up. Said he died in a mine cave-in. He was a man like you, Mister Coopersmith. You know, steady and reliable, a man who's there when you need him. Truth is, I was thinking about that made-up daddy when I brung Tommy to your ranch and told him to set things right with you. I figured he'd listen to you and get hisself straightened out. . . ."

"Find Anderson," Gideon interrupted.

"Huh?"

"Ben Anderson will lead you to Whitlock."

"Well, how're we gonna locate him?" she asked.

Gideon put his feet up on the seatback in front of him and pulled his hat down on his forehead. Eyes closed, he said: "Sheriff Tyler might help you . . . if you're civil to him."

After a silence she said: "Mister Coopersmith, I got a

feeling you're quitting the hunt."

He did not answer. He was thinking about a boy walking over bleak sandhills in the oppressive heat of midsummer, a boy alone and wondering about life and death, a son trying to understand his mother's decision.

"I'm right about that, ain't I?" Ruth asked. "Soon as we get to Laramie, you're riding back to your ranch. Ain't that for a fact?"

Chapter Fourteen

Dear Maggs,

This is the first letter I have ever wrote to you. I never even wrote love letters when we courted. I figured a letter scrawled from me would spook you, so I never put pen to paper with a Dear You on it. After we got hitched there was no reason for letters because we have been side by side ever since. Anyway now I dont worry about spooking you. You are wearing my brand and it is permanent.

Maggs, I saw my pa's grave in the Red Cliff Cemetery. I dont know how he died or when. Wasnt nobody left in that town to tell me. He is buried alongside of my ma. Bet you are wondering how I know all this and how I came to hike up the side of Boothill over in Nebraska. Well, as you probably guessed, it started with that danged Ruth Logan. . . .

While Gideon relieved some of his loneliness by penning his first letter to Maggs, thoughts of his father sailed through his mind. No man should have to die alone, and he wondered if his father had. He figured R.J. was friendless. Maybe he took ill and managed to get to town. . . . Likely, such questions would never be answered. But knowing that did not stop the questions.

A few days after he returned to the home place, he was in the horse barn with Patrocino when the braying of donkeys reached their ears. The two men had been filling canvas nosebags with oats, and Gideon stepped outside with an empty one slung over his shoulder. Patrocino came after him, a look of anticipation bringing a smile to his lined face.

With a shout and one arm raised in his exuberant greeting, Mills Pillow came striding into the snow-covered yard. He was followed by the pair of mouse-gray donkeys. His face reddened from the glare of the snow, the city man looked toughened by the elements.

"Gideon, you've been in the company of horses too long," Pillow said.

"What do you mean?"

"You're taking your meals out of a nosebag now," he replied.

Gideon pulled the bag off his shoulder. "Mister Pillow, didn't you know? That's how we get our horse sense out here in the West."

Pillow laughed as they walked into the barn. After the donkeys were stabled, the three of them went into the house for coffee.

Mills Pillow propped his Sharps against the wall by the door, and shed his coat and hat as he headed for the kitchen. He thrust his hands out to the cookstove. "Can't get enough heat in me," he said, shivering. "Lord, this region is cold."

Gideon grinned. "You look a mite weathered, but none the worse for wear. Did you climb Deadman?"

He shook his head. "Too much snow draping that mountain. I worked my way around the base of it, making camps as I went along. It's a tremendous sight . . . a silent and white world under the bluest of blue skies I've ever seen." He paused, rubbing his hands together. "I ran out of food. The Blake brothers were kind to feed a poor beggar like me. I hiked back here with a proposition for you."

"What do you have in mind?"

"I will drive your ranch wagon to Buckhorn," he replied, "to fill your list and restock my own larder. Save you a trip. How about it?"

While Gideon considered that, Pillow went on: "If you lack confidence in a novice like me, Patrocino can accompany me . . . with your permission, of course."

Gideon nodded slowly, thinking about his letter to Maggs. He decided to write another to Annie. Pillow could post them both.

"Reckon I could use a few items. Go ahead and ask Patrocino if he wants to ride with you. He hasn't been off this place for weeks. Every man needs a change of scenery now and then."

"*¡Si, señor, sí!*" was the wrangler's answer when Pillow spoke to him in Spanish.

The city man turned to Gideon. "You're right, *padrone*. He's eager to go."

For the next three days Gideon was alone on the ranch, alone and lonely as he had not been since he built the house. He had plenty of chores and kept busy every waking hour, but at night the house was quiet with a strange emptiness as though someone had died. Not entirely quiet, though. He had never noticed the plank flooring creaked and popped as it cooled in the night.

Before falling asleep his thoughts invariably went to Maggs and Annie and the baby. He wondered about them—what they were doing and how they were doing. The thought crossed his mind that, if Annie grew accustomed to living in a mansion in the big city, she would never be satisfied with ranch life again.

Wondering turned to concern the moment Mills Pillow and Patrocino returned. Gideon saw Pillow sprint through the snow to the house, a telegraphed a message in his gloved hand. It had been sent by wire a week and a half ago, addressed to **Double Circle C Ranch, To Whom It May Concern**.

"That deputy, Ollie Moore, flagged me down," Pillow said, "as soon as I stopped the wagon in front of the hotel. He said he'd been watching for someone from the ranch. . . ."

Gideon barely listened as he unfolded the paper and read the words printed in pencil:

GIDEON COME TO DENVER RIGHT AWAY
WE ARE ALL RIGHT BUT WE NEED YOU HERE
MAGGS

She was not a woman to panic. Gideon took solace in that fact as he struggled to keep his gut-knotting worry in check. But clearly something had happened. He read and re-read the message. Was it the baby? No, Maggs had said they were all right. She would not have written the message that way if a family tragedy had occurred.

Sleepless the last night before leaving the ranch, he got up earlier than usual, ate a full breakfast, and saddled the paint in sub-zero darkness. He rode the mare to Buckhorn, wired a reply to Maggs, and in the morning boarded the train.

All manner of dark thoughts coursed through Gideon's mind while he sat in the passenger coach, staring out the window. Winter scenes slid by, from ice-covered creeks twisting through cañon bottoms to snowy forests of pine and spruce trees, and finally the open prairie at lower altitudes. By the time he reached Union Station in Denver, he had decided Lucretia must have fallen ill or suffered a serious injury. He could think of no other reason for Maggs to summon him with such a cryptic message.

Carrying his valise, Gideon walked hurriedly from the train station through town. He jogged up the slope of Capitol Hill. A turn of the brass bell handle brought Maggs running. He heard footfalls, and then she flung the door open. Gideon dropped the valise and took her in his arms. She was followed by Annie.

"Daddy! Daddy!"

Gideon lifted her up and held her. When he put her down, he turned to Maggs. She spoke breathlessly.

"Gideon, the bank is taking everything, the house, the furnishings, everything . . . !"

"Slow down," he said. "What does the bank have to do with it? Is your mother hurt? Is she all right?"

Maggs shook her head. "No . . . yes . . . oh, I don't know. She . . . she won't come out of her room. . . ."

Emotions too long suppressed burst forth, and Maggs sobbed with a child's abandon. Gideon held her while Annie hugged her waist, the daughter telling the mother: "Everything will be all right. You'll see." Then they went into the library and sat on a cushioned sofa with Annie snuggling between them. The baby was asleep in a crib that had once been Maggs's.

"Oh, Gideon, it's all so . . . so shocking. I don't know what to do. I truly don't. Talking to you was all I could think of. I thought . . . somehow . . . if you were here, we'd solve this problem."

Gideon was still confused, but in the next few minutes he understood all too well. Ezra Allen Stearns had invested in Colorado silver mines, a sound practice that had continued to pay dividends after his death. But when the government declared an end to bimetallism, Lucretia did not rein in her spending. Intent on her climb to the highest rung of Denver's social ladder, she continued living in luxury, traveling to Europe, and generally out-spending her friends just to prove she could do it.

"Destitute," Maggs whispered in disbelief. "My mother is destitute." She drew a deep breath. "Mama feels publicly shamed. Says she can never show her face in Denver, and will not leave her bedroom. The Colorado State Bank and Trust represents the creditors. Gideon, the bank president came here himself, and Mama would not see him. He told me the city marshal will evict her, if she doesn't vacate the premises."

"There's only one thing to do," Gideon said.

"What?"

"Take her to the ranch with us," he said.

Gideon's voice and presence in the mansion influenced Lucretia. From first denying the truth, she now accepted it. A task that would have been well nigh impossible before his arrival was easier now than anyone could have predicted. The next morning Lucretia emerged from her bedroom. Haggard but dressed, she stood before Gideon on the landing overlooking the marble entryway. She grasped the railing with both bony hands like the claws of an eagle on her perch.

"Margaret tells me," she said in a subdued tone of voice, "that you have invited me to visit your ranch."

"Yes, ma'am," he said, seeing a lowered gaze no longer haughty. "We welcome you. Stay as long as you want."

"We'll pack our clothing in time to meet the next train to Buckhorn," Maggs said, taking her mother's arm while casting a grateful look at Gideon.

Lucretia paused and turned to Annie. "My dear, I'm so sorry you'll miss school."

"I'm not!" Annie said.

Maggs looked at her in surprise. "Why do you say that? You love school."

"I love the teachers," Annie said. "Those girls tease me."

"Tease you. In what way?"

"They call me a bumpkin," she replied. "They say I am a cowgirl who smells like manure. They say I have hayseeds in my hair. I don't stink, do I?"

Lucretia gasped as she stared at her granddaughter.

Maggs said: "Honey, you never told us. . . ."

"I can handle those mean girls," Annie interrupted. "I have a plan."

Maggs cast a sidelong glance at Gideon. "Where do you suppose your daughter gets that attitude?"

Gideon shrugged.

"Besides," Annie said, "I miss Brownie. And Patrocino. We're going to train my pony, Grammy. Just wait until you see him! He's beautiful!"

"My dear," Lucretia said in a tone of voice barely above a whisper, "you are the one who is beautiful."

After spending the rest of the day and that night in the Colorado Hotel—declared to be "primitive" by Lucretia— Gideon rented a covered coach and drove her and his family to the Double Circle C. The next day he came back to Buckhorn and loaded the ranch wagon with his mother-in-law's possessions. The wagon was full, stacked high with trunks, crates, and hard leather hatboxes secured by ropes. It all seemed so impractical to him, bringing ostrich plumed hats to the ranch, but he knew Maggs was humoring her mother by packing all of her clothing, white kid gloves, high-button shoes, and hats included.

Before departing for the home place, he crossed Front

Street and found Nate Clarke in the sheriff's office. Settling into a captain's chair, he spoke to him while stretching his booted feet out to the potbelly stove. Clarke listened intently.

"You opened that grave?" he asked, eyebrows arching in surprise.

"Wasn't anybody alive in Red Cliff to stop me," Gideon replied with half a grin.

"And you figure Whitlock faked his death."

"He's not buried in that cemetery," Gideon said. "I know that much." He paused and asked: "Has Ruth Logan been in town?"

Clarke shook his head. "Haven't seen her."

"I don't know where she went when I left Laramie," Gideon said. "She's determined to run Whitlock down."

"With that woman dogging him," Clarke said, deadpan, "it almost makes you feel pity for the man."

The irony of that comment and vivid details from those moments of conversation with Nate Clarke were fixed in Gideon's memory. He forever remembered the suit Clarke wore, his short-cropped graying hair and neatly trimmed mustache, the friendly glimmer in his eyes. Gideon would always wish he had stayed longer, that he had spoken to him at greater length, that he could have somehow changed the course of events after he had driven his Studebaker wagon out of Buckhorn that morning.

Three days later word reached him on the home place: Clarke had been lured out of town by a phony cattle theft report and shot from ambush—one bullet dead center through the forehead that had taken out the back of his skull like a blow from a sledge-hammer. A search had been launched after the riderless horse came in. Tracks led Ollie Moore and several townsmen to the body that they found sprawled in the bloodied snow a mile out of Buckhorn. Boot prints and packed snow in the bottom of a draw three hundred yards away revealed the spot where the killer had waited. A single set of horse tracks led from the draw to a wagon road, and were lost. The account came from Roy Ellersby. The saloonman had made the ride to the Double Circle C at Ollie Moore's urging, knowing the two men were longtime friends.

Gideon listened. He stood still for a long moment. Then he yanked his hat off his head and slapped it against his leg. He needed some time alone, and sent Ellersby to the bunkhouse. Later, when he strode out of the barn to the main house, he had made his decision. Before dawn the next morning, he kissed Maggs good bye and gave Annie a last hug. Accompanied by the somber-faced Ellersby, he rode out of the ranch yard on the paint, fast, his thoughts racing ahead.

Gideon wondered who had convinced Clarke to investigate cattle rustling alone. According to the account Ellersby had heard from Deputy Moore, one fact was certain: Clarke had been slain by a single bullet fired from long range. Gideon thought about that. He remembered the rifle in Sam Whitlock's saddle scabbard. With the long barrel and a telescopic sight, it was a sharpshooter's weapon.

Liked or disliked, admired or despised, no man was better known in the county than Nate Clarke. Even though he was a bachelor without surviving family members in Colorado, his funeral drew mourners from all points of the compass. They ranged from dignitaries to saloon swampers, from gamblers on the fringe of the law to county commissioners who drafted laws. A city marshal from Denver arrived on the train, black armband around his coat sleeve.

Another lawman, Sheriff Henry Tyler, traveled down from Laramie to pay his respects.

With the exception of Gideon, North Park ranchers were absent. Far-flung across the frozen plain, most cattlemen would not learn of the sheriff's death for days or even weeks after the funeral service.

Clarke's favorite horse, the gray, was led into the cemetery by Moore, stirrups hooked over the saddle horn. A Methodist minister read from Ecclesiastes. He spoke of Clarke's life, and prayed over the freshly turned soil.

Hat in hand, Gideon stood in silence, considering the irony of life and death. Nathaniel James Clarke was laid to rest in the cemetery space next to Tommy Logan.

"Mister Coopersmith?"

Heading for town after the graveside service, Gideon heard his name called. He turned to see Tyler walking swiftly to catch up. They shook mittened hands.

"You recall that woman by the name of Ruth Logan?"

"I can't very well forget her."

Tyler eyed him. "She tells me you do not believe Sam Whitlock is interred in that grave in Red Cliff."

"I'm sure of it," Gideon said.

"How can you be?"

"Didn't Ruth tell you?"

Tyler shook his head. "She asked me if it was a crime to open a coffin. I advised her grave desecration certainly is a crime punishable by law, and she told me she had nothing more to say."

Gideon smiled. "Then I reckon I don't, either, Sheriff."

"Mister Coopersmith, as you know, I do not represent the law in the state of Nebraska," Tyler said. "But I am interested in the facts of the case."

Gideon told him what he knew about the corpse buried

in Red Cliff's boothill, adding his belief that at some time in his life the man known as Griffith had worked on a ranch. Gideon was familiar with that unique injury, having barely escaped it himself a time or two. Cowhands, roping a steer, hastily wrapped the lariat around the saddle horn, sometimes catching a thumb in a loop at the exact moment the cutting horse planted his hoofs and the steer reached the end of his rope. As the critter was thrown, the rope sang taut, cutting the thumb off, not as slick and quick as a slash from a blade, but more like a blow from a sledge-hammer.

"Miz Logan asked me where she could locate Ben Anderson," Tyler said. "I heard Whitlock and Anderson hailed from Omaha, Nebraska. Could be rumor, for all I know. I told her that, but the next morning she boarded the eastbound train, valise in hand. . . ."

"Gideon!"

He turned and saw Ollie Moore amid a cluster of mourners leaving the cemetery. The deputy led the smoke-gray horse through the wrought iron gate. When he drew near, he held the reins out to Gideon.

"Nate did not leave a will," Moore said, "but I know he wanted you to have his horse and gear, if anything ever happened to him."

Gideon stared at him for a moment. Caught by surprise, grief welled up, choking off his voice as he fought tears.

Moore went on: "This horse is strong and quick, and Nate always figured he had the makings of a good cutting horse. He often said you should have him, if there came a time when he didn't need him."

Gideon took the reins. He stroked the horse's neck while trying to regain his composure. He heard Tyler ask the deputy the question that had been on his mind, too: "Who drew Sheriff Clarke into an ambush?"

"Nobody knows," he replied. "Find out, and we'll hang the bastard."

Gideon cleared his throat. "Nate was alone?"

He nodded. "On his way out of town he mentioned to Silas that he was going after rustlers. It isn't unusual for either one of us to investigate a crime report alone. We're short-handed . . . just like you are up there in Laramie. Right, Sheriff?"

Tyler nodded. "I could use a hand. Just about the time I find a good man and get him trained, he figures out he can double his wage by working for the railroad."

"I wonder who talked to Nate in the hours before his murder," Gideon said. He added: "Ben Anderson could have planted that story."

Moore asked: "Who's he?"

"All I know about him is that he works for Sam Whitlock," Gideon said. "They could have cooked up the scheme to draw Nate out of town."

Moore stepped closer. "You'd better explain where you get that notion."

Standing beyond the gate in a fence with vertical bars of wrought iron encircling the cemetery like upturned spears, Gideon filled in background information. He finished by describing the high-powered rifle in Whitlock's saddle boot.

"Whitlock faked his own death," Gideon said. "And I figure he's a sharpshooter capable of killing a man from a considerable distance."

Both lawmen listened, and both posed the same question: Why would Sam Whitlock kill him?

"Revenge," Gideon said, recalling Clarke had run him out of town along with Ben Anderson and Griffith.

Without a co-operative witness or physical evidence, Tyler said, the case would be impossible to prove in a courtroom trial. Ollie Moore agreed. Besides, Whitlock's whereabouts was unknown. If he was wealthy, as folks claimed, he could be a long way from here by now.

In the afternoon Gideon was nursing a shot of the smoothest Kentucky bourbon stocked in the back bar of the Crystal Pistol when he overheard the news: Moore had been appointed interim sheriff by the county commissioners. Gideon figured Ollie Moore was far and away the best candidate for the job of top lawman. Not everyone agreed. Grudgingly respected in Buckhorn and Columbine, as well as by the outlying ranchers who knew him, Moore lacked the gentlemanly polish of his predecessor. Now Gideon overheard men, leaning against the bar, complain of Moore's eagerness to use his weighted sap. The deputy was known for breaking up drunken disputes by clubbing men to the floor whether they were combatants or not. Clarke, on the other hand, had possessed a quiet authority. His smile and soft-spoken manner had commanded respect. He could generally talk men out of trouble without showing a weapon.

Gideon figured any comparison between the two lawmen was unfair. They were opposites. As sheriff, Moore would enforce the law and keep the peace, and that's what folks demanded.

Gideon lifted his shot glass. He paused in a silent toast to the memory of a good man. Life in Buckhorn would go on. Somehow. But everyone knew Nate Clarke was one of a kind, and this was a day for grieving.

Chapter Fifteen

On the Double Circle C, Patrocino went to work on the gray. By spring, the horse would be ready for range work, if he had what it takes. For a rancher the most valuable animal in the string was his cutting horse. Fast and short-coupled, a trained cutting horse, once shown a particular steer, would chase that critter through an entire herd of hundreds or thousands, dashing, dodging, turning on a dime until the animal was cut from the others—whether the cowhand was still in the saddle or not.

Through that month of training a horse for range work and keeping up with winter chores, Gideon watched Lucretia's slow transformation from tearful self-pity to hot anger and finally to morose resignation. He was caught by surprise one night when Maggs slipped into his arms in bed and whispered: "Mills Pillow has taken an interest in my mother."

"Oh, no," Gideon said.

"Oh, yes," Maggs said.

"Oh, no."

"Gideon, she's my mother, but she's also a woman. When I see that certain look in a woman's eye, I know. And her mood is improved. Surely you've noticed that."

"No," Gideon lied.

"My first inkling came when I overheard the two of them talking about renaming Deadman. Mama thought nothing of the idea when she heard it from me. But when Mister Pillow spoke to her about it, she decided it was the greatest idea she's ever heard."

Mills Pillow and Lucretia Stearns? Gideon pondered that one. He had never thought about a relationship flowering between them, but he supposed they were about the same age and maybe they had found some common interests. Even so, he wondered if he had gone snow-blind or if his wife was deceived by an overactive imagination fueled by novels of romance.

Upon her arrival, Lucretia had retired to the spare bedroom and seemed determined to stay in there for the rest of her life. For trips to the outhouse, she donned her black woolen cape, a hooded, ankle-length garment trimmed with fine silver thread. When she padded in and out of the house with her head covered, Gideon thought all she lacked was a long-handled scythe to be transformed into the Grim Reaper.

At last she had been coaxed out by Annie. They bundled up and went to the barn to admire Brownie. Lucretia soon returned, shivering and rosy-cheeked and complaining of the sub-zero cold—but clearly invigorated. At Annie's urging, they went to the great room where they sat by the fire and read aloud poems by Walt Whitman.

At first Lucretia expected to be waited on like the Queen of England, Gideon observed, but as the second week led into the third, she took a greater hand in meal preparations and even helped Maggs and Annie with kitchen chores— this from a woman who'd had servants at beck and call for all of her adult life.

Gideon had seen Mills Pillow come and go, donkeys in tow, in his explorations of North Park in winter. These treks were short, and Pillow soon returned. Gideon noticed that. And now he was aware of uproarious laughter when Pillow and Lucretia got together and exchanged tales of life in Washington.

When Pillow talked her into a sleigh ride, though, and Lucretia did not complain of the cold, Gideon knew Maggs's antennae had sensed signals of the heart that he had missed. One sleigh ride led to another, then a longer trek in their visit to the homesteads of the Blake brothers, and finally to a proposed wagon trip to Buckhorn—for the two of them.

That was timely. When Pillow and Patrocino had gone to town last month, Gideon had expected the three of them to be alone on the ranch all winter and had sent a short list. Now when he opened the trap door in the kitchen floor and descended the narrow steps to the root cellar, he raised his lantern to cast light on plank shelves almost depleted of flour, sugar, salt, and other staples.

Gideon gladly let Pillow take on the job of restocking, and gave him a new list. Seeing him gently hand Lucretia up to the wagon seat and then fuss with her lap robe and foot warmer made him realize Maggs had been right. The man had taken a liking to Lucretia. How or why, Gideon could not fathom.

Their return brought disturbing news—disturbing to Gideon, once he had time to reason it all out. Lucretia rushed into the house, animated as never before, and sky high with talk of an "important man in Buckhorn." This man waved a telegraphed message, a petition signed by every United States senator calling for the nation's imminent return to bimetallism. The document was headed straight for President Cleveland's desk.

On Front Street Lucretia and Pillow had joined a crowd of townspeople gathered on the snow-packed street in front of the sheriff's office. They listened to this orator argue passionately for a worker's right to earn a living wage mining silver—"our sacred, God-given right"—were thunderous words that drew hearty applause.

"Oh, think of it!" Lucretia said to Maggs and Gideon. "When the federal government comes to its senses, my property will be valuable once again!"

Gideon started to tell her the truth, but was silenced by a look from Maggs. Truth was, Lucretia was broke. Rock bottom busted. She had nothing, other than elegant clothes stored in brass-cornered steamer trunks out in the barn, and those hats in leather hatboxes. The mining properties purchased by Ezra Allan Stearns were long gone, sold for dimes on the dollar at auction. To satisfy the rest of the creditors, the Stearns mansion high on Capitol Hill had been sold, too.

The transfer of deeds and other paperwork authorizing sale of properties had been signed by Lucretia in the presence of her daughter. Maggs had reminded her of all this— more than once. Each time, Lucretia listened and seemed to understand. Still, she would sometimes close her eyes and tip her head back while expressing hopes of returning "home" one day. Rather than argue, Maggs let her cling to the fantasy. Gideon's jaw-clenched silence made him a co-conspirator. Rich or poor, by his reckoning she was an impractical woman.

"Who is this important man?" Gideon asked now, turning to Mills Pillow.

"The new sheriff of Buckhorn," he replied.

"Ollie Moore?"

"No, the new sheriff."

Gideon stared at him.

"Deputy Moore was not promoted to sheriff," Pillow went on. "A new man was appointed by the county commissioners. A barman told me Moore packed up his family and left town, leaving his house standing empty."

Gideon was too amazed to speak, but he was even more surprised when Lucretia added to the news from Buckhorn: "The new sheriff works for a salary of one dollar a year," she said. "Can you imagine? One dollar. And he hires deputies at his own expense. He predicted Buckhorn will boom again, and professional deputies will be needed to protect the citizenry from the criminal element."

"What's this gent's name?" Gideon asked.

"Mister Sam Walker," she replied.

"A short man," Gideon asked, "with a long black beard?"

"No, he's clean-shaven," she said.

Pillow interjected: "He is short of stature. And he's always accompanied by a big man with a gun, a deputy by the name of Anderson."

Lucretia threw her head back and drew a deep breath. "Oh, isn't it exciting? Men like him will force the government to come to its senses!"

Pillow said: "He struck me as a bit pompous."

"Oh, he is not!" Lucretia scolded.

"Bimetallism is a dead issue," Pillow said with a shrug. "Everyone in Washington knows it."

She pouted. "I am disappointed in you. Mister Walker is a man for our time! The man of the hour!"

Gideon looked at Maggs. He knew she was not thinking about gold and silver any more than he was. His thoughts were on this important man, Sam Walker. Same first name, same initials. He figured Sam Whitlock was wearing his gun belt again.

Late that night in their bedroom Maggs's whisper came out of the darkness: "I've always known you're a man who must go his own way in life, and I've never stood in your way. But before you go riding off to Buckhorn, I want you to think of your family."

"Buckhorn," he said, turning in the bed. "What makes you think that notion jumped into my head?"

"I know you. And I know how you felt about Nate. You want to settle the score. Don't you?"

"Reckon so."

"Gideon, think of your family," Maggs said. "That's all I ask."

The riders came a week later. Under a bright sun, eight armed men on horseback swept into the ranch yard, their horses kicking up fresh snow and exhaling white plumes like fiery beasts of mythology. Gideon stepped out of the ranch house to greet them. He had been eating dinner. Still chewing, he moved to the edge of the verandah, hands on his hips. He recognized the stocky rider in the lead—Ben Anderson.

"Mister Coopersmith?" Anderson said.

"You know me," he replied, and swallowed that last bite of his noon meal. He looked past Anderson at the horsemen; a few he remembered from Whitlock's posse. All were well mounted and armed with holstered pistols and repeating rifles in saddle scabbards.

Movement beyond them caught Gideon's eye. The door to the bunkhouse eased open. The riders heard a hinge squeak and turned in their saddles to see Patrocino step into the doorway with the Remington revolver in his hand. Gideon had given him that gun along with the cartridge belt.

"I'm bringing information from Sheriff Walker to ranchers in the county."

"You mean Whitlock."

"I mean Walker . . . Sheriff Sam Walker."

"You can lie to folks who don't know better," Gideon

said, "but don't count me among them."

Gideon saw the man's hand drift toward the grips of his pistol. He wondered if Anderson would bring up their set-to in front of the Colorado Hotel that night. Clearly, he expected trouble.

Gideon asked: "Just what kind of information are you spreading around these parts like so much manure?"

Face darkening with anger, Ben Anderson stared at Gideon. "The sheriff guarantees strict law enforcement throughout the county. Ranchers and businessmen are paying a monthly fee for protection against the criminal element."

"The county levies taxes for that," Gideon said.

"This fee is separate," Anderson explained. "The money goes directly to law enforcement. You are guaranteed protection by armed and mounted deputies."

Gideon paused. "We don't have much trouble with outlaws out here." He added: "Nothing I can't handle."

"Sir, would you change your mind, if you lost cattle or horses to rustlers?" Anderson asked. "Or if something else happened . . . ?" His voice trailed off.

Gideon squinted against sun-glare. "Such as?"

"A barn set afire," Anderson replied. "Or nesters damming your creek upstream." He paused for a long moment. "Or harm coming to a member of your family."

"Sounds like a threat, mister."

"You asked a question," Anderson replied, "and I answered it. With protection from the sheriff, you won't have to worry about outlaws. Your fee is one hundred dollars per year. . . ."

Gideon broke in: "A hundred!"

"The fee is reasonable."

"How in the world do you figure that?"

"According to the *Breeders Gazette*," Anderson replied, "one bull calf worth five dollars at birth will fetch fifty, sixty dollars after three seasons." He then asked: "How many breeding bulls are under your brand?"

"That's like asking a man how much money he's got in the bank," Gideon replied. "None of your danged business."

"Seems to me, Coopersmith, any sensible rancher would want to protect his investment."

"And if some unreasonable cuss like me won't pay?"

"As I just explained," he said, "you won't be protected by the sheriff."

Gideon heard the door open behind him. Maggs came out of the house. She moved to his side and slipped her arm through his. In a glance back, he saw Mills Pillow step into the doorway with his Sharps rifle cradled in the crook of one arm. Lucretia and Annie were close behind him until he motioned them into the house and closed the door.

Anderson's gaze went to Maggs and then back to Gideon. His hand moved away from his pistol and came to rest on the saddle horn. "Think it over, Coopersmith. This is a fine ranch, the finest in North Park, according to your neighbors. It only makes good sense to protect your livestock and property. And your family. . . ."

Gideon interrupted: "I don't have to think it over. I'm not paying any fee. Go tell that to your sheriff, whatever name he's going by now."

"I haven't forgotten our last meeting," Anderson said with a lingering glance at Maggs. "You're reckless. Don't add stupid to the list. . . ."

Gideon pulled away from Maggs and charged down the steps of the snow-dusted verandah. He halted at the shoulder of Anderson's horse.

"Keep up that kind of talk, mister," Gideon said, "and

you'll have to climb off your saddle and face me like a man."

Anderson made no move to dismount. He studied Gideon. Then, shaking his head once, he neck-reined his horse around and rode out of the yard.

Gideon watched the riders leave. He turned and raised his hand in a gesture of gratitude to Patrocino. The wrangler acknowledged it with a wave and stepped back into the bunkhouse, closing the door. Gideon mounted the steps as Pillow leaned his Sharps against the log wall and came out to the edge of the verandah.

Maggs said: "Looks like the new sheriff found a way around the taxation problem."

Gideon scowled. "Nothing but a hundred dollar hold-up."

Pillow said: "The practice of tribute is illegal in America."

"Tribute," Gideon repeated. "What's that?"

"In Old World Europe," he said, "vassals paid tribute in gold or food or livestock to feudal lords for protection."

"Vassals?" Gideon said.

"Farmers and villagers," Pillow explained. "Those who refused to pay were severely punished, even executed, whether the offender was an individual or an entire village. One hundred and twenty years ago our forebears waged a revolution against the King of England to put a stop to that kind of treatment from the highborn."

"If the county commissioners hired Sam Whitlock," Maggs said, "they must have found a way to make the practice of paying tribute legal."

"Ah, yes," Pillow mused in his professorial tone. "The regal commissioners. Reminiscent, isn't it, of the princes of Europe creating laws to suit their interests."

Gideon was unclear on all the historical references, but he knew his mind. "The way I figure this thing, Whitlock killed a good lawman and ran off the deputy so he could take over Buckhorn. Now he's after the whole county. . . ."

"Gideon," Maggs interrupted.

He turned to her, aware Pillow looked on with interest.

She said softly: "Your family still needs you . . . now more than ever."

"Maggs," Gideon said, "I've worked beside men all my life, and, if I've learned anything, I know a man like Whitlock feeds on weakness. If no one stands up to him, he'll push and shove, taking more and more. . . ."

She drew a deep breath to battle surging emotions. "Gideon, you are a husband, a father, a rancher . . . not a sheriff." She paused. "If you must do something, go to the county commissioners. Tell them everything you know about the vigilantes and Sam Whitlock. They hired him . . . they can fire him."

"If I may add a thought," Pillow said, "you are within your legal rights to report him to the federal marshal in Denver. You may request an investigation."

Gideon recounted his conversation with Ollie Moore and Henry Tyler after the funeral service in Buckhorn. Both of them were convinced the case against Whitlock was not strong enough to stand up in court.

Now he met his wife's gaze. He saw fear in her eyes. She was not a fearful woman, and she rarely questioned his decisions. But this was different. He turned to her and put his arms around her.

"I'll stay on the home place," he whispered.

It was a promise he aimed to keep until he drove the hay sled to the hollow the next morning. Accompanied by Pillow and Patrocino, he looked ahead and saw blood on the snow near French Creek. Horse tracks showed where a critter had been encircled by riders—and roped, likely. Gideon urged the team ahead. He followed a trail of frozen blood. A mature bull, wounded, had staggered down the bank of the creek. Dropping in his tracks on the ice, the big animal had rolled onto his side and bled to death.

Gideon halted the team and jumped off the sled. He jogged through the snow to the carcass. Kneeling, he saw a gaping wound. The underside of the bull's thick neck had been slashed open at the jugular.

Gideon stood. "Looks like Ben Anderson left a message." He turned to Patrocino and saw the *viejo*'s face distorted in anger. Mills Pillow was silent. No translation was needed.

Pillow asked: "What are you going to do?"

"Make him pay," Gideon said.

Chapter Sixteen

Gideon saddled his paint for the ride to Buckhorn, and then he threw a saddle over Clarke's gray and drew the cinch tight. Last night Maggs had tried again to persuade him to stay home, but no amount of reasoned debate or heartfelt pleas in the intimate darkness of their bedroom would change her husband's mind.

"Gideon, the thought of losing you . . . it's more than I can bear."

He held her. "You won't get rid of me that easy. You'll have to do more than just think on it."

"Oh, Gideon."

In the end, she had to be satisfied with two compromises. After both Mills Pillow and Patrocino had volunteered to ride with him, Gideon insisted Patrocino stay on the home place, armed. He allowed Pillow to ride with him. Second, all of them agreed not to reveal the reason for this trip to town to Lucretia or Annie.

On the ride to Buckhorn, Gideon held the mare to a slower pace than he liked. Pillow had once said he was no horseman, and he wasn't, not even mounted on a horse with a smooth gait like the gray's. But he was not a man to complain, and, after stopping to adjust his stirrup lengths a second time, Gideon noticed Mills no longer grimaced while gripping the saddle horn for dear life. Gideon spurred the paint. Pillow managed to keep up at the faster pace.

In that last hour before dawn the sky was star-bright. Riding horseback at night was mesmerizing, and stars in a black sky amid the squeak of saddle leather and clink of bridle chains lulled Gideon into the past. As a youth he had learned a great deal from an old, battered cowhand who went by the name of Kansas. Whether spinning bunkhouse tales or tossing a loop from a cutting horse, Kansas showed hard-earned skills. And he was the only hand Gideon had ever met who owned up to a dislike for horses.

"Damned if them four-leggers ain't on the look-out fer new ways of killing me," Kansas often said. "You'd think they'd have something better to do, wouldn't ye? In my time I've been throwed, kicked, bit, stepped on, head-butted, tail-slapped. One outlaw even knocked me off my feet in a corral, stood over me, and peed. I didn't drown in that gushin' yellow river, but I'm here to tell ye, boys, I'm one lucky cuss to be alive to speak of it."

As a youngster riding night herd during spring branding or autumn roundup, Gideon had learned from Kansas how to use the Big Dipper for a timepiece. The constellation rotated around the North Star, completing one full turn every twenty-four hours. On clear nights a seasoned cowhand measured his shift by those stars, and knew when to return to camp to awaken the next night hawk.

With the stars fading in dawn's early light, Gideon stopped to rest the horses. Mills Pillow groaned when he dismounted. The big Sharps was slung over his shoulder. He left the weapon hanging from the saddle horn while he walked stiff-legged in a wide circle through boot-high snow. When he came back to the horses, he arched his back to relieve his soreness. Then he looked at Gideon across his saddle.

"You're quiet. What's on your mind? Or should I say, who . . . Whitlock?"

He shook his head. "I was just thinking about the old days."

"Which are better . . . old or new?"

"New."

Looking back through a haze of time, those cowhand days seemed simple and carefree. But the constant company of men had filled Gideon with desolate feelings, as though life held no greater reward than the next Saturday night binge in town. He never forgot that emptiness of spirit, even in later years when memories were clouded by nostalgia. Kansas was a good and likable man, a trustworthy pard. But Gideon did not want to end up like him. A chill coursed down his back when he feared he would become one of those homeless horsebackers who traveled with the seasons, one more cowhand with nothing to show for a life in the saddle but the contents of his war bag, busted bones healed crooked, and cow know-how.

The prospect of such a fate deepened Gideon's determination to prevent it from befalling him. Then came the day when he bought land in North Park, built the home place, and married the woman he loved. His wife and children brought a spark to his life, an inner warmth to ward off the cold. Commonplace routines on the ranch gave Gideon the heart-swelling pride of home and family, a joy he had never known as a cowhand.

Even though Gideon had lived in North Park for fifteen years, he was still an outsider in Buckhorn. Acquainted with a bank clerk or two, a few shopkeepers, Silas, the liveryman, and saloonmen like Roy Ellersby, Gideon could claim only Nate Clarke as a friend. To most of the town's residents, he was not well known. For that reason he had no feel for the prevailing mood, no sense of the reaction of townsfolk to the new regime.

Lucretia had described local folks enthused by a promise

of coming prosperity. Maybe she was right. Gideon figured she had witnessed a reaction to a desperate wish, a collective hope for prosperity, and she had been caught up in it. She had exclaimed over the sight of people elated by new hopes for the future, as though somehow she would bask in the coming glory.

Gideon thought about Lucretia. To him, she was as impractical as she was odd. Maggs had once explained why her mother rarely spoke to him—aside from the fact that to her he was a shiftless cowboy, and always would be. Lucretia at sixteen had hardly been more than a child herself when she married the wealthy Ezra Allan Stearns. A strong-minded man, he was both father and husband to her, at once a disciplinarian and lover. She obeyed him without question, and for that reason never learned how to carry on a normal conversation with a grown man who was not a servant. No other children were born to Ezra and Lucretia, and in a strange way the mother came to regard the daughter as dress-up doll, playmate, best friend, most valued possession. She lost them all to Gideon.

On the ride to Buckhorn he thought about asking Mills Pillow how he was getting along with Lucretia. He even mentioned her name as they rode southward. But when the city man volunteered nothing, not one word about her, Gideon took the hint. He would not explore that subject until Pillow opened the door and invited him in.

After a night in the Colorado Hotel and a breakfast that was late by ranch standards, Gideon took Mills Pillow aside in the hotel lobby. "I appreciate your offer to ride to Buckhorn with me. You helped settle Maggs's nerves. But from here on, let me handle things."

Pillow shook his head. "I'll see it through."

"This is not your fight," Gideon said.

"I backed you up when those armed riders came to the ranch. I shall do it again. Too bad we do not have time to construct a Trojan horse. . . ."

"I have a plan. . . ."

Pillow interrupted: "I don't suppose the strategy would work in this situation, though. Troy was a walled city that seemed impregnable. Many people mistakenly believe the whole Greek army hid in the wooden horse as it was towed into Troy. Greek scholars, however, tell us only a few men hid inside the horse, enough to open the gates that night after the drunken celebration by Trojans believing they had triumphed in a ten-year war against Greece. . . ."

Jaw clenched, Gideon said: "Damn it, Pillow! Shut up long enough to hear what I'm saying. Stay the hell out of my way. I've got enough to worry about without keeping an eye on a greenhorn."

Normally cheerful, Mills Pillow's round face stiffened. He stared at Gideon, at once surprised and offended, clearly feeling betrayed by a friend.

"Stay in the hotel until I come for you," Gideon repeated. Clapping his hat on his head, he turned swiftly and left the lobby. Mills Pillow did not follow.

On his way to the livery, Gideon saw a charred building. He paused there, noting broken plate glass and blackened boards. The empty storefront had once housed Mrs. Baity's Millinery. The fire had not spread to neighboring shops, even though they were separated by a gap of only six or eight feet. If other wood structures had ignited, the whole block would have gone up.

In the livery barn, Silas told Gideon that as far as he knew, every business owner in Buckhorn was paying a fee of five dollars a month for "protection against the criminal element." The man tried to put a brave face on, but, when

Gideon pressed him with questions, Silas would say nothing more, and shied like a whipped horse when asked what had happened to the blackened building across the street and down a few doors.

Gideon left the livery. He walked the length of Front Street to the saloon and dance-hall district. Peering through a frost-framed window of the Crystal Pistol, he saw Roy Ellersby. He tapped on the glass. The gentleman's club was not open for business at this early hour, but Ellersby let Gideon in and locked the door behind him. He poured coffee for him. They talked while he cleaned the mirror and back bar.

Ellersby waved his bar rag in a sweeping gesture around the interior of the place. "Before the silver crash, I hired a man to do the scrubbing. Now I do it."

Gideon sprinkled in questions with idle conversation. According to Ellersby, Ollie Moore had departed in anger. The sheriff's position had been offered to him, and then it was yanked away when the man calling himself Sam Walker rode into town. Walker and his gunmen made a big show of maintaining law and order in Buckhorn, claiming "justice" would come at no financial cost to the county. Once appointed, Ben Anderson and the seven other deputies had taken up residence in Ollie Moore's house off Front Street while the new sheriff moved into a corner suite in the Colorado Hotel—rent free. As word around town had it, the deputies shared equally in fees demanded by the sheriff. After the fire in the old millinery, the pay was good.

Gideon watched Ellersby gaze at his own image in the back bar mirror for a long moment, as though seeing a stranger there, drooping mustache and all.

"This place is all I've got," Ellersby added as though to be certain Gideon understood. His voice matched his dour expression when he described his initial refusal to pay the sheriff's fee. The fire in town and a persuasive visit by lawmen had inspired prompt payment from the Crystal Pistol and other businesses in Buckhorn.

"Maybe he's right," Ellersby conceded. "If this district booms again like he claims it will, we'll need every deputy we can find to protect us against the criminal element." He added: "I was robbed at gunpoint a while back. . . ." His voice trailed off.

"What makes anyone believe the Columbine district will boom?" Gideon asked.

"The sheriff showed me a petition to the President of the United States himself," he replied. "It's signed by senators, all of 'em. Those politicos are demanding the government return to a policy of bimetallism. He figures they will carry the day, and I'm not one to argue."

Ellersby was no taffy-pulling push-over, and Gideon was surprised to see this man cowed, reduced to mouthing the words of Whitlock—all tall tales and false hopes, according to Mills Pillow. But folks who are rabbit-scared for the future cling to hope tighter than usual, Gideon figured. When he asked where Ben Anderson could be found this morning, Ellersby cautioned him against tangling with the man.

"He pistol-whipped Silas," he said. "Hauled him into the livery barn and did the job in there where nobody could see." He added: "I'd stay clear of him."

"Thanks for the advice," Gideon said.

Ellersby eyed him. "You aren't gonna take it, are you?"

Gideon smiled. "Where is he?"

The saloonman paused before replying. "Anderson takes his breakfast in the hotel." His gaze moved from the wind-up clock on the wall to street-facing plate glass windows where backwards letters spelled out the name of this place.

"I generally see him walking past here on his way to meet the sheriff in the café."

Hunched against the cold, Gideon stood on crusted snow between the Crystal Pistol building and Fortune, a gambling hall next door. Even in cold weather, this narrow space smelled of urine. In the darkness, men who could not or would not wait in line at the four-holer behind the saloon came here for bladder relief. Now he waited in the stench and the quietude of morning. The sun was up, but Front Street was empty. The town's shops had not yet opened for business.

His wait was not a long one. Muffled footfalls on the snow-covered boardwalk gave him all the notice he needed. He shed his coat and yanked off his hat. Kneeling behind a fire barrel, he saw Ben Anderson stride past, and lunged after him.

Grabbed from behind by the coat collar, Anderson went down like roped steer. Gideon dragged him off the boardwalk out to the middle of the street, and let go of his collar. Cursing and at once confused, the big man rolled over and came up on all fours.

"You owe me one hundred dollars," Gideon said.

Ben Anderson scowled. "What the hell are you talking about, Coopersmith?"

"Payment for the bull you killed," Gideon answered. "That critter was the best of my breeding stock. Take a hundred dollars out of your wallet, or I'll take it out of your hide."

Ben Anderson raised up on one knee. "I knocked you on your ass once. You gonna make me to do it again?"

Gideon kicked snow in his face. "I'll give you as much chance as you gave my bull."

Angered, the big man got to his feet. Before he could charge, Gideon drew his foot back and kicked him between the legs, the pointed toe of his riding boot punching into the man's crotch. Anderson gasped, color draining from his face.

"You gave me a kicking," Gideon said. "Your turn now."

Gideon kicked him in the crotch again. Mouth stretching open in agony, the big man grabbed himself with both hands and sank to his knees. When Gideon kicked him in the gut, he toppled over on his side, legs drawn up, elbows pulled in.

"You killed my bull. Didn't you?"

"Go to hell. . . ."

Gideon kicked him in the ribs, and heard Anderson cry out. Circling the man, he methodically kicked him in the belly again, in the back, in the ribs, each blow from his boot harder than the last.

"There's nothing pretty about you," Gideon said, "but, when I kick your face in, you'll be uglied-up proper."

The threat brought a mumbled confession. "Ordered . . . I was ordered to do it . . . if you made a stand."

"Whose orders . . . Whitlock's?"

"Yeah," Anderson said through clenched teeth.

"Next time, remember," Gideon said.

"Huh?"

Gideon kicked him until he cried out. "Taking orders from Sam Whitlock is painful."

Anderson whimpered. Rolling onto his back, he begged for mercy.

"The price of mercy today is one hundred dollars."

Holding a quivering hand out to ward off more blows from the toe of the riding boot, Anderson reached into his trouser pocket with his other hand. He brought out his wallet. It fell from his shaking grasp.

Gideon leaned down and picked it up. Ben Anderson carried a wad, he discovered—several hundred dollars.

"Looks like you've been out collecting your danged fees," Gideon said, peeling off two fifties from the thick stack of greenbacks.

Gideon tossed the wallet to the snow-packed street. In the next instant, he was startled by a familiar voice.

"Law and order, Coopersmith. That's the rule in Buckhorn now."

Gideon looked around to see a clean-shaven Sam Whitlock standing in the middle of Front Street, gun drawn. A five-pointed, silver star on the lapel of his coat caught the morning sunlight. A dozen townspeople stood in the street half a block away, watching.

Whitlock went on: "This time you don't have a friend hiding behind the badge. You won't walk away from this crime."

"Crime," Gideon repeated. "What crime?"

"Beating and robbing a man," Whitlock replied, motioning to the prone figure of Ben Anderson.

"Handing this joker a whipping wasn't a crime," Gideon said. "It was a pleasure."

"You will be punished under the law."

"Hangman's law?"

"If the noose is required by the demands of justice," he said, "we shall use it. Buckhorn is a peaceful community. . . ."

"Whitlock, I know of two men and one boy you lynched," Gideon said. "But when it came to someone who could fight back, you bushwhacked him. You murdered Nate Clarke, killed him from a safe distance. Didn't you?"

"Your accusations have no basis in fact," he said. For the

benefit of the townspeople, he added louder: "I suggest you stop spreading lies about me."

Gideon raised his voice, too. "The way I add this up, the only reason for you to fake your death, shave your beard, and take a new name is to stay ahead of lawmen."

"If there was a law against a man changing his name, every jail in the West would be full." Whitlock moved a pace closer, leveling the revolver at him. "Now drop that gun belt."

Gideon did not comply.

"Or be a damned fool and reach for your gun."

Gideon still did not move.

"Take your pick," Whitlock said. "A jail cell, or the cemetery plot next to your dead friend."

Chapter Seventeen

Gideon did not believe in ghosts, but he felt the presence of Nate Clarke in the sheriff's office. He found himself hoping—while knowing at once the notion was foolish—to find Clarke seated in his swivel armchair, leaning back with his feet propped up on the desktop, and smiling as he took his pipe out of his mouth to greet a friend.

That moment passed in the blink of an eye. The chair was empty. Nate Clarke was not here. His remains were buried in the Buckhorn cemetery. Even so, overriding that reality, Gideon felt a familiar presence, a strange sensation, a certain odor. . . .

Maybe that was it. The fragrant smell of pipe tobacco still filled the office when Gideon came in at gunpoint. Whitlock escorted him past the desk through the office to the cell block. Ben Anderson hobbled along behind them, grabbing a ring of skeleton keys off a hook on the office wall.

"You are charged with assault against a peace officer and strong-arm robbery," Whitlock said as they came to a bank of eight-by-ten cells, each one barred like a cage. Anderson shoved Gideon into the first one, slammed the door, and locked it.

"When is my trial?" Gideon asked sarcastically.

Anderson grabbed the steel bars. "You can rot in here, Coopersmith."

"You'll have to let me out, big Ben," Gideon taunted, "if you want a rematch."

"You bastard. . . ."

"Come with me, Ben," Whitlock said, turning away. "Justice will be done in due time."

"No matter what happens to me," Gideon said, "you'll have to answer to the circuit judge."

"Coopersmith," Whitlock said, whirling to facing him, "we are operating under full authority of this county. Remember? *Posse comitatus* . . . power of the county. As a resident, you are required by law to obey all laws and ordinances. Violate them, and you will face the consequences."

"You've got your own little kingdom set up here, don't you?" Gideon said, and taunted him with a question: "When is your silver boom coming?"

Whitlock eyed him. "That's up to the politicians. All you need to know is that you will stay in this cell until you decide to obey the law . . . starting with the law enforcement fee paid by ranchers who are honest and have nothing to hide."

The remainder of that day and a long, cold night passed without water or food. Windowless, the cell was equipped with a steel bunk and bedpan, nothing else. As the sole prisoner, Gideon wondered if Whitlock aimed to let him die here. He doubted that. Whitlock was a man to do his dirty work in hidden places.

Gideon judged the hour to be mid-morning when the door to the sheriff's office swung open. Whitlock entered the cell block, alone. Except for a sheath of papers, he was empty-handed, carrying neither food nor a dipper of water.

Gideon left his bunk and moved to the barred door. The papers in Whitlock's hand were crime reports penned by Clarke.

"I'm using these documents to stoke the fire in my office stove," Whitlock said, holding out the top one for Gideon to see.

Jaw clenched, Gideon recognized the report on Whitlock's posse, the words he had dictated to Nate Clarke. "Burning papers won't change anything."

"You're living in the past, Coopersmith. Everything has changed here in Buckhorn and in the whole county. I have established law and order. With obedience, men live in peace. Obey, and you will share in the prosperity of our labors, whether the bounty is in minerals, crops, or livestock. You can go along or be left behind, left to choke in the dust of our progress."

"You're some fancy talker," Gideon said.

He watched Sam Whitlock leave the cell block. An hour later he returned with the ring of keys in his hand. "You're free to go."

Gideon cleared his dry throat. "You mean, I'm just going to walk out of here?"

"Mister Anderson decided not to press charges," Whitlock said, his small black eyes fixed on him. "I'm giving you some time to think over the law enforcement fee. Now, after you pay the fine for disturbing the peace, you may leave town. . . ."

"Fine," Gideon repeated. "I won't pay your trumped up fine."

"Sounds like you need a few days in this cell to clear up your thinking," he said. "You know, a man deprived of water suffers terribly."

Gideon drew a deep breath. "I'll take a wild guess, Whitlock. The fine for disturbing the peace is the hundred dollars I took off your man, Anderson, along with all the cash I'm carrying."

"Fair guess," Whitlock said.

"Let me out of here," Gideon said hoarsely.

Whitlock unlocked the cell door. He led the way into the

office and opened the cabinet. Gideon took out his gun belt and strapped it on. Picking up his wallet, he pulled out the two fifties he had taken from Ben Anderson, along with a dozen greenbacks.

"Here's your tribute," Gideon said. He tossed the cash down on the big rolltop desk. Then he stared at it, as though he had sullied the memory of an honest man. Nate Clarke had never used the badge to line his pockets, and in Gideon's mind this big desk was still his.

"The money is not for me," Whitlock corrected him. "I merely represent the people of this county."

"Maybe you've got some folks believing that," Gideon said. "Truth is, you're holding them hostage."

"You damned fool," Whitlock said. "Without strict law enforcement, the citizenry will lose everything they own to the next two-bit outlaw who comes to town."

"Is that why you hanged Tommy Logan?"

"You're headstrong, Coopersmith. Like most ranchers, you live by your own rules. If I must use strong measures to bring you into line, I will do it."

"You aren't man enough for that job," Gideon said.

His small eyes narrowed. "Need I remind you of the dangers to your property . . . your livestock . . . your family?"

Gideon had had enough. His hand lashed out, grasping Whitlock's shirt front. He nearly lifted the smaller man off his feet when he yanked him close.

"You lynched two men on my land, you killed a boy, and you ordered Anderson to kill a Double Circle C bull. I've told you before, Whitlock, if anything else happens on my range, I'll come after you."

"Get out," Whitlock said, face reddening. "Get out of Buckhorn."

★ ★ ★ ★ ★

Gideon downed two full glasses of water in the café in the Colorado Hotel. Then he ate a breakfast of scrambled eggs, fried potatoes, and ham. He paid his bill at the desk. A neat signature in the hotel register indicated Mills Pillow had checked out. He figured the man had left town until he stepped into the livery barn. The gray was stabled in the stall next to his paint mare. Pillow was in Buckhorn, somewhere.

Aware of Silas standing in the near-darkness at the far side of the runway, Gideon paused before stepping out of the barn. He thought he had heard his name called, and turned. The liveryman's voice came out of deep shadows.

"He says he'll kill you."

"Who?"

"Ben Anderson. Walk careful."

Pulling his Colt from the holster, Gideon checked the loads in the cylinder and thrust the revolver into his coat pocket. Hand on the grips and finger on the trigger, he left the livery and walked along the boardwalk to the far side of town.

Few people were out, and no horse-drawn vehicles traveled snow-rutted Front Street. Anywhere along here Anderson could be waiting between two buildings. Hatred in the man's eyes told Gideon the man was not above backshooting him as an act of revenge. Or Whitlock might have sent him to gun down an "escaped prisoner."

After walking the length of Front Street with no sign of Anderson or any of the other deputies, Gideon breathed easier. He located Mills Pillow. The city man was in the train dépôt, seated on a high-backed bench.

"Gideon!" Pillow exclaimed, leaping to his feet. "Are you all right?"

"Yeah," Gideon replied, holstering his revolver. "I'll be even better when we ride out of this town."

"I saw the sheriff march you into the jail at the point of a gun," he said. "I tried to get in to see you and post bail, but he turned me away. In fact, he threatened to jail me, too."

"Obliged," Gideon said, offering his thanks. "Reckon I was a little rough on you in the hotel yesterday. I apologize."

"You were merely attempting to protect me, weren't you?"

Gideon nodded.

"I harbor no ill will toward you," Pillow said. "The way you man-handled that big deputy, you clearly did not need me to back you up."

"You saw that little set-to?"

"From the hotel window," Pillow said. "I opened it and aimed my Sharps rifle at that lawman after he drew his pistol. I decided not to pull the trigger when he took you into his office. As I said, I had hoped to post bail until I discovered this so-called sheriff operates well outside the bounds of law."

"He has these folks buffaloed."

"Everyone except you," Pillow said.

Gideon disagreed. "I've got a feeling North Park ranchers won't pay his law enforcement fee."

"If that's the case, may I posit a theory?"

Gideon was not certain what he meant, but he nodded.

"Speaking as a newcomer who has traveled the length and width of North Park," he said, "I can say with certainty that your reputation in this entire region is sterling." He added for emphasis: "Absolutely sterling."

Gideon stared at him. In a land of long and severe winters, he rarely saw his neighbors, and he had no awareness of his reputation among them. He had no way of knowing.

The ranchers of North Park had never formed a cattlemen's association. The subject had been casually discussed over the years when a few ranchers happened to meet in town or on occasion out on the range, but in fair weather they were too busy to get together for meetings, and in winter travel was risky, often impossible. Besides, no North Park outfit had experienced enough rustling or robbery to warrant an organized effort at self-defense.

"Therefore, my theory is this," Pillow went on. "Whitlock will force you to pay tribute as an example to your neighbors. In other words, as Coopersmith goes, so goes every other rancher in this county."

"Then I'd say he's wrong about that," Gideon said. "Ranchers are an independent bunch."

"True or not," Pillow went on, "if my theory is correct, Whitlock will come after you because he believes resistance will break after you pay his fee." He added: "Gideon, even if he shoots you, he has achieved his goal. Other ranchers will be intimidated as never before."

Gideon considered that notion, recalling Mike O'Connor's characterization of Whitlock as the most ruthless man he had ever encountered. And Gideon remembered the building on Front Street that had burned—an example of "criminal activity" that he saw as nothing more than a threat. Townsfolk might have seen it as a scare tactic, too, if their judgment had not been clouded by the promise of the federal government adopting the gold and silver standard again.

"Let's get out of here," Gideon said, and saw Pillow cast a glance toward the telegrapher's cage. Now he noticed the city man clutched half a dozen penciled messages in his hand.

"I'm awaiting three more messages," Pillow said. "They

should come over the wire in a few hours."

"I've been invited to leave town by his highness," Gideon said. "I'd better ride before he turns his dogs loose on me."

Pillow looked toward the telegrapher's cage again, pausing as he made his decision. He shrugged. "I can retrieve my messages another day, I suppose."

The late start put them in sight of Dutchman's well after dark. Clouds swept in with a warm breeze, a winter chinook blotting out stars. The spring season was a long way off, but chinook winds floating through North Park signaled the first crack in winter's iron grip. It was a tantalizing promise of warm days and cool nights, a reminder of knee-high grasses and blooming wildflowers in a season marked by the return of migratory wildlife.

Gideon had planned to rest an hour at Dutchman's, melt snow for water, and ride on. His plan changed suddenly when the breeze brought a scent of woodsmoke. It came from the direction of the cabin.

He reined up. By cloud-dimmed starlight the log cabin was a boxy shadow on the snow against a dark background of leafless cottonwood trees. Jumpy after threats from Whitlock and a warning from Silas, he leaned close to Mills Pillow and whispered instructions: "Hobble your horse. We'll move ahead on foot, guns at the ready."

They approached the cabin with no sound louder than snow packing under their boots. When they reached it, Pillow brought his Sharps to bear on the closed door. Gideon leaned closely, listening. He heard a scraping sound inside the cabin. With a nod to Pillow, he reared back, raised his boot, and kicked the door in. Shrill curses met them, and then a shotgun blast in a flash of flame leaped toward the rafters.

"One step closer, and it'll be your last! One damned step!"

Gideon stood in the darkened doorway, lowering his Colt revolver. The sound he had heard through the door was snoring. "Ruth, why is it every time you get a tad agitated, you shoot another danged hole in the sky?"

"Mister Coopersmith? Is that you? Is that you, Mister Coopersmith?"

"Yeah, it's me."

She took a ragged breath. "You scared me half to death, Mister Coopersmith. What the hell are you doing here? Say, who's that with you?"

After introductions and explanations, Ruth Logan made coffee by candlelight. She served it in tin cups she brought from her wagon, along with canned milk. The ore wagon was behind the cabin, the pair of mules tethered nearby.

"My trip to Omaha," she said, "was a wild-goose chase. I searched ever'where, even farms outside of town. Whitlock wasn't there. Onliest thing I found out was that big feller, the one calling hisself Ben Anderson, he's wanted in Omaha, wanted fer bank robbery. Did you know that?"

Gideon shook his head. "No, I didn't."

"In the Omaha city marshal's office I seen a reward dodger with his picture on it," she went on. "Plain as day. He goes by half a dozen different names, Ben Anderson being one. There's a five-hunnert dollar reward on him. I sure could use that money. . . ." She paused. "Mister Coopersmith, how about you and me bringing him in? We'll turn him over to Sheriff Tyler in Laramie. That lawdog will ship the prisoner to Omaha, and you and me, we'll split the reward fifty-fifty."

Gideon declined the offer, aware of Mills Pillow watching in quiet fascination. "I've got a ranch to run,

Ruth." He added: "It'll be a long time before I set foot in Buckhorn again."

Ruth's eyebrows arched with that last remark. "You can tell me the truth, Mister Coopersmith."

"About what?"

"Sam Whitlock."

"What about him?"

"Your lovely wife, she done told me," Ruth said. "That new sheriff in Buckhorn, he matches the description of Whitlock without his beard." She added somberly: "I heard about Clarke. I know you two was friends. . . ."

Ruth slapped her hands together and abruptly changed the subject. "Mister Coopersmith, I met your mother-in-law at the ranch house. Lucretia. Now she's a dee-lightful lady."

Gideon forced a smile.

"It's true, ain't it?"

"About my mother-in-law?"

"No," she said scornfully. "About Sam Whitlock. He's in Buckhorn, toting a badge, and calling hisself sheriff. That's the Lord's truth, ain't it?"

Gideon recounted events in Buckhorn, and offered a caution: "Ruth, if you go charging into that town firing off your shotgun, he'll cut you down."

She cocked her head in a mannerism that reminded him of Tommy. "Listen, Mister Coopersmith, I know I've been whumped by the ugly stick, but that don't mean I'm stupid."

Gideon did not reply.

"Let me handle that man in my own way, Mister Coopersmith." She repeated: "In my own way."

Gideon did not know what she had in mind, and did not ask. He knew her well enough to be certain he could not talk her out of going to Buckhorn. She was set on avenging Tommy's murder. No matter what he said or did, she would confront Whitlock in some way—or ambush him.

He thought about accompanying her, but knew his presence in Buckhorn would only add fuel to an explosion. He had done as much as he could to help her. Besides, he remembered Maggs's tone of voice in the darkness of their bedroom. She was right. His family needed him. Now that he had made his point to Whitlock, all he could do was hope the man would think twice before sending deputies to the Double Circle C again.

"I brung in the blankets, Mister Coopersmith," Ruth said, swiftly unbuttoning her dress front. "I'll blow out the candles, and we'll get close on this here bed. Come on, now. Pull off your pointy-toe boots and shed them clothes."

As she stepped out of her long dress, Gideon saw a wide-eyed expression on Pillow's round face, an expression that somehow reminded him of a peeled apple. When the man drew back, Ruth turned to Gideon.

"Don't he know about our sleeping arrangement, Mister Coopersmith?" she asked.

"A gentleman doesn't tell," he replied.

She laughed. "Reckon I've never been with one of them. Men hear about me, they do, and they must like what they hear." With another laugh, she added: "I just now thought of it . . . Pillow. Get it? Pillow! Mister Coopersmith, you done brung us a pillow for our bed!"

Gideon had never seen Mills Pillow flustered, but this remark and the sight of Ruth Logan laughing as she disrobed made him sputter, his face white.

"Oh, it's all right," Ruth said, untying the laces of her underclothes. "Don't shy off. That lovely Missus Coopersmith, she knows me and her mister snuggle up." She turned to him for confirmation. "Don't she?"

Before Gideon could explain, Pillow said: "Uh, Gideon, we uh . . . we were planning to ride to the ranch tonight."

Gideon nodded as Ruth's gaze moved to him, disappointment creasing her scarred face. "Ruth, we aimed to stop here long enough to rest and water the horses."

She ducked her head and turned away. "Well, then I reckon you'd better do them chores so's you can move on."

"Reckon so," Gideon replied.

For a talkative man, Mills Pillow was uncharacteristically quiet after they left the cabin. Finally Gideon noted his silence.

"I suppose I have fallen into a pensive mood," Pillow said.

"Yeah," Gideon said. "Pensive."

They rode through snow-reflecting starshine for two hundred yards before either man spoke again.

"As I mentioned a while back, Gideon, I have found the West to be as wild as they claim back East. Every bit as wild with rugged beauty, wild and. . . ." He paused, searching for the right phrase. "Socially unfettered. Yes, that's it."

"Socially unfettered," Gideon repeated. "Pensive, too," he added, intending to ask Maggs exactly what all those words meant.

"Yes," Pillow mused as they rode into the night. "By my witness, frontier existence brings out raw danger and every thrill possible in life . . . more than can be imagined by a man who has never experienced the phenomenon. Yes, much more."

Gideon grinned.

Chapter Eighteen

Tears of relief mixed with sobs of joy when Maggs wept in Gideon's embrace. She cupped her husband's face in her hands and gazed up at him.

"You know I'm not a worry wart," she said, "but this time, when you rode out, a chill ran up my back as though death's hand had touched me. I was afraid I'd lose you."

By a blazing fire in the great room, Gideon and Mills Pillow told Maggs and Lucretia what had happened in Buckhorn. Annie sat nearby, holding the baby. All of them listened in rapt attention until Lucretia gasped as though jabbed by a hot poker.

"I can bear no more!" she said, rising. "How dare you speak of Mister Walker in this way!" Turning, she hurried out of the room to her bedroom.

"What's wrong with Grammy?" Annie asked.

Maggs went to her and stroked her blonde hair. Andrew was awake, his brown eyes following shadows from the fire.

"Your father and Mister Pillow are speaking the truth," Maggs said, "but Grammy won't listen."

"Why?"

"It's painful for her."

"Oh," she said, and turned to Gideon. "Daddy, will you have to go to that jail cell again?"

"Nope."

Mills Pillow said nothing in response to Lucretia's outburst. Gideon thought about his earlier conversation with him. The more he went over Pillow's theory, the more sense it made. If Whitlock could not break Gideon Coopersmith, how could he hope to collect fees from other North Park ranchers?

Through the next week Gideon patrolled rangeland as a precaution, working around his daily chores in shifts with Mills Pillow and Patrocino. Riding through snowfields near and far, they searched for tracks or any signs of horsemen. It was not a difficult task with fresh snow falling most nights. Nothing out of the ordinary was spotted until Patrocino came galloping back to the home place on a Double Circle C saddle mount.

Mills Pillow translated his rapid Spanish for Gideon: "A lone horsebacker, a townsman is coming."

Gideon met the rider in the ranch yard. It was Royal Ellersby. After stabling his horse, Gideon and Pillow took him into the bunkhouse. Patrocino made coffee, and the four of them sat around the stove, with the carved faces looking on. Ellersby stretched his hands to the warmth and cast a furtive glance at the figures before turning to Gideon.

"Every business owner in Buckhorn is paying the law enforcement fee," Ellersby said. "I recall talking it over with you."

Gideon eyed him. "That tinhorn sheriff sent you, didn't he?"

"He knows we're friends," Ellersby conceded, running a hand through his drooping mustache. "He asked me to help out. I will, if I can."

"If you want to help," Gideon said, "ask Whitlock why he faked his own death and changed his name. Ask him why he lynched two men and a boy. Ask him why he dry-gulched Nate Clarke."

Ellersby stared at him, obviously unprepared to defend the man against these charges.

Gideon went on: "I'll tell you the answer to that last one. He murdered Nate so he could take over Buckhorn and Columbine. Now he's working on the rest of the county, carving out a little kingdom for himself."

"If there's proof. . . ."

"He's wearing the badge, isn't he?" Gideon broke in. "He's lording his authority over everybody."

"But do you have proof he committed murder?"

"Look at that sharpshooter's rifle of his," Gideon replied, aware his own voice swelled in anger. "Pace off the distance of the shot that knocked Clarke out of the saddle, blowing half his head off. Not many rifles could throw a slug that far with that much power, and not many riflemen could make a dead-on shot from that distance."

Ellersby did not answer. "Gideon, the sheriff's telling folks in town you won't pay the law enforcement fee. He says you don't want deputies poking around the Double Circle C because this is an outlaw haven."

"That's a bald-faced lie," Pillow interjected.

Ellersby glanced at him. "Either way, there could be trouble out here. Real trouble. That's what I came to tell you, Gideon. We've known each other for a long time, and I wouldn't want to see anything happen to you or to your wife and children."

"Stay the night, Roy," Gideon said, standing. "After breakfast, you can ride back to Buckhorn and tell the sheriff my answer hasn't changed." He walked out of the bunkhouse with Ellersby gazing after him, his mournful expression showing helplessness.

For the next five nights Gideon did not sleep well. He knew Whitlock faced two choices: take him on, or back off. Gideon figured Whitlock would take him on. But when? How? Would he be dry-gulched like Clarke was?

For a time, Gideon felt disgust for Roy Ellersby. In the guise of friendship, the man played the rôle of lackey to Whitlock. But after talking to Mills Pillow about it later, Gideon realized townsfolk had a far different view of the situation than he did. The man calling himself Sam Walker brought a promise of wealth and security to the people of Buckhorn, and now—"He enjoys a measure of legitimacy."—in Pillow's words. If this new sheriff claimed Gideon Coopersmith was harboring outlaws, most folks would believe him because the two men who knew the truth—Nate Clarke and Ollie Moore—were gone. Now Whitlock called the shots. Not only was there no one to oppose him, but from the county commissioners on down to the saloon swampers the townsfolk either supported him or feared him enough to keep quiet.

Long after midnight on the sixth night, Gideon was awakened from a fitful sleep by a heavy wagon rumbling into the ranch yard. He pulled a window curtain aside and looked out. The moonlight cast stark shadows across the yard. In answer to his wife's mumbled question, he replied: "Ruth Logan."

He put on his clothes and boots and hurried outside, oil lamp in hand. Ruth stood beside her mule-drawn ore wagon. Gideon invited her in, but she beckoned to him.

"Step over here, Mister Coopersmith," she said, moving to the rear of the wagon. She added: "Sorry to be a bother."

Gideon descended the verandah steps and crossed the yard. He heard the door to the bunkhouse open and close. Mills Pillow and Patrocino, hastily dressed and hatless, stepped outside into the cold. They met him at the wagon's tailgate.

"Howdy, Mister Pillow," she said. "And *buenos noches* to you, *Señor* Patrocino."

"*Señora*," he greeted her.

Gideon lifted the lamp higher as Ruth reached into the wagon box. She pulled back a heavy tarp covering her worldly possessions. Now the tarp covered something else—her prisoner.

Trussed up like a hog on a one-way trip to market, Ben Anderson lay on his side, haphazardly covered by quilts and blankets. He swore, demanding to be set free.

Ruth ignored him and turned to Gideon. "You always said my cut-down shotgun gets me into trouble, Mister Coopersmith, but you should have seen the respect I got down in Buckhorn after I fired off one shell in a houseful of deputies. I took this outlaw out of there, slick as a whistle, with them other growed men running for their lives in their underwear. One shell!"

"Set me loose!" Anderson repeated.

Ruth gazed at him indifferently, and said to Gideon: "I need cash money real bad, and I aim to collect that reeward. Now, if you and the missus can possibly put me up for the night, I'll be Laramie-bound at dawn." She repeated: "Sorry to be a bother."

She was a bother, Gideon thought, more than she knew. He sent her into the house to get warmed up. While Patrocino unhooked the mules and led them to the barn, Gideon untied Anderson's legs. With Pillow's help, he pulled the cursing man out. Anderson was bruised and sore from hours of travel in a wagon box with no cushions or springs. Gideon took him to the bunkhouse where he and Pillow lashed him to a bunk.

"You're in over your head," Anderson said to Gideon. "Let me go, or you'll pay one hell of a price. . . ." When Gideon turned away and strode toward the door, Anderson said louder: "Damn it, Coopersmith! Loan me a horse.

Soon as I get back to Buckhorn, I'll call Sam off. You won't have to worry about that fee." He added: "I'll pay you for that steer, too!"

Gideon came back and stood over the bunk. "There's only one thing I want from you, Anderson."

"What?" he demanded.

"The truth about the dead man."

"What dead man?"

"Griffith," Gideon replied. "Who killed him . . . you or Whitlock?"

"Hell, we never killed him," Anderson said.

"What did he die of . . . bad luck?"

"We got caught in a hell of a blizzard," he said. "Couldn't see. Griffith rode off the side of a bluff. Somersaulted down to the bottom. He was dead when we got to him." The memory of it brought a shudder.

"Go on," Gideon said.

"Sam and me, we pulled the horses into an overhang at the bottom of that bluff," he said. "Found some old Indian blankets and a stack of sage roots in a fire pit. Got a fire going, and that's how we survived. When the storm broke, we took the body to Laramie. Sam got the idea to make it look like he was the one who died. Even strapped his gun belt on the corpse. Sam paid me to bury the body in Red Cliff, Nebraska, where no one would investigate, and to make sure the sheriff in Laramie knew about it."

"Why?"

"He figured his death would be recorded in one state," he said, "and the body buried in another with nobody to check up on it."

"Why did he want the records to show he was dead?"

Anderson drew a breath. "Sam paid me to do the job,

like he paid me to call you out. I done the work. That's all I'm saying."

"Ben," Gideon said, addressing him by his first name, "you picked a hell of a man to throw in with."

"Just because you've got the upper hand," Anderson said slowly, "that don't mean I'm gonna turn on him."

"Tell me something."

"What?"

"During that storm, did you see a man driving a ranch wagon?"

Ben Anderson shook his head. "Hell, no. If we had, we'd have got help. Why are you asking?"

Gideon turned and walked out of the bunkhouse without answering. He was followed by a stream of curses and threats from Anderson. He barely heard. His thoughts were on the storm—and Whitlock. Their paths had almost crossed that night of the blizzard, and Gideon wondered if he would be alive today if they had encountered one another. Had Whitlock spotted Gideon in the swirling snow, he might well have gunned him down just to settle the score after their fight in Buckhorn.

Mills Pillow joined him. "Perhaps we are thinking along the same lines."

Gideon turned to him, seeing his round face by white moonlight. "Wouldn't surprise me. You seem have a way of knowing what's going on."

"I'm thinking about Whitlock," Pillow said.

"Reckon I am, too," Gideon allowed.

To be exact, he was thinking about the slow pace of that mule-drawn ore wagon Ruth drove from Buckhorn north to the Double Circle C—and how easily the big iron-tired wheels could be tracked through fresh snow.

"He's coming, isn't he?" Pillow said.

Gideon nodded. "I figure Whitlock and his deputies aren't far behind Ruth Logan."

They came after dawn, eight armed men riding out of the cold fire of sunrise. Alerted by Patrocino, Gideon watched them from the verandah, his Winchester in the crook of one arm. His sheepskin coat was pulled open, showing the Colt holstered on his cartridge belt.

Uncertain how the confrontation would unfold, he had sent Maggs and Lucretia into the cellar under the house with Annie and the baby. Awakened, Ruth refused to go with the other women, but agreed to stay inside the house until Gideon signaled her to come out. Lucretia had complained, but obeyed a terse command from Gideon. He had watched them descend the steps into the darkness and had closed the trap door, pulling the small rug over it.

Earlier Gideon had told Pillow and Patrocino to leave the ranch—for their safety. Pillow translated this advice into Spanish, and both men promptly declined. They brandished weapons, Patrocino the Remington and Pillow the Sharps. This morning, when armed riders were sighted on the lane, neither man had shown fear. Gideon positioned Pillow in the horse barn, Patrocino in the bunkhouse. If gunfire erupted, men bunched in the yard would be caught in a crossfire.

"Coopersmith!"

Sam Whitlock called out to him as his mount cantered into the snow-covered yard. The deputies grouped behind him when he reined up. One man led a spare saddle horse.

"Where's Anderson?" Whitlock demanded.

Gideon had made no effort to hide the ore wagon, and now he saw Whitlock's gaze sweep past the vehicle.

"In my bunkhouse," Gideon replied.

"Did that crazy woman shoot him?"

"Nope. Your man's roughed-up a little, that's all."

"I brought his horse," Whitlock said. "Let him go."

"Can't do that," Gideon said.

"You damn' well can," he said, "and you will obey a lawful order to do so."

"As a lawman," Gideon said, "you want to see justice served, don't you?"

"What the hell are you talking about?"

"Anderson's wanted for knocking over a bank," Gideon replied. "Sheriff Tyler will take him into custody."

"Like hell he will," Whitlock said, drawing his revolver. The men behind him reached for their guns.

In a prearranged signal, Gideon raised his rifle and fired one shot into the air. It was immediately answered by a deep *boom* from the Sharps in the barn. Then the Remington pistol fired from the bunkhouse doorway. Ruth rushed out of the house, sawed-off shotgun in her hands as she moved to the end of the verandah. She leveled the barrels at Whitlock.

With each gunshot, the horses pranced and their riders fought to control them. Sam Whitlock's head snapped around, his gaze darting from the barn to the bunkhouse. His eyes came to rest on Ruth Logan when she cursed him.

"I oughta gun you down right now," she said. "Payback for lynching my son."

"Lady, I have no knowledge of any such crime. Lower your shotgun, or my deputies. . . ."

Gideon cut off the threat by jacking a fresh round into the chamber of his Winchester. "If you want gun play, you gents came to the right place."

"You are providing safe haven for an outlaw, Coopersmith," Whitlock said with an angry gesture to Ruth.

"And you are holding my deputy prisoner. You will be prosecuted for these crimes."

"You've had your say," Gideon said. "Now get off Double Circle C range."

A long moment passed before Whitlock holstered his revolver. He glowered at Gideon. Then, reining his horse around, he rode out of the yard with the deputies following.

Ruth swore softly. "Lord, how I wanted to give that murderin' bastard both barrels."

"For a minute there," Gideon said, "I thought you would."

"As I was squeezin' the triggers," she said, holding up her double-barreled Greener, "I thought about your family in the house. I don't care about myself, but somebody else might have got killed in a shoot-out." She looked at the departing gunmen and let out a whoop. "We ran 'em off! Didn't we? We done a proper job of it!"

Gideon raised his rifle again. At that signal, Mills Pillow emerged from the barn with his Sharps rifle in hand. A moment later Patrocino stepped out of the bunkhouse, holstering the Remington. Now the two men headed for the house in long strides through loose snow.

Pillow grinned at Ruth's shouts of exultation until he noted Gideon's grim expression. Climbing the verandah steps, he said, "I see you are not celebrating your victory."

"That was no victory," Gideon said.

"What the hell do you mean?" Ruth demanded. "We ran 'em off. . . ."

Gideon broke in: "They'll be back."

"They're scared outta their britches!" Ruth said. "We'll cut 'em to pieces if they set foot here, and they know it!"

Pillow agreed. "Whitlock beat a fast retreat."

"Reckon we'll find out," Gideon said. "Soon."

"Why do you say that?" Pillow asked.

"None of those men led a pack animal."

"Meaning?"

"Meaning they can camp in the snow and live off supplies in their saddlebags for a day, maybe two," Gideon said. "That doesn't give Whitlock much time to decide."

"Decide what?" Ruth asked.

"Hit us," Gideon said, "or go home."

Pillow considered that. "What should we do?"

"Get ready for a fight," he said, and rushed into the house. In the kitchen he pushed the rug away with his foot, leaned down, and raised the trap door. From the bottom step Maggs looked up at him. She handed the baby up to him and climbed out.

"I heard shots," she said.

"No harm done," Gideon said. "Whitlock and his riders are gone . . . for now."

Maggs helped Annie and her mother out of the cellar. Wearing her black hooded cape, Lucretia was pale and drawn as though she had risen from a cold hell. She hurried to her room. When Annie was reassured everyone was all right, she did as she was told and carried the baby into the great room. Maggs stepped into Gideon's embrace.

"Hell, I'm leaving."

Gideon and Maggs turned at the sound of Ruth's voice. The big woman stood in the kitchen doorway, heavy coat on, out-size miner's boots on her feet.

"You don't have to go . . . ," Maggs began.

"I've been thinking," Ruth said. "I'm the one who put Whitlock on your trail. Didn't aim to, but, when I brung Anderson here, that nest of hornets follered me, didn't they?"

Gideon nodded.

"So if I clear out," she went on, "Whitlock won't have no call to shoot up your place. That's why I'm heading north. I'll collect my ree-ward in Laramie. Then I'll go after Whitlock."

"Ruth," Gideon said, "Sam Whitlock wants my hide, not yours. If he comes back, he'll settle his score with me."

She shook her head. "Maybe you're right about that, Mister Coopersmith, and maybe you're not. That man killed my son. He knows I'm coming for him."

Gideon heard the tone of stubbornness in her voice and saw her scarred face set like cement, an expression he had first seen when she had defended Tommy against any and all accusations.

Maggs moved closer to her. "Ruth, at least stay overnight. Then if you feel you must leave, you'll have a fresh start in the morning."

"You're kind to offer, Missus Coopersmith," she said, "more kinder than I deserve after the trouble I brung you. But, thank you, no. Time's a-wasting. I'm pulling out."

Ruth Logan left the Double Circle C with Ben Anderson bound hand and foot in the wagon bed. Gideon heard the man curse, uttering threats as the wagon lumbered down the lane.

For the rest of the night Gideon kept watch in shifts with Patrocino and Pillow. When it was his turn to sleep, he lay in bed in the darkness, eyes open. With every creak and pop of the flooring, he felt alarm, knowing at once there was no danger in pine planks cooled by nighttime temperatures. That was not what kept him on edge. He knew if Whitlock mounted an attack, day or night, his armed riders would overwhelm three guns on the ranch.

The sounds of cooling floorboards in the house gave him an idea. Unable to close his eyes, much less sleep, he decided to quit trying. He dressed and fired a lantern. In the kitchen he opened the trap door and went down the steep steps into the cellar.

The old miner's tunnel was lined with shelves bearing canned goods, store-bought tins, crates of staples, and venison hanging from a timber. Gideon had long ago boarded up the mouth of the tunnel. It was timbered, and he had nailed scrap boards over the outer frame of six-by-sixes, covering the opening to keep rodents out. Then on the slope outside he had shoveled dirt, heaping soil and rocks against the boards. Over the years weeds and grass had overgrown the opening. Now, from the inside, he tried to loosen the boards with his bare hands.

He was a better carpenter than he knew. The boards did not budge. He left the house. Checking with Patrocino on guard in the bunkhouse, he went on to the barn. To his surprise, he found Pillow there, awake. The city man was bundled up with blankets over his shoulders, huddled just inside the doorway with his rifle at the ready.

"You can't sleep, either?" Gideon asked.

Pillow grinned and shook his head.

"Might as well give me hand, then," Gideon said, and took a pry bar and hammer out of the tack room.

Pillow followed him to the house and down into the cellar. By lantern light the two men pried out nails and pulled upper boards away from the tunnel mouth. Knocking away dirt and tangled roots, they punched out a hole large enough for a man to crawl through. Then they replaced the boards and tapped the nail heads with the hammer, driving them in just enough to keep them in place. Outside they shoveled snow over the opening, concealing it.

"There's an escape route," Gideon said, "if it's needed."

In the morning Gideon spotted a wagon coming. He hollered for Pillow and Patrocino to be ready, and took up his gun. Squinting against the snow glare, he recognized the out-size ore wagon. As the lumbering vehicle drew closer, he made out two figures perched on the bench seat—the Blake brothers, scrawny even in their winter garb.

"What happened?" Gideon asked as the wagon rolled into the yard.

"We heard . . . heard shootin' . . . found. . . ." Excited, Clarence ran out of breath.

"This here woman," Charles said, finishing the sentence.

"Uh . . . uh . . . two-thirds dead."

Gideon hurried to the wagon box, joined there by Pillow and Patrocino. The brothers swung down from the wagon seat as Gideon pulled back a corner of the tarp. Ruth Logan lay there, stringy hair matted, and her eyes closed as though asleep. Gideon saw blood seeping through holes in her coat.

"She's shot up fierce . . . uh . . . uh . . . thr . . . thr. . . ."

"Three bullet holes in that coat she's wearing," Charles said. "She was gunned down. We seen horse tracks. . . ."

"Help me carry her into the house," Gideon broke in, yanking the tarp away. Supplies, the tattered buffalo robe, bedding, and the old trunk were there. A cut rope was the only sign of Ben Anderson.

Chapter Nineteen

One brother started, the other finished. In the great room Gideon listened to the Blake brothers recount events leading to their discovery of Ruth Logan sprawled in the snow, bleeding. Unaccustomed to being in the main house as they were now, the brothers stood close together, nervously shifting from one booted foot to the other as they warmed themselves before the leaping flames in the fireplace.

Clarence and Charles had heard shots—rifles firing and two blasts from a shotgun. Grabbing up their guns, they left their dugouts and hiked through the snow. They soon discovered the woman lying under the ore wagon, left for dead. Around the wagon were numerous tracks, half a dozen horses by their estimate. When Gideon told them Sam Whitlock and his band of eight, armed deputies had returned to North Park, the brothers agreed those men must have attacked Ruth Logan.

"You don't know that!" Lucretia interrupted. "How dare you defame a good man, one who's not here to defend himself!"

The Blakes had been introduced to her, and now they stared in amazement at her outburst. So did Mills Pillow. Displaying a haughtiness Gideon had not seen recently, Lucretia stood and turned her back, neck bowed, as though giving him and everyone else in the world one last chance to grovel and beg for her forgiveness.

In that moment of silence Gideon could have cited chapter and verse, starting with Whitlock's firing a bullet into the boardwalk at Maggs's feet and ending with the man's latest threats to harm the Coopersmith family. But he let it go. The truth had never punctured Lucretia's fantasies before, even when it came from Maggs, and there was no reason to expect the words of a shiftless cowboy would change her view now.

That day, Gideon learned Mills Pillow, among his other adventures, had once spied a career as a doctor. In first-year medical school classes the man had acquired basic skills in treating injuries and wounds. With Ruth lying on a cot in a spare bedroom, he helped Maggs pull off the bloodied coat and then cut away dress fabric and underclothing with sewing shears. Using hot water from the stove in the kitchen, they washed Ruth's wounds. Two bullets had passed through her upper body, and one had creased her ribs—rifle fire at close range. Properly bandaged by Pillow, the bleeding abated, but did not stop.

Ruth was breathing, barely, Maggs reported as she came out of the room, her shoulders sagging. A somber Mills Pillow followed. He closed the door after them.

"That is the grand reason I chose not to pursue a career in medicine," he said to no one in particular. "One does all one can, but it's never enough."

Annie rushed to her mother. "Will she live?" she asked, her eyes reddened from tears. "Will she?"

Maggs shook her head slowly and replied in a low voice: "I don't know. I just don't know."

Annie sobbed, and Maggs knelt and put her arms around her daughter.

A sudden crash of breaking glass caught Gideon by surprise. In the next moment shards from a second window fell to the plank floor and shattered. Gideon saw two bullet holes in the opposite wall, only then realizing someone ha shot out the windows from a distance so great that the booming of a rifle was almost swallowed by it. If Maggs had not knelt at that instant to comfort Annie, the first bullet would have found her.

"Get down!" Gideon shouted. "Down on the floor!"

Everyone went down. In the next moment the front door banged open. Gideon drew his revolver and brought it to bear on the doorway just as Patrocino dove in. He came up on his knees, shouting a terse warning in Spanish.

Pillow turned to Gideon and translated: "Riders coming."

In the next few minutes ten more bullets from the high-powered rifle slammed into the great room, the shooter moving closer, judging from progressively louder reports reverberating through the air. Every time glass shattered, Lucretia covered her face and sobbed.

Gideon turned to his wife. Her eyes were fixed on him. She held the crying baby and rested her free hand on Annie lying on the floor beside her.

Gideon said: "Get in the cellar."

He turned to the Blake brothers. "Stay low and follow Maggs into the kitchen. She'll lead you to safety."

Clarence and Charles lay still—whether out of fear or defiance, Gideon did not know. Maggs carried the baby and kept Annie close to her as they crawled across the floor strewn with broken glass. Lucretia held back, dazed, ignoring her daughter's pleas. She came up on her knees as though praying, and sobbed mightily until Annie called to her.

"Grammy!" Annie shouted, when they reached the ___. "Grammy! Come on! You'll be safe with us!"

___-like, the older woman dropped to all fours and fol-
___ in disarray, her face wet with tears.

The front door stood half open. Gideon and Mills Pillow belly-crawled to it. Patrocino came after them, the Remington revolver clenched in his hand. They were joined by the Blake brothers.

Clarence stammered: "Five . . . eight. . . ."

Charles finished his brother's thought: "Five of us . . . eight of them."

"Them's good . . . good . . . ," Clarence sputtered.

"Good odds," Charles said.

Gideon raised up far enough to look out across the verandah. The riders had halted on the lane more than a hundred yards away from the bunkhouse and horse barn. Even so, Gideon recognized the heavy-set man in the lead—Ben Anderson.

"I don't see Whitlock," Gideon said. "He's out there somewhere with that big rifle of his. Reckon he aims to keep us pinned down in here while his gunmen move in for the kill."

Patrocino spoke rapidly, with Pillow translating: "He says we should mount an attack. If we fail to take the offensive, he says they will burn us out and shoot us one by one, like dogs."

Gideon acknowledged that assessment with a nod. From his reading of Europe's historic land battles in the RIDPATH volumes, he knew the best defense was an aggressive offense. What he did not know was how to implement it. He was no general. He had been a worker all his life, often solitary, certainly never a strategist or even a leader of men. Patrocino must have sensed that, and was alarmed by Gideon's hesitancy.

"Reckon we can slip out of the house through the cellar," Gideon said. "Those jokers won't expect that."

Pillow repeated this in Spanish, and translated

223

Patrocino's reply: "He says those gunmen will decide to stay together or divide their forces to attack on more than one front . . . the eternal question in warfare. He says large battles and small skirmishes alike are won or lost on that command decision alone."

Gideon looked from him to Patrocino. "Ask him how he knows that."

Pillow relayed the question, listened to the reply, and translated Patrocino's words: "For many years he was a sergeant in the Mexican cavalry. In a battle with revolutionaries in Puerto Vaca, his company was nearly wiped out. After he was forced to witness the execution by firing squad of his beloved *capitán,* he took the peasant clothing of a dead revolutionary, and fled northward across the border. The fighting was pointless, he says. He left a homeland he calls murderous . . . *del meurto* . . . knowing he could never return to Mexico, never see his family again. Gideon, he says your family is his family."

Gideon remembered Patrocino's tears when Annie left the ranch to go to Denver. He also recalled Maggs's contention that the self-described *viejo* had aged prematurely, bent by the weight of life's burdens, a man driven from home and hearth by tragedy. . . .

Now his eye was caught by a trio of Patrocino's carved faces, three life-sized busts Maggs had taken a liking to and lugged into the house. Down the hall the door to Lucretia's bedroom stood open. He saw hatboxes in there, and an open trunk.

Gideon looked at the gunmen on the lane again. Four had edged closer. They dismounted and in pairs ran through the snow to the outbuildings. Two men searched the horse barn while the other pair looked into the bunkhouse and cow shed. They returned to their mounts. All of the gunmen gathered around Anderson, no doubt working out a plan to attack the house, as Patrocino believed.

Standing, Gideon rushed out of the great room to Lucretia's bedroom without drawing fire from the high-powered rifle. He came back with a handful of silk scarves and three hats—one ostrich-plumed, the other two more modest with felt brims stiffened by a ring of wire. The hatbands were decorated with colored glass baubles, and the rounded crowns sported silver hatpins with small handles of crystal cut to resemble diamonds. He dragged a table to a window that had been shot out.

"What are you doing?" Pillow asked.

"Giving those gunmen something to think about," Gideon replied.

While Patrocino and the others lay flat on the floor and watched, Gideon stood the carved busts up on the table, facing the window side by side, and crowned them with fine hats. He wrapped the scarves around the base of each one, and ducked down as another bullet crashed into the wall behind him.

"What's . . . what's . . . your . . . ," Clarence stammered.

"Plan?" Charles said.

Gideon turned to the brothers. Clarence gripped a twelve-gauge pump shotgun in his hands. Charles held an old Navy pistol, a heavy, reliable weapon.

"I didn't aim to drag you gents into my fight," Gideon said. He repeated: "You two head for the cellar. You'll be safe. . . ."

"Mister Pillow, he done told us what happened in Buckhorn," Charles interrupted. "This ain't just your fight. It's ours, too . . . a fight for North Park."

Clarence drew a deep breath and launched a complete sentence: "Gideon, we stand shoulder to shoulder with you against Whitlock." He grinned, at once surprised and pleased with himself.

"*Padrone*," Patrocino said urgently as he crawled closer. He spoke quickly. Pillow translated: "We must execute our plan immediately . . . or those men will surely kill us."

Gideon nodded agreement, but a troubling thought came into his mind: "What about Ruth Logan?"

"Carrying her out of that room," Pillow said, "and lowering her into the cellar poses a greater risk to her life than leaving her where she is."

Gideon drew a deep breath and exhaled. Outside he saw the riders turn their horses. Now each man held a repeating rifle at the ready. With Anderson in the middle, they spread out and advanced in a line, their mounts walking slowly through the snow.

"They're bunched," Gideon said.

Once again Patrocino spoke urgently through Pillow: " 'We must fire on them! All together!' "

Gideon turned to the others. "Reckon that's the plan. Here's how I figure it. Each of you fire six rounds, fast as you can. Don't take time to aim. Make a hell of a racket. Then run for the cellar. Pillow and I opened it up last night, and we'll come out behind the house. Those jokers will think we're out of ammunition, and hunkered down in here. I figure they'll be watching the front of the house, and that's our chance to surprise them when we bust out of the tunnel."

The Blake brothers nodded agreement. Pillow translated the instructions for Patrocino.

The *viejo* nodded approvingly. He spun the cylinder of the Remington revolver and checked the loads. Patting a full cartridge belt, he spoke again—"Do not forget to reload . . . even seasoned soldiers sometimes forget in battle."—was the sentence translated by Pillow.

Gideon turned to Mills Pillow. "Sorry you got yanked into this little war. If you. . . ."

He interrupted: "I'm as ready as I'll ever be. Do not try to talk me out of it. You just might succeed."

Gideon managed a smile. Then he turned to the others. "Gents, find your places." He turned and looked out the doorway. He waited until the riders passed the bunkhouse. When they approached the verandah, he moved to the door jamb and swiftly raised his Winchester to his shoulder. He drew a deep breath. Slowly let it out. Squeezed the trigger. The butt plate of the Winchester punched his shoulder.

A tremendous din erupted with all of them shooting through broken windows and the open doorway. Gideon levered a fresh round into the breech and pulled the trigger again. The noise of five guns rapid-firing inside the great room was deafening, and by the time thirty rounds were expended, the room had filled with a haze and the acrid smell of powder smoke.

Ears ringing, Gideon did not wait to see if any of their bullets had found a mark. After jacking the seventh round into the breech, he lowered the hammer to half-cock, and ran to the kitchen. Throwing open the trap door, he rushed down the steps into the cellar, rifle in hand, with the others close behind him.

"Stay here!" Gideon shouted to Maggs and Annie. As he ran past them, he noted Lucretia huddled on the tunnel floor, her bony hands covering her face.

Gunshots came from outside—one volley and then more volleys with the gunmen concentrating their fire. From above, Gideon heard *thunk-thunk-thunk* as bullets struck the inside walls of the house. A fleeting worry about Ruth came to him again, but he knew he could do nothing to help her now. He sprinted to the end of the tunnel, stopping long enough to reload his Winchester. Then he punched out the loosened boards with the butt of the rifle.

Knocking snow away, he created an opening large enough to pass through. With the great peak, Deadman, looming out there, he squinted against the full sunlight on white snow. He started to crawl out, but halted abruptly and pulled back. He had spotted a lone figure—a man of short stature standing beside a saddle mount, rifle braced for distance shooting.

Sam Whitlock. Even from here Gideon knew it was him. Whitlock peered through his telescopic sight. A wisp of smoke plumed from the barrel as he squeezed off another shot, the report delayed by distance. Glass shattered as the bullet broke out a rear window. Closer at hand, the deputies continued firing into the front of the house.

Amid all this gunfire, Gideon halted in a moment of indecision. From the angle of the bullets fired from the high-powered rifle, he had not expected to see Whitlock, not out there. The man must have moved to a new position when the attack began. Now he was ready to kill anyone who fled from the rear of the house. Gideon was certain of one thing—Whitlock would spot the tunnel opening when movement caught his eye. They were trapped.

"What's wrong?" Pillow asked.

"Whitlock," he said.

"Where?"

"Out there," Gideon replied. He motioned with his rifle, and added: "He's out of the range of my Winchester." The caliber of the octagonal-barreled rifle was .32-40, a good all-purpose weapon, but ineffective for long-range shooting.

Gideon glanced back at Pillow. The others were bunched behind him, weapons up, each man ready to take the fight to the gunmen. Gideon hesitated longer, in those moments feeling responsible for their lives. He could not allow them to be cut down here. He took a second look at the Sharps in Pillow's hands.

"Ever made a long shot with that big gun?"

Pillow considered the question. "About two years ago, I knocked down a bull moose in Maine from a distance, perhaps, of three hundred yards."

Gideon edged back from the tunnel opening. He pointed outside. "See if you can make a believer out of Whitlock."

Mills Pillow moved to the opening and positioned his rifle. "How great is the distance, would you say?"

"One hell of a long ways," Gideon replied.

"Can you be more precise?"

"Nope."

Pillow paused. "Four hundred yards, possibly more. Gideon, I've never attempted to hit a target from this distance, much less a human being."

"All I want you to do," Gideon said, "is to shoot him before he spots us and starts pouring lead in here."

Gideon watched him flip up the rear sight and adjust the crosspiece. Cocking the hammer, Mills Pillow pressed the stock against his shoulder, and carefully drew aim. Gideon covered his ears and was looking past him when he squeezed the trigger. The big rifle bucked like a mule and roared like a dynamite charge through the old tunnel, and a moment later snow plumed a dozen feet away from Sam Whitlock.

Gideon grinned when he saw the horse rear up. Whitlock grabbed for the reins, at once looking all around as he was obviously baffled by the origin of a bullet coming that close to him.

"I seem to have missed completely," Pillow said. "My apologies. . . ."

"That was a hell of a shot," Gideon interrupted. "He doesn't know where we are. Lower that rear sight a notch, and let go with another one."

The next roaring shot must have sent a round whispering past Whitlock's ear for the man went down and immediately scrambled to his feet. He pulled his frightened horse back and fled to escape a shooter who was invisible to him.

"Come out of there!" Ben Anderson's shout was close, so close that Gideon first thought they had been discovered.

"Drop your guns and come out of the house!"

Gideon inched through the opening in the tunnel. Hatless, he poked his head outside. No one was in sight. He crawled farther out, rifle in hand.

"Come out of there! Give it up, or you'll die!"

Gideon saw no one and realized the deputies were still in front of the house, unaware of the tunnel. They must have figured Whitlock covered the rear, mistaking the two shots from the Sharps for his high-powered rifle. Now Anderson believed his prey was at bay, cornered with nowhere to go.

"If I have to burn you out of there, I will!"

"Let's go," Gideon whispered over his shoulder, and belly-crawled out of the tunnel into the sun-bright snow.

Chapter Twenty

Gideon got to his feet. Snow fell from the front of his coat and trouser legs as he cocked the rifle and looked around. No sign of Whitlock. He had either fled, or had pulled back far enough to be concealed behind a rise. Gideon kept watch while Mills Pillow crawled out of the cellar, followed by Patrocino and the Blake brothers. The shooting had stopped. From the front of the house came hushed voices mixed with the sounds of stamping hoofs from the nervous horses. Then Anderson shouted, again demanding surrender under threat of death.

Gideon turned to Patrocino as all five of them silently checked weapons one more time. He gave instructions in a low voice. Three—Patrocino and the Blakes—would advance on one side of the house, Gideon and Pillow on the other. They would converge at the verandah.

"Don't show yourselves or shoot until you hear me holler," Gideon whispered. "We'll give those jokers one chance to give it up. If they don't, fire away."

Mills Pillow translated for Patrocino. The *viejo*'s whispered reply came back through Pillow: "That is more respect than they gave us, *padrone*."

"We're not like them," Gideon said, and gestured for the Blakes to follow Patrocino.

The brothers turned and walked behind Patrocino through the snow, disappearing around the corner at the west side of the house. Gideon led Mills Pillow to the east side. They moved quietly along that log wall. Gideon edged to the corner and halted. Leaning his rifle against the wall, he drew his Colt. At close quarters the revolver would throw out more lead, and faster than his lever-action Winchester.

Still hatless, Gideon eased around the corner for a look. He had thought about this moment, knowing it could be quick and deadly, a life-changing confrontation for every man here. His hope was to get the drop on the gunmen and end it peacefully. But if this came to a fight, he had no qualms about shooting them out of their saddles. Ben Anderson knew women and children were in the house when he gave the order to shoot. Gideon figured he knew why. Anderson had some scores to settle with the Coopersmiths—Maggs had dropped him with that pry bar, and Gideon had publicly kicked him into submission on Front Street. By Gideon's estimate, those eight men brandishing repeating rifles had fired at least a hundred rounds into the house. Anderson meant business and would see to it that his gunmen would not leave until their work was done.

Gun up now, Gideon inched forward. He peered around the corner. He saw six gunmen. They sat their horses in an uneven line, facing the verandah, rifles ready for the next volley at Anderson's command. Four horses bled from wounds, but were still on their feet. Two gunmen were down, lying in the snow and bleeding from wounds inflicted by Gideon and the others firing from the great room. Despite taking casualties, Anderson and his men looked determined, no doubt believing their superior firepower would overwhelm anyone in the house.

"Drop your guns!" Gideon shouted.

Startled, they all turned to him, amazement flashing across their faces. A horse reared, spooking a second mount. While those two riders fought for control, the others instinctively swung toward the sound of Gideon's voice, bringing their guns to bear on him. Anderson fired first, swiftly aiming and pulling the trigger of his rifle in one smooth motion.

Gideon drew back the instant before Anderson squeezed the trigger. With that shot, the other gunmen loosed a volley at him. They had been trained like soldiers, and each man fired accurately. Bullets splintered pine at the corner of the home place.

When Gideon had told Patrocino and the Blake brothers to wait for his shout, he figured his voice would draw the gunmen's attention to himself, and none of them would be looking at that far corner of the house. If there was gunfire, Patrocino and the Blakes were to lean out from the corner and blaze away before the gunmen knew what hit them.

That was his plan. Now with his back pressed against the log wall, Gideon did not have to look out there to know how events were unfolding. He heard two revolvers firing, the Remington and the old Navy pistol, and then came mighty blasts of the pump shotgun, one deafening shot after another until the weapons were empty. Then silence.

Gideon and Pillow jumped out from their corner of the house, both leveling their guns at four men still on their horses. Gideon's finger was tightening on the trigger when they threw down their rifles.

"Don't shoot!"

"We give up!"

Urgently shouting their surrender again, the men thrust their hands skyward. Four others lay sprawled in blood-stained snow now, dead or dying, Ben Anderson among them. The big man lay on his back, looking up through slowly blinking eyes.

Gideon stepped away from the corner of the house. He approached the gunmen cautiously, followed by Pillow who

233

leveled his Sharps at them. On the other side of the house, Patrocino and the Blake brothers eased out from that corner, guns reloaded, cocked and ready.

Gideon kicked Winchesters away from the downed men. Their fight was over. The four still on horseback sweated in the cold air, involuntarily perspiring from the shock of escaping death by the narrowest of margins. Their gazes darting left and right, they clearly feared swift revenge.

Patrocino and the Blake brothers disarmed them, taking away sidearms and cartridge belts. A wounded man lying in the snow began crying in child-like sobs, his eyes squeezed shut against the pain of the bullet-shattered bones in his left shoulder. Two others, alive moments ago, lay sprawled in the grotesque poses of the dead. Anderson had been hit twice, one bullet through his chest, a load of buckshot in the belly.

Gideon moved to his side and knelt in the snow. He heard the big man's voice, surprisingly calm and strong as he spoke.

"I ain't . . . I ain't got long . . . do I?"

Gideon shook his head.

"That's a blue sky . . . ain't it blue?"

"Yeah."

"You whipped me, Coopersmith. Nobody ever whipped me. . . ."

"You have time to set things right."

"Huh?"

"You have time to tell the truth," Gideon said.

"Truth," he repeated. "You mean, about the bank?"

"About Nate Clarke," Gideon said.

"Huh?"

"You drew him out of Buckhorn into Whitlock's ambush," Gideon said. "That's the truth, isn't it?"

Anderson paused. "Yeah . . . I told Clarke where he'd

find rustled cattle. . . . Sam was waiting. . . ."

Hearing the man's voice weaken and trail off, Gideon went on: "And Whitlock lynched Tommy Logan in Buckhorn. Didn't he?"

Anderson nodded once. "Yeah, but I had no hand in that one . . . I ain't going to hell for killing a kid. . . ."

"Why did Whitlock do it?"

"Saloonman . . . told us the kid robbed him. . . ."

"Which saloonman?"

Ben Anderson tried to speak, but no words came. He sighed, and Gideon heard a soft whisper like a breeze high in the pines.

Gideon closed the man's eyes. He stood, turning to the four gunmen on horseback. They stared at him, ill concealing their fear. Gideon looked each man in the eye. Then he spoke, raising his voice over the sobbing cries of the wounded gunman.

"Load your dead on the horses and lash them to the saddles. Ride out. All of you. Ride out, and don't come back here."

The damage and the sheer viciousness of the attack took a toll on everyone. Gideon helped Maggs and the baby out of the cellar, and then gave Lucretia a hand up as she climbed the stairs leading out of the cold darkness.

Maggs barely controlled her rage when she walked through the kitchen to the great room with the baby in one arm and Annie's hand clasped in her free hand.

"Oh, Gideon . . . ," her voice broke. "Gideon, what did we do to deserve this?"

Gideon thought about that. "We stood up to a man who figures he can whip us."

The others were struck silent by the sight of the interior

walls peppered with bullet holes. Even stones in the fireplace chimney were scarred where bullets had hit and careened off. A RIDPATH volume on the mantle bore a round hole.

Annie asked quietly: "Are the badmen gone?"

"Yeah," Gideon said. "They're gone."

"Will they come back?" she asked.

Hands on his hips as he surveyed the damage, Gideon turned to his daughter. "Nope."

Gideon's eyes went to the three figures carved by Patrocino, sculptures that had been shot off the table and now lay on the floor like upended statues. Elegant hats and fine silk scarves were strewn across on the floor, along with the hatpins and baubles belonging to Lucretia.

Maggs's mother stared at her jewelry scattered across the plank floor amid shards of broken glass. She seemed dazed, unable to comprehend what had happened here, how her scarves and pins had come to be tossed to the floor like discarded trash. She bent down and picked one up.

"Gideon."

He turned toward Maggs's voice. She had moved to the spare bedroom where Ruth Logan lay on a cot.

Hurrying across the room, Gideon joined his wife at the doorway. The plank door bore bullet holes, too, as though it had been hammered open. They stepped inside, relieved to discover Ruth Logan was alive. None of the rifle bullets had struck her. The big woman's head slowly turned to them as they approached the side of the cot. Her voice was thin.

"What . . . what in hell happened, Mister Coopersmith? I heard shooting . . . where's . . . where's my man-tamer?"

Gideon started to tell her about the attack, but her eyes closed, and she snored.

At the sound of voices, Mills Pillow rushed in. He examined Ruth, and hurried out. After heating water on the stove, he returned to tend her wounds and change the bandages. He reported the bleeding had nearly stopped and her breathing was heavy, a good sign.

"She seems to be on the mend," he said, unsmiling.

"Thanks to some good doctoring," Maggs said to him.

Pillow answered with a grim shrug.

In the great room, Gideon saw Lucretia gathering up her baubles. At the same time Patrocino lifted his sculptures off the floor. Gideon watched him examine the bullet holes in each one while speaking softly in Spanish, as though addressing the faces carved into wood. Gideon beckoned to Mills Pillow. Maggs stepped into the room behind him.

"What's he saying?" Gideon asked in a low voice.

Pillow listened. "*Viva*. It means life."

"What's he saying about life?"

Pillow spoke to Patrocino, and then translated. "He says the figures possess life."

"But what does he mean by that?" Maggs asked.

Pillow questioned Patrocino further, and turned to Gideon and Maggs. "He says he carves the faces of the dead. By creating these images, the souls of soldiers slain in battle at Puerto Vaca live on. Says his masterpiece will be the face of his captain. He has not found the wood for it yet."

To make the home place habitable again, the floor was swept and mopped, cleaned of glass shards and countless slivers of window glass. Broken windows were boarded up, a temporary measure to hold heat. By noon, fires in the hearth and kitchen stove had warmed the house.

Maggs insisted the Blake brothers stay for a simple midday meal at the Coopersmith table, along with Pillow and Patrocino. Pillow declined, and headed for the bunkhouse without a word of explanation. The Blakes shyly accepted as though their heroism of the day had been an ordinary event, one overshadowed by the privilege of taking a meal in the dining room on a real linen tablecloth with china and silverware. Afterward, they thanked Maggs in unison, and waved off Gideon's expression of gratitude.

"Them gunhands . . . won't come back . . . to North Park," Clarence said.

Charles grinned in agreement, and the brothers set out for their homesteads.

Lucretia soon recovered her sense of outrage. She did not believe Sheriff Sam Walker had anything to do with this attack. More importantly to her, she wanted to know how her "gems" had come to be flung across the floor of the great room. Some of the gold settings had been damaged, and she demanded an explanation.

Her concern for baubles seemed trivial to Gideon after what had taken place here today. "You mean painted lead, don't you?"

"I mean gold!" Lucretia insisted. "Gold!"

At her insistence, Gideon described his last-minute plan for decoying the gunmen with the sculptures wearing scarves and hats. Unimpressed, Lucretia cast a haughty look at him and announced the decorative pieces were not colored glass at all. Red rubies and green emeralds were genuine, and the "cut glass" pieces mounted on long silver pins were diamonds. The jewels had been purchased at Tiffany & Company in New York many years ago, gifts for Lucretia from the late senator.

"Mama!" Maggs said, shocked at this revelation. "They are worth a fortune!"

"Of course, they are, my dear," Lucretia said, cupping

the gems in her hands. "I have more in my luggage. You didn't think for one moment, did you, that I would turn over everything of value to that mean banker?"

After the Blakes departed, Gideon shouldered into his coat and headed for the bullet-pocked door. Maggs crossed the great room and met him there.

"Gideon, where are you going?"

"I don't know where Whitlock rode off to," he replied, "but I know where to pick up his trail."

"He won't give up," she said. "He may still be out there."

"If he is, I'll find him."

Her eyes searched his as she was clearly at war with her emotions. She hugged him. "Oh, Gideon. We've been through hell today, haven't we?"

"Close enough to feel the heat," he replied.

She whispered so only he would hear: "We're not out of it yet, are we?"

"I love you, Maggs," he whispered, and held her for a long moment.

She pulled away and looked up at him. "Take Patrocino with you."

Mounted on the paint, Gideon led the way out of the ranch yard, Patrocino following on the gray. They both carried .30-30 Winchesters left behind by the gunmen, magazines fully loaded. Angling away from the wheel ruts with Deadman off to their left, they approached a line of willows. That slash of orange branches ahead marked French Creek.

Gideon peered ahead. He glimpsed a puff of smoke. In the next instant he was punched out of the saddle. A rifle sounded, the deep boom of its report delayed by distance. Gideon lay sprawled on his back in the snow when the next bullet blew off Patrocino's hat.

"¡Señor! ¡Señor!"

Chapter Twenty-One

The bullet had been aimed on a perfect trajectory, and once again Gideon had the sheepskin to thank for saving his life. So said Mills Pillow after he had extracted the bullet lodged under Gideon's breastbone. The round would have penetrated his chest cavity and killed him, if not for the heavy leather of the coat overlapping where it buttoned, extra layers of clothing, and, perhaps, the distance the bullet had traveled. The second round came within an inch of taking off the top of Patrocino's head.

The shots had come from a distance so great that neither Gideon nor his wrangler had caught sight of the ambusher. The shooter was well hidden, no doubt picking his spot after the gunmen had been routed from the Double Circle C, a killer content to wait.

After dragging his *padrone* through the snow back to the home place, Patrocino had galloped away on the gray. He circled a bend in French Creek, dismounted, and moved in cautiously with the Remington in hand. Among the orange-branched willows bordering the frozen stream he found a pile of horse droppings where the bushwhacker had concealed his saddle mount. A short distance away, packed snow marked the spot where he had lain in wait. From there, tracks led south toward Buckhorn.

Patrocino returned to the home place and reported this to Mills Pillow. By this time Gideon was bandaged, lying in his bed. Like a man coming out of a deep sleep, he slowly regained consciousness, his memory of recent events fragmented. Pillow repeated the wrangler's account.

Struggling to sit up in bed, Gideon threatened to go after Sam Whitlock right away. Pillow scowled. He ordered him to stay put. Lucretia had overheard, and she tossed in her two-cents' worth by reiterating her assertion that "Sam Walker" was a great man, a law-abiding peace officer innocent of any crime.

Gideon was not surprised to hear her defend the man, but he had been startled by Pillow's gruff tone of voice: "Stay put."

Hours later, when Pillow did speak at length again, he expressed his bone-deep disgust over the carnage he had witnessed in the American West, his anguish over the wounded he had treated, and his anger at the arrogance of violent men imposing their will by force of arms. Gunning down a woman was the worst of it. Spoon-fed by Annie, Ruth could sit up, but was unable to leave her bed. Under Pillow's care, she had regained enough strength to rant about Whitlock when awake, and snore when asleep.

Mills Pillow demanded: "How can these beasts call themselves civilized? How?"

"They cannot," Lucretia replied to his rhetorical question. "Mister Pillow, having lived in Washington as a point of comparison, we both know precious little culture exists on the frontier. Out here, we are far, far removed from civilization."

"I have seen for myself," he said slowly, as though reluctant to agree, "that without the strictures of societal traditions, the law of the jungle prevails."

Gideon did not understand all of that, until Pillow concluded: "I must say, that great mountain is aptly named, after all. Deadman."

Later Maggs observed privately: "Mister Pillow has lost

both his verbosity and good cheer."

"Verbosity," Gideon repeated thoughtfully. Having seen a scowl in the round face of the man, he figured he knew what she meant. "Yeah, all that verbosity is gone from him."

Gideon closed his eyes. He felt as though he had taken a blow from a sledge-hammer. As much as he wanted to be up and around, he slept more than he was awake the next day. He consumed chicken soup spooned into his mouth by Annie.

"The more you eat, Daddy," she said in her adult voice, "the sooner you'll mend."

Maggs changed his bandage and cleaned the wound according to Pillow's instruction. Under the city man's direction she also treated Ruth's gunshot wounds. Maggs received a great deal of medical instruction from him. The reason was soon apparent.

The following morning Gideon had regained enough strength to eat solid food and walk unassisted into the dining room. That was the day surprising news came from Maggs: Mills Pillow and Lucretia had left the Double Circle C.

In the night, Pillow had loaded the ranch wagon with two of Lucretia's steamer trunks and then at dawn he had driven away with her on the seat beside him, donkeys in tow. The wagon and team would be left at Silas's livery, to be picked up later by Gideon or Patrocino.

Gideon listened, amazed, yet no more surprised than Maggs had been. She told Gideon of her mother's announcement that she would travel by train to Washington, escorted by Mr. Mills Pillow. Lucretia had learned his departure was imminent, and was forced to make a quick decision—go with him, or stay on the ranch indefinitely. Accompanied by someone she trusted on the long eastward journey, this was her chance to travel in safety.

Lucretia had confided to her daughter that a budding romance with Mills Pillow had faded as quickly as it had blossomed. She offered no details, other than to say that she respected the man for his gentlemanly demeanor, but not his politics. Or his religion, either. As a good Methodist, she had been horrified when Pillow described a religious sect's conviction that blackbirds do not exist, but are merely the shadows of invisible birds. With that, Pillow declared religions of the world to be pretty much alike, differing only in details.

"Heresy," Lucretia whispered as though Satan might overhear. "I do believe that man's a heretic."

She had devised a plan. Back East she would sell her gems and invest the bulk of the money in bonds. Perhaps someday she would return to Denver, she said, an entrance to be made in high style. In the meantime, she still had many friends in Washington, and assured Maggs she would be all right on her own back there. Once settled, she would send for her remaining trunks, hatboxes, and hand luggage. Mother and daughter would keep in touch through letters, just as they had when she lived in Denver. Then with hugs and hurried good byes to sleepy grandchildren, Lucretia Stearns was gone.

Shaking his head in wonderment, Gideon took all this in, feeling as though he had slept long and awakened to a changed world. He wondered aloud why the city man had not said good bye to him. Mills Pillow had told Maggs he did not wish to awaken Gideon and disrupt the rest he needed for a complete recovery from his gunshot wound.

She suspected otherwise. When she had questioned him, she'd quickly discovered he did not wish to discuss his decision. "He's soured," Maggs said. "Soured, and simply eager to leave. Talking to you would have only made parting more difficult."

Gideon shrugged. "Maybe so."

All he knew for certain was that Mills Pillow had landed here with a ready smile and boundless enthusiasm, and departed with a tight-lipped scowl while expressing his disgust for the bloodshed he had seen in the West.

Gideon mentioned to Maggs and Annie that he felt strong enough to ride to Buckhorn and pick up the ranch wagon. He would purchase window panes and putty, and fill out their list at the general store.

Maggs eyed him, knowing his casual tone was for Annie's benefit. With a glance at her daughter, she nodded silently, and made no protest. Even in the privacy of their bedroom Gideon had never said it in so many words, yet, he and Maggs both knew the day would come. Sam Whitlock would be held accountable. Gideon's best chance was to track him down before he had time to hire and train more gunmen.

Restless now, Gideon denied feeling any pain in his chest when questioned by Maggs. She did not believe him, having seen him grimace in their embrace, but knew at once that she could not stop him. She got one compromise out of him: unlike the time he had ridden in hard pursuit of Tommy Logan, he promised he would set a slow pace, even stopping at Dutchman's to rest. With that one concession to his bandaged wound, an early start from the home place was not necessary.

On the verandah he kissed his wife and daughter good bye under a bright noonday sun on a cold day. He held the baby one more time, pulling the blanket open as he gazed at the small face stilled by sleep. When Patrocino brought the paint mare up, saddled and bridled, Gideon handed Andrew to Maggs. He descended the steps, thrust a boot into the stirrup, and swung up.

"Are you going after the badmen, Daddy?"

Gideon looked at Annie in surprise. "Just one," he replied.

"Annie, how . . . how did you know . . . ?" Maggs's voice trailed off as Annie turned and hurried into the house. She came running back, holding the Greener in both hands.

Maggs exclaimed: "Be careful with that thing!"

"Miz Logan told me," Annie said.

"Told you what?" Gideon asked.

Annie jumped down the steps and thrust the sawed-off shotgun at him. "She said you have no quit in you. You'll need 'this here man-tamer.' That's what she said, Daddy. You'll need 'this here man-tamer.' "

Gideon grinned. He leaned down from the saddle and took the weapon from her. With a last look at Maggs, he turned the horse and rode out of the snow-covered yard while Annie called after him: "Good bye, Daddy! Good bye, Daddy! Good bye, Daddy!"

Gideon had seen tears shining in Maggs's eyes, and now, with Annie's good byes reverberating through his mind, he did not have to look back to know his wife and daughter would watch from the verandah until he was out of sight.

As quiet and menacing as a stalking cougar, the snowstorm came on padded feet during the night. Aware only of an overarching silence when he awoke in the Dutchman's cabin, Gideon pulled open the door to find three feet of fresh snow on the ground. The plank door crafted long ago by the Dutchman swung inward for that very reason. A heavy snowfall in the night would trap anyone inside if the door was hinged to swing out.

Gideon headed south on the wagon road, wheel ruts obliterated by the heavy snowfall. At least he hoped he was on the road. The thick cover lent a rounded sameness to the vast terrain. Once familiar, the land was strange now, a white-on-white expanse from horizon to horizon. Even a rider who knew the way could become lost in snow deep enough to blot out landmarks.

Unlike the day Gideon had driven his ranch wagon into the teeth of a howling blizzard, this storm was gentle and quiet, almost alluring. No wind. The air temperature was not bitterly cold, and the mare slogged through powder as white and fine as sifted flour. Horse and rider were soon coated with snowflakes drifting to earth from a low, iron-gray sky.

In this storm, like a stalking cougar, danger was quiet and ever-present. A man alone could wander to his death. If his mount went down, the snow would soon rob body heat and the rider would lose consciousness, slipping into "the mighty quietude" as Mills Pillow had once described his view of the hereafter.

The snowfall waned as he rode farther south. In clearing weather, this horse and rider found their way. On the outskirts of Buckhorn, Gideon caught the scent of coal smoke in the air. Riding past the crushing mills on the steep hillside, he heard a locomotive before he saw the great, dark beast. Looming ahead, the engine breathed fire and shot steam into snow-filled air. He was surprised to find a locomotive with a gondola, three freight cars, a passenger coach, and red caboose at the dépôt. The engine, he realized now, was building a head of steam, and that was the source of the coal smoke he smelled.

Knowing something out of the ordinary had happened for the train to be here on this day, and knowing Lucretia and Pillow should have been on it, he rode straight to the dépôt. He tied his mare at the rail, and swung down.

Brushing snow from his coat, he slapped his hat against his chaps as he crossed the platform. He opened the door and entered. The waiting room was empty.

"Snowslide buried the tracks," was the ticket agent's answer to his question. The train had departed on schedule, but had soon returned, backing up to the dépôt where the two passengers, a man and a woman, disembarked.

"Telegraph line's still up," the agent went on. "I got word yesterday of a snowplow and crew dispatched from Denver. They'll punch it through and clear the rails. . . ." His voice trailed off as he studied Gideon. "Say, aren't you Coopersmith?"

"Yeah," Gideon said, and gestured to the message board. "Anything for me?"

The agent shook his head. He swallowed hard, his eyes darting about nervously.

"Something wrong?"

"No, sir," he replied quickly.

Riding through the fine snow, Gideon followed Front Street to the center of town. He passed the Colorado Hotel. A familiar figure stood at the bay window in the lobby—a man dressed in a vested gray suit, wearing a derby. Mills Pillow seemed to look directly at him, but gave no sign of recognition as Gideon passed by.

"Walk careful." Speaking in a low voice, Silas again issued that warning to Gideon in the semidarkness of the livery barn.

From Silas he learned the sheriff had accused him of ambushing four deputies and running the other "lawmen" out of the county. The Double Circle C Ranch was a nest of outlaws that needed to be cleaned out, once and for all, Whitlock proclaimed, like a den of rattlers. Residents of Buckhorn and Columbine had received his flyer calling for the killer to be brought to justice. As an incentive a $500 reward would be paid to any citizen who brought in Gideon Coopersmith, dead or alive.

Now Gideon opened his coat. He drew his Colt and checked the loads. Thrusting the revolver into his coat pocket, he tugged his hat down on his forehead and left the livery.

A wagon rumbled past, the wheels churning snow. He saw no one else. With no livestock or barn chores to drive them from a warm hearth, few townspeople braved even mildly snowy weather. Head bowed, Gideon walked swiftly along the boardwalk to the sheriff's office. Pulling out his Colt, he threw the door open and lunged in, gun up.

The outer office was unoccupied, the stove warm, not hot. That meant Whitlock had been out of the office for an hour or so. Gideon unlocked the steel door to the cell block and looked in. All the cells were empty.

He figured his only chance was to close in fast. Holstering his gun, he jogged across the street, coat open. He entered the lobby of the Colorado Hotel and shook the snow from his coat and hat. He figured Whitlock was in his room upstairs, alone, he hoped. He crossed the lobby toward a wide-eyed desk clerk, intent on finding out which room was Whitlock's. Like the ticket agent, the desk clerk recognized him, and drew back.

For the moment Gideon did not draw his gun. But with no time to explain the circumstances, he was prepared to force the issue if the clerk refused to give out Whitlock's room number. Striding toward him, Gideon halted when he heard a feminine peal of laughter. It came from the café.

No mother and daughter could have been more dissimilar than Lucretia and Maggs, but their laughter was identical. If Gideon had not known better, he'd have sworn

Maggs was in the café. He crossed the lobby to the French double doors, and stepped over the threshold. He looked around. The café was half-filled with townspeople, a warm place to meet on a cold and snowy day. In the far corner Lucretia Stearns shared a table with Sam Whitlock.

Her laughter was cut short when she saw him. Gideon moved in long, swift strides through the café. Whitlock turned, his face registering alarm at the sight of the rancher rushing toward him, jaw set.

Gideon saw Whitlock grab for his hand gun. He lunged. Grasping his ruffled shirt front, he yanked the smaller man to his feet. Lucretia shrieked as the chair tumbled over. Whitlock struggled to pull away, his shirt tearing. Diners left their chairs and backed away, many with white linen napkins in hand, their mouths open in amazement.

Gideon drew his fist back and threw a short punch to the jaw. Whitlock's head snapped back, eyes rolling as his knees buckled. Holding the man upright with one hand, Gideon disarmed him with the other, shoving the small caliber pistol into his waistband. Whitlock tried to knee him in the crotch. Gideon cocked his fist, and hit him again, harder.

Whitlock staggered. He wobbled and fell back, sprawling across the table. Water glasses, dessert dishes, and china cups and saucers crashed to the floor, shattering amid two slabs of dried apple pie and two cups of hot coffee. Hands to her face, Lucretia screamed at her son-in-law, demanding to know what he thought he was doing.

Gideon did not reply. He bent down and hoisted Whitlock over his left shoulder like a sack of grain. Aware of cooks and servers peering around the edge of the kitchen doorway, he turned and strode out of the café, leaving the diners standing there, agape in a tableau of shocked silence.

Across the lobby, movement near the staircase landing

caught Gideon's eye. Leaning right to balance Whitlock's weight on his left shoulder, he drew his Colt. He took aim at the shadowy figure there, his finger tightening on the trigger. Then he saw Mills Pillow. The man stepped out of the shadows and turned his back to him as he mounted the stairs.

Gideon holstered his gun. He could have called to him, but he was not inclined to push him. By Gideon's reckoning, Mills Pillow was a man who had seen trouble and wanted no more.

Opening the front door with his free hand, Gideon stepped outside. Light snow still drifted out of the overcast sky. In the distance a train whistle penetrated winter silence with three shrill blasts from an approaching locomotive. The snowplow had made it. Gideon looked left and right. Except for a pair of freight wagons a block away, the street was empty. He stepped off the boardwalk. With the weight of the man bearing down on him, his boots slid in the snow, and he nearly went down.

He caught his balance. Half turning, he leaned and let Whitlock slide to the ground. He grabbed the back of his collar and dragged the man through the snow on Front Street to the sheriff's office.

Gideon stepped up on the boardwalk and opened the door. He yanked Whitlock inside. The cold air and bumpy ride must have revived him for he cursed. Gideon dragged him past the rolltop desk, grabbed the ring of keys, and pulled him into the cell block. Opening the barred door of the first cell, he man-handled Whitlock into it. Then he backed out and locked the door, leaving him sprawled on the cement floor, moaning.

In the sheriff's office, Gideon shouldered out of his sheepskin, hanging it on the coat tree by the stove. He drew a deep breath and exhaled, feeling pain in his chest. His fingers touched the bandage, and came away bloody. Gideon opened his blood-stained shirt. The bandage looped over his shoulder, around his back, and under one arm. Hefting Whitlock had moved it, and blood had seeped out of the wound. He put the bandage back in place, his fingers fumbling with the strip of fabric. He tightened it as best he could, and buttoned his shirt.

The bleeding was not serious, but the pain of the wound had sapped his strength. Fatigue caught up with him. He tossed Whitlock's pistol onto the desk. Sitting heavily in the swivel armchair, he put his booted feet up and leaned back, eyes closing while he awaited the inevitable. He heard the wall clock ticking minutes away one second at a time.

He drew another deep breath. The room still bore the subtle odor of pipe tobacco, soft as a whisper from the past. With his eyes closed in a moment of rest, Gideon's thoughts went to Nate Clarke. He still visualized the man as clearly as if he had seen him moments ago, but he had no time to reflect on memories. A low rumble of voices came from the street. As he had expected, word had spread from the hotel through the town.

Gideon opened his eyes. His gaze went to a locked gun case. Whitlock's custom-made rifle was racked in there with half a dozen Winchesters and other makes. Turning in the swivel chair, he looked out the window.

A dozen townsfolk gathered outside, bundled up against the snow. A few were men he recognized—Johnny Ferree, the gunsmith, Silas, the liveryman, Will Highfield, store proprietor, and saloonman Roy Ellersby among them. Others he vaguely recalled seeing over the years when he came to town on buying trips, nodding acquaintances whose names he had forgotten if he had ever known them.

Now a dozen grew to fifteen, fifteen to twenty-five with more coming, most of the men carrying hand guns, rifles, or old shotguns.

Gideon stood. He saw Lucretia across the street. She stood under the hotel's covered entry, hands clasped under her chin. Movement behind her caught his eye. Pillow came out, carrying his carpetbags with the big Sharps slung over his shoulder, derby hat on his head just as he had appeared the first day Gideon had laid eyes on him. Now the city man paused before moving past Lucretia. Gideon could see she was distraught as she spoke to him. Their brief conversation ending, Pillow turned and left her there as he strode down the boardwalk toward the dépôt.

Gideon moved to the door and opened it. He unbuckled his gun belt and deliberately hung it from the brass door-knob, aware that all eyes were on him. Then he turned to face the crowd, hands on his hips.

"Howdy, gents."

Chapter Twenty-Two

In those moments the crowd swelled by twos and threes as more townsfolk joined their friends and neighbors standing in the snow on Front Street. The name "Coopersmith" was whispered among them. Tensed and unmoving, they stared at this rancher in the doorway to the sheriff's office. The sight before them was bizarre, almost beyond comprehension—a wanted man, unarmed, blood seeping through his shirtfront, grim determination etched into his face. They stared at him warily, regarding him with an uncertainty that might have been reserved for a madman. Nearly filling the snow-covered street now, they were startled when angry shouts came from the cell block.

Gideon heard Whitlock's voice behind him. The man called out, demanding to be set free at once. With every shout from him, murmurs from the crowd grew louder.

Gideon held up the ring of keys to the cell block. "Reckon your sheriff doesn't like the view from jail."

A thin townsman whose beard was trimmed into a goatee, his name unknown to Gideon, raised his rifle until the barrel was leveled at him. "Whattya you aim to do, mister?"

"Say my piece," Gideon replied.

Like the other townsfolk, the man stared at him, baffled.

Gideon went on: "I've got a thing or two to say about this gent who calls himself Sam Walker."

A man wearing a narrow-brimmed hat and wolf-hide coat demanded: "Such as what?"

"When I first met him last month," Gideon said, "he was leading a bunch of gunmen from Wyoming. He wore a full beard and mustache, and went by the name of Sam Whitlock." He paused. "Makes a man wonder why he changed his name and shaved his face clean, doesn't it?"

The townsman wearing the narrow-brimmed hat asked: "What're you driving at?"

"The truth," Gideon said. "I'm here to tell you he's a good deal more than a liar." He recounted his discovery of the hanged men at Dutchman's, and related Mike O'Connor's eyewitness account of the murders committed by Sam Whitlock.

Gideon was surprised to see the townsmen inflamed by his words. They protested loudly, a number of them raising weapons and labeling Gideon as the liar, accusing him of the murder of four deputies. Off to his left and to his right, several men stepped up on the boardwalk and edged closer, guns in hand.

"Sheriff Walker, he brung law and order to our town," one man said, and others echoed their agreement.

"How did he do that?" Gideon asked. "By putting a price on my head?" When no one answered, he posed another question: "How would Nate Clarke have handled this thing?"

"All I know is," another man said, "until silver comes back, we cain't afford a slew of deputies."

"You went and shot 'em to pieces!" a third one called out. "Can you deny that fact?"

Another cupped his hands to his mouth and shouted: "You can be sure outlaws will be scared off by Walker, deputies or no deputies!"

"Outlaws," Gideon repeated. "Strange, isn't it, that in all the years I've ranched in North Park, I wasn't an outlaw until he landed here." While the townspeople considered that, Gideon added: "All I'm asking is a chance to say my piece. What you folks do after that is up to you."

A man who had inched closer to Gideon's left raised his revolver. "Now, you listen here, cow-chaser. Hand over that key ring. When the sheriff's set free, you can stand out here in the snow and jaw all you want. . . ."

Suddenly Silas shoved his way through men standing elbow to elbow. He turned to face them. "Let him talk!" When other townsmen shouted their objections, Silas yelled louder: "Coopersmith's right! It's time to tell the truth! All of us!"

Gideon saw the men look at the liveryman in surprise, as though seeing him for the first time. Silas was a quiet man, not outspoken, a man no doubt more comfortable in the company of horses than two-legged critters. But now he was caught up in the moment, and commanded their attention.

The thin townsman with the trimmed goatee regarded Silas. "Just what do you mean by that?"

"Am I the only man in this town who was pistol-whipped by Ben Anderson?" he said. "I caved in to a bully. I'm not proud of it, but I was scared, scared for my life." The liveryman drew a breath. "As long as we're telling the unvarnished truth, how many of you was bullied and threatened by that gang of toughs the sheriff brung to town?"

No one answered.

Gideon gestured to Ellersby. The saloonman had not added his voice to one side of this dispute or the other. Gideon believed he knew why. "Roy, what about you?"

His hat white with snow, the saloonman brushed a hand through his drooping mustache. "What about me?"

"You caved in to Whitlock and Anderson, didn't you?"

"Well, after the fire in town," he said, "I was persuaded. . . ."

"No," Gideon broke in. "After the kid was hanged."

The townspeople turned to him. They stared in silent curiosity.

"What're you talking about?" Ellersby demanded.

"You were robbed by Tommy Logan," Gideon said. "You told Whitlock about it, and he hanged that kid."

Ellersby lowered his gaze.

Gideon hoped he sounded like he knew more than he did. Remembering Ben Anderson's last words, he figured this sequence of events was the only way the lynching made sense. Ellersby had turned the *posse comitatus* loose on the boy.

"Roy," Gideon went on, "if you don't get the truth out where everyone can see it, Whitlock will put his slant on it. Cross him, and he'll make it look like you're guilty of hanging a fifteen-year-old kid."

"Gideon, I never had a thing to do with killing him . . . ," Ellersby's voice choked.

"I'm not saying you tightened the noose with your own hands," Gideon said. "I'm saying you struck a deal with Whitlock. . . ."

"But I never knew he'd do that!" Ellersby blurted. "That's the honest truth! Nate Clarke and Ollie Moore, all they did was run that kid out of town. I complained about it to several men standing at my bar. When the boy's body was found, strung up in the mill like it was, I was shocked like everybody else in Buckhorn."

A long silence was broken when the townsman with the goatee posed a question: "Roy, did you actually see who lynched him?"

Ellersby shook his head. "No! I'm telling you, I wasn't there."

The bearded man turned to Gideon. "You claim to be

fair-minded, Coopersmith. Wouldn't you say our sheriff has a right to defend himself?"

"After you folks hear me out," Gideon said, "I'll turn over these keys to you. You can set Whitlock loose . . . if you still want that man walking your streets."

Loud protests were met with a challenge from Silas: "Are you men afraid of the truth? Are you?"

This time the crowd fell silent.

Not given to oratory, Gideon related his experiences with Sam Whitlock in a straightforward recounting of events, from their first meeting on Double Circle C range to his discovery of the hanged men at Dutchman's. He laid out evidence that Whitlock had killed Nate Clarke from ambush, and then offered proof the man later faked his own death. After recounting the shooting of Ruth Logan, Gideon described the attack on his ranch. It was, he said, an assault by gunmen led by Ben Anderson and backed up by the distant sharpshooter—Sam Whitlock.

His speech was met by silence. As he looked at the gathered townsmen, he felt satisfied. He had done what he came to Buckhorn to do. The facts were laid out, confirming Whitlock's guilt. Now these townsfolk could see the man for what he was.

Disgruntled murmurs rose in volume as several townsmen spoke at once, their voices rising. The man with the goatee raised his voice above the others. "All right, Coopersmith. We've heard you out. Now, you hear us. A bunch of us, we're thinking the same way. You never saw Sheriff Walker commit any crime, did you?"

"Not one!"

Before Gideon could answer, another man shouted: "You got witnesses?"

Gideon eyed him. "Several of us saw your sheriff firing

from a distance. Like I told you, he and his gunmen danged near shot my ranch house to pieces without regard for the lives of women and children. . . ."

"It's his job to root out lawbreakers," one man pointed out.

Gideon countered: "If you're telling me the sheriff's star is a license to kill, I want to know one thing . . . who's next?"

"Well, there's been talk of outlaws," said another, "and Ruth Logan ain't exactly as pure as the driven snow, now, is she?"

The man with the goatee advanced a pace. "Sounds to me like you got fair warning, Coopersmith."

Another shouted: "You don't want deputies coming around your place because you're hiding longriders. That's why you won't pay the fee, ain't it?"

"The only outlaws I saw were those so-called deputies," Gideon replied angrily. He drew a breath and added: "Ben Anderson cleared his conscience when he was dying. He told me that your sheriff ambushed Nate Clarke, gunned him down with that big rifle of his. And he said Whitlock left Tommy Logan's body hanging in the crushing mill. That was a threat against all of you, just like the millinery shop he set fire to."

The townsman wearing the narrow-brimmed hat said: "Those are your words, Coopersmith."

"Who's gonna back you?"

"You got witnesses?"

"Or are they all dead?"

Across the street, the desk clerk from the hotel called out: "She's a witness, isn't she?"

Gideon had not seen him come out of the hotel, but he spotted him at the back of the crowd now, pointing at

Lucretia. "This is the mother of Coopersmith's wife."

The crowd turned to her. Lucretia stood as still as a dark statue in the covered entrance to the Colorado Hotel, hands pressed to her mouth, whether in a pose of fear or fascination, Gideon could not determine.

"Reckon she can tell us what happened on the Double Circle C," the clerk said.

After a moment of hesitation, two men went to her. She pulled up the hood of her black cloak, covering her head as each townsman took an arm and helped her across the snow-rutted street to the boardwalk in front of the sheriff's office. She turned to face the crowd, avoiding Gideon's gaze. Then she cleared her throat.

"Gideon forced me and my daughter and grandchildren into a cold and dark root cellar during the . . . fracas. I heard shooting. . . . Gideon had refused to pay the law enforcement fee, and I am told Sheriff Walker sent out deputies. . . ." She cleared her throat again and glanced at Gideon. "I am sorry to say this, but the truth is the truth. I never saw the sheriff that day. I do not know who started the shooting. All I know is . . . some men died, and it was a terrible sight with . . . with blood soaking into the snow."

Gideon stared at her while voices in the crowd swelled in collective outrage. With the black hood concealing most of her face, all he could see in profile was the end of her nose reddened by exposure to the cold air.

Lucretia lifted her hand, quieting them. "I have spoken to Sheriff Walker myself. He assured me his sworn duty is to uphold the law. We were conversing in the hotel café when my son-in-law . . . well, when Gideon acted in an ungentlemanly manner." She paused. "Now, regarding the character of Sheriff Walker, in my estimation he is a fine man. I cannot say I've been introduced to a man touched by such greatness since the day I met the love of my life, the gentleman who would become my husband, Ezra Allen Stearns, so many years ago. Like my late husband, Sheriff Walker possesses a vision of the future, a vision of peace and prosperity that is inspiring, simply inspiring."

Gideon felt as though he had been slugged, struck silent with the breath driven out of him. A townsman pulled Lucretia aside while others grabbed Gideon, two men on his left, two on his right. They quickly overpowered him.

The thin, bearded man rushed up and yanked the key ring from his hand. He hurried into the sheriff's office, and presently came back with Whitlock following. The sheriff had buckled his monogrammed gun belt around his waist, and now he stepped outside, carrying wrist irons.

Gideon met the man's angry gaze. He did not resist when townsmen pulled his hands behind his back and Whitlock shackled him. He took some satisfaction in seeing a purpled knot the size of a walnut on Whitlock's clean-shaven jaw. Onlookers were quiet and watchful as their sheriff turned to face them.

"Justice will be done," he said. "All of you who helped me dig those four graves know Coopersmith is guilty of murder. This rancher killed four deputies, killed them in cold blood. He ran the others off after stealing their weapons and ammunition. There is little doubt Coopersmith intends to arm longriders . . . thieves and killers who will terrorize all of us."

Gideon stared at him while he spoke, now turning to Lucretia. "You know better than that. Tell them."

"I . . . I don't know what to believe any more," she whispered.

Surveying the faces of the townspeople, Whitlock went on: "Do we need a trial to discover the truth?"

Several men shouted at once: "No!"

"Do we need to build a gallows for justice to be done?"

"Yes!" came shouts in a rising chorus.

Lucretia stood mute, her eyes downcast.

"As you know," Whitlock said, "I posted a reward at no cost to the county . . . five hundred dollars for the capture of Gideon Coopersmith. Looks to me like you good folks of Buckhorn have done exactly that. With your permission, I shall donate the reward money for the hiring of a teacher and the purchase of school supplies. Next September, the door to the Buckhorn school will be open!"

A cheer went up, but only for a moment. The exuberant cry of townsmen was cut off by a thunderous gunshot. Along with everyone else, Gideon was startled by it. He whirled and peered through the fine snowflakes drifting out of the overcast sky.

Mills Pillow, bare-headed now, started across the street, his Sharps rifle pointed skyward with powdersmoke drifting out of the barrel. Coming from the direction of the train dépôt, he was followed by a well-dressed man wearing a suit, topcoat, and derby hat. The man halted on the board-walk by the hotel while Pillow continued on.

"As Sophocles, the dramatist of the ancient Greeks wrote," Pillow announced loudly while making his way through the crowd, " 'No one likes the bearer of bad news.' Prepare to dislike me."

Whitlock demanded: "What do you want?"

Pillow ignored him and stepped up onto the boardwalk to address the townsmen. "Some of you know me. For those of you who do not, my name is Mills Pillow. I traveled here on holiday from Washington, D.C. where I am employed as a government cartographer. I happened to be here in Buckhorn in the company of Missus Stearns the day your sheriff claimed United States senators had petitioned the president for a return to bimetallism. That claim seemed to me to be extravagant. So I sent off some inquiries by wire. Now I have answers." With his free hand, Pillow reached into a coat pocket. He pulled out a handful of telegraphed messages, and held them up for all to see.

"These are replies to my inquiries," he went on. "You may read them, if you wish. They confirm my initial suspicion, namely, the bad news I mentioned . . . no *ad hoc* committee of senators has ever petitioned President Cleveland or anyone else for a return to a gold-silver policy. No such petition exists. Your sheriff's claim, while dramatic, was a lie."

Whitlock shouted: "I spoke the truth! For all I know, the mealy-mouthed politicians changed their tune since I learned of that petition."

With every townsman listening intently, Pillow added: "Bimetallism is a dead issue in Washington. I know everyone here places high hopes on the price of silver skyrocketing. It won't. Whether we like it or not, the gold standard will carry our currency into the Twentieth Century." He glanced at Whitlock. "That is the truth."

"I give you my word!" Whitlock called out. "There was such a petition!"

"Perhaps you will give your word just as readily on another matter," Pillow said.

"What the hell are you talking about?" Whitlock said, red-faced in anger.

"While snowbound here in Buckhorn, I sent inquiries by telegraph to the United States Marshal's office in Denver." Pillow gestured to the man standing at the corner of the hotel across the street. "Marshal Roger Gaines just arrived on the snowplow train. He is interested in questioning you about your involvement in the embezzlement of bank funds."

"Embezzlement!" Whitlock exclaimed. "First you call me a liar. Now what are you accusing me of?"

Pillow turned and addressed the gathered townspeople: "Your sheriff matches the description of one Samuel Whitlock, an officer of the Nebraska State Bank and Trust who resigned in the aftermath of a hold-up. That crime was committed by Ben Anderson and Tom Griffith."

Murmurs from the crowd rose in volume as Pillow let this information register with them. For the moment Whitlock was silent, his gaze darting to the townsmen as he tried to read their mood.

"In point of fact," Pillow went on, "that hold-up was merely a diversion. Bank examiners discovered more money was missing . . . some twenty-three thousand dollars. An investigation was launched. The bank officer disappeared." Pillow turned to Whitlock. "Until now."

"Your accusations are false!" Whitlock said. "All of them!"

"Marshal Gaines will give you the opportunity to clear yourself," Pillow said, lifting his hand to the man across the street.

Whitlock called out to the townsmen: "Don't you see? Pillow and Coopersmith are in this together. They're trying to railroad me."

"If that is the case," Pillow said, "then it will be an easy task to prove your innocence in a statement to the United States Marshal."

Whitlock turned to the crowd. "This is wrong . . . all wrong! Haven't we worked together to make our town safe and prosperous? As long as you good folks back me up, no lawman can cross state lines and haul me off to Omaha on falsified charges."

Hatless as he stood in the light snowfall, Pillow's eyebrow lifted. It was the expression of a man who has set a trap and watched it spring shut.

"Who said anything about Omaha?" Pillow asked.

Whitlock sputtered. "You did!"

Pillow shook his head. "Everyone here heard me say Nebraska. How did you know the bank in question was in Omaha?"

The crowd parted as the man wearing the topcoat and derby angled across Front Street toward Whitlock. As though thunderstruck, they watched in silence. Moments ago they had been willing to hang Gideon Coopersmith. Now their attention moved from the man crossing the street to their sheriff, distrust stealing over them like cloud shadows.

Gideon glimpsed sudden movement. Whitlock dashed to his left, drawing his revolver. He grabbed Lucretia. She shrieked when he pulled her in front of him and backed toward the wall of the sheriff's office with her as a shield.

Barely tall enough to see over her shoulder, Whitlock shouted: "I came here to help Buckhorn grow into a peaceful and prosperous community. . . ." He drew a ragged breath while Lucretia struggled against his grasp. "Robbery! Murder! Rampant lawlessness! Is that what you want?"

Silas shouted: "You've lied to us! You'll face the gallows, not Coopersmith!"

The townsman with the goatee advanced a step. "Now, hold on here. Just hold on. Sheriff, a bunch of us are behind you. You don't need that gun. Face the circuit judge. He's a good man. You, too, Coopersmith. We'll get to the bottom of this."

Breathing heavily, Whitlock shouted: "You fool! Don't you see? It's too late for that! I used the money for your benefit, your protection from the criminal element, but now no man among you has the courage to back me up. . . ."

His words were cut off when Silas leaped onto the board-walk and charged him. Still standing behind Lucretia, Whitlock swung the revolver around. He snapped off a shot, the barrel angling downward when the bullet struck Silas at point-blank range. Lucretia screamed as the liveryman spun and crumpled to the boardwalk.

Several men standing nearby on the street panicked. They turned and tried to flee, but collided with others who stood rooted in fear. In the confusion of the moment more guns were fired, curses shouted, and bullets and buckshot flew harmlessly into the sky or lodged in storefronts facing Front Street.

Gideon saw Whitlock bring his gun to bear on him. In that instant he knew the man had nothing to lose now and sought one last victory. In that nightmarish moment Gideon knew he could neither defend himself with his hands bound behind his back, nor dodge the next bullet from Whitlock's revolver.

"This is what I should have done a long time ago," Whitlock said.

A small man, he was no match for Lucretia Stearns. She suddenly bent at the waist and threw herself backward, her weight driven by piston-like legs slamming her girdled but-tocks into his chest. She jammed him against the brick wall with enough force to snap ribs and knock the wind out of his lungs.

Arms sinking to his sides, Whitlock's revolver dropped to the boardwalk. When Lucretia stepped away, he slid to the walk and sat there, wide-eyed and struggling for air. Half-turning, she looked down at him, hands pressed to her mouth as though fearful of what she had done.

Gideon kicked the revolver into the street. The

townsmen rushed forward to free him while Pillow knelt to tend to Silas's wound. The liveryman was conscious and alert when Roy Ellersby came forward, dropping to one knee while Pillow pulled his coat open in search of a gun-shot wound.

"You said you caved in," the saloonman said, "but I think everyone in this town knows you've got more sand than any of us."

Silas looked up at him and managed a smile.

"No blood," Pillow said in surprise.

"My leg hurts something fierce," Silas said. Grimacing, he sat up. He gingerly felt his thigh where the woolen trouser leg bore a hole. Then he reached into his trouser pocket. He pulled out a bent silver dollar and held it up. "Lucky coin," he said with a grin.

Pillow stood. "Lucky, indeed. You'll be sore for a good long time, but you're not injured."

Lucretia edged close to Gideon and whispered through her fingers: "I . . . I'm sorry . . . so sorry."

"Reckon we all owe you an apology, Coopersmith," the thin townsman with the goatee added. "Guess we got caught up in Whitlock's promises. We were quick to turn on you, and I'm not proud of it."

"None of us are," a man added with others murmuring their agreement. "Not one bit."

A pair of townsmen flanked Whitlock, grasped his arms, and hauled him to his feet. He breathed raggedly, grimacing against the pain in his ribs.

Will Highfield turned his attention to the man wearing the topcoat and derby. "Mister Pillow, he's no U.S. Marshal. I didn't recognize him under that derby until he got close, but I've seen him before. He's a section hand for the railroad in the Denver yards."

A grin creased Pillow's round face. "You are correct, sir. He was on the snowplow train. I paid him two dollars to wear my hat and put on my spare suit down in the train station. I told him all he had to do was stand across the street by the hotel and walk toward me when I signaled him."

Whitlock swore in anger. He resisted briefly and mixed threats with curses as he was taken into the sheriff's office and on to the cell block.

"I still don't get it," the townsman in the narrow-brimmed hat said.

Pillow held up the telegraphed messages. "While snow-bound in your town, I've been on the wire from here to Denver. On my previous trip to Buckhorn I had notified federal marshals of a lawman exceeding his authority here. Then by wire I found out about the charge of bank fraud in Omaha, Nebraska. Federal marshals knew your sheriff as Samuel Whitlock, and believed he was dead and buried. A lawman named Tyler in Laramie, Wyoming knew the full story, having heard it from Gideon after the funeral of Nate Clarke." Pillow paused. "An arrest warrant is on the way from Denver with Marshal Gaines, but he will not arrive until the next train. So, humbly borrowing from the master, Sophocles, I used a bit of drama to force Whitlock's hand."

Pillow turned to Gideon. "Speaking of hands, I must shake yours and add my apologies to the others here."

Gideon grasped his hand, looking at him curiously.

"I regret my behavior," Pillow said. "Common courtesy dictates a proper farewell, and I should have spoken to you before leaving your ranch. From the day we first met you took me in, a stranger. You and your family were good to me, and for that I shall always be grateful."

"You earned your keep," Gideon said, "and then some."

Pillow said: "The only excuse I can offer for my boorish

behavior is that I had never been close to a gun battle before and, seeing those men die shook me to my core. I was shocked into a dark view of life in the West until I had time to think things over in the confines of a room here in the Colorado Hotel. My view has changed, Gideon. You and everyone else living out here are creating your own societal traditions. Certainly I am in no position to criticize you Westerners."

Gideon nodded slowly. "Societal traditions. Yeah, I reckon we're working on them."

The snowstorm broke in the night as slowly and quietly as it had crept into North Park. With the sky clearing, Gideon found his way to Dutchman's by the light of stars. He rested the paint, and then rode on.

The rhythmic motion of the horse and the vast silence of this starry winter night lulled his mind, pulling him into an emotional landscape on the edge of sleep. As though peering into the past, Gideon found himself reflecting on his life, from his childhood days on the sandhills homestead to discovering his father's grave in the cemetery of a dead town. He thought of a cowhand named Kansas and all those years in the saddle before he met Maggs.

Then for some unaccountable reason a vivid image of Tommy Logan came to mind—the kid warming himself at the stove in the lobby of the Colorado Hotel, pleading to Gideon: *What am I gonna do now?* Gideon had once been a kid on his own, too, but he had always known what to do.

Both Nate Clarke and Tommy Logan had crossed the divide too soon. A man in his prime, Nate deserved better. So did the kid, despite his crimes, Gideon thought as the image of Ruth came to mind. She would heal from her gunshot wounds in due time and leave the ranch, he figured, but the pain of a mother's loss would never heal.

Gideon thought of Maggs and her beckoning smile that reached to his soul. Images of Annie and Andrew seeped into his mind, lingered, and faded. He thought of Patrocino, carving the images of his dead comrades, a man coming to terms with his past, an artist searching for that one length of pine or aspen worthy of his *capitán*.

Deadman cut the starlit horizon in the distance. Gideon wondered if the name of that rugged mountain would ever be changed, or if the quest was even important to Maggs any more. Maybe Pillow had been right. In a strange way the name was fitting, crossing an era from the lone trapper killed by a grizzly to violence among men half a century later. Yet, to Gideon, the peak was not a symbol of death by any name. It was a landmark, a great towering presence representing strength and endurance, qualities needed for survival here.

He thought about Annie's schooling. Maybe a father's wish would be answered, after all, and she would be educated not by teachers in a formal way, but by the people who passed through her life—Patrocino, Ruth Logan, Mills Pillow, and even Tommy Logan—with book learning from her mother and a measure of horse sense from her father. When Annie came of age, she could go to a university. Well, that's a long way off, he thought, but immediately corrected himself as he recalled skating on the frozen beaver pond with his daughter. Time flies, he had thought then, and now remembered his nightmare while asleep in the U.P. passenger coach bound for Red Cliff, a mad dream of clocks speeding out of control like a night train hurtling through space and time. . . .

Not hurtling now, Gideon's thoughts drifted to ranch chores as the paint crossed the frozen creek named for

French trappers. He rode on, a lone horseman crossing a field of snow by starlight. When the mare tossed her head and pranced, Gideon stood in the stirrups. He peered ahead at the dark, angular shapes on a south-facing rise—the home place.

DARK EMBERS AT DAWN
STEPHEN OVERHOLSER

Like many a veteran of the Civil War, Cap McKenna went west to the Rockies to build a new life. But that new life changes forever the day he comes across an abandoned infant, whom he takes in and cares for until the baby's Cheyenne mother appears at his door. Alone and terrified, all the woman wants is to find the baby's father. Cap helps her locate him at the U.S. Cavalry encampment, but Colonel Tom Sully stands defiantly between the father and his family. When the desperate man deserts to be with his wife and child, Sully sends a detail after him and suddenly Cap finds himself caught in a deadly pursuit—ready to risk all for what he knows is right.

___4657-1 $4.50 US/$5.50 CAN

Dorchester Publishing Co., Inc.
P.O. Box 6640
Wayne, PA 19087-8640

Please add $1.75 for shipping and handling for the first book and $.50 for each book thereafter. NY, NYC, and PA residents, please add appropriate sales tax. No cash, stamps, or C.O.D.s. All orders shipped within 6 weeks via postal service book rate. Canadian orders require $2.00 extra postage and must be paid in U.S. dollars through a U.S. banking facility.

Name_____
Address_____
City_____State_____Zip_____
I have enclosed $_____ in payment for the checked book(s).
Payment <u>must</u> accompany all orders. ❑ Please send a free catalog.
CHECK OUT OUR WEBSITE! www.dorchesterpub.com

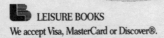